ADVENTUREGAME COMICS

1

LEVIATHAN

JASON SHIGA

AMULET BOOKS • NEW YORK

Library of Congress Control Number 2022932384

ISBN 978-1-4197-5779-2

Copyright © 2022 Jason Shiga
Book design by Andrea Miller

Printed and bound in U.S.A.
10 9 8 7 6 5 4 3 2 1

ABRAMS The Art of Books
195 Broadway, New York, NY 10007
abramsbooks.com

For Kazuo

LEVIATHAN
3
INSTRUCTIONS
BEGIN
5

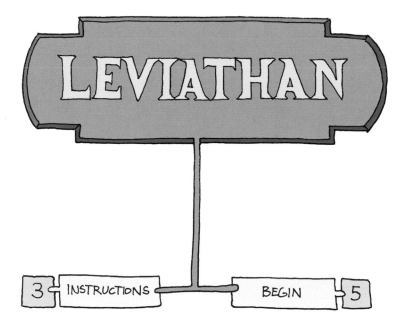

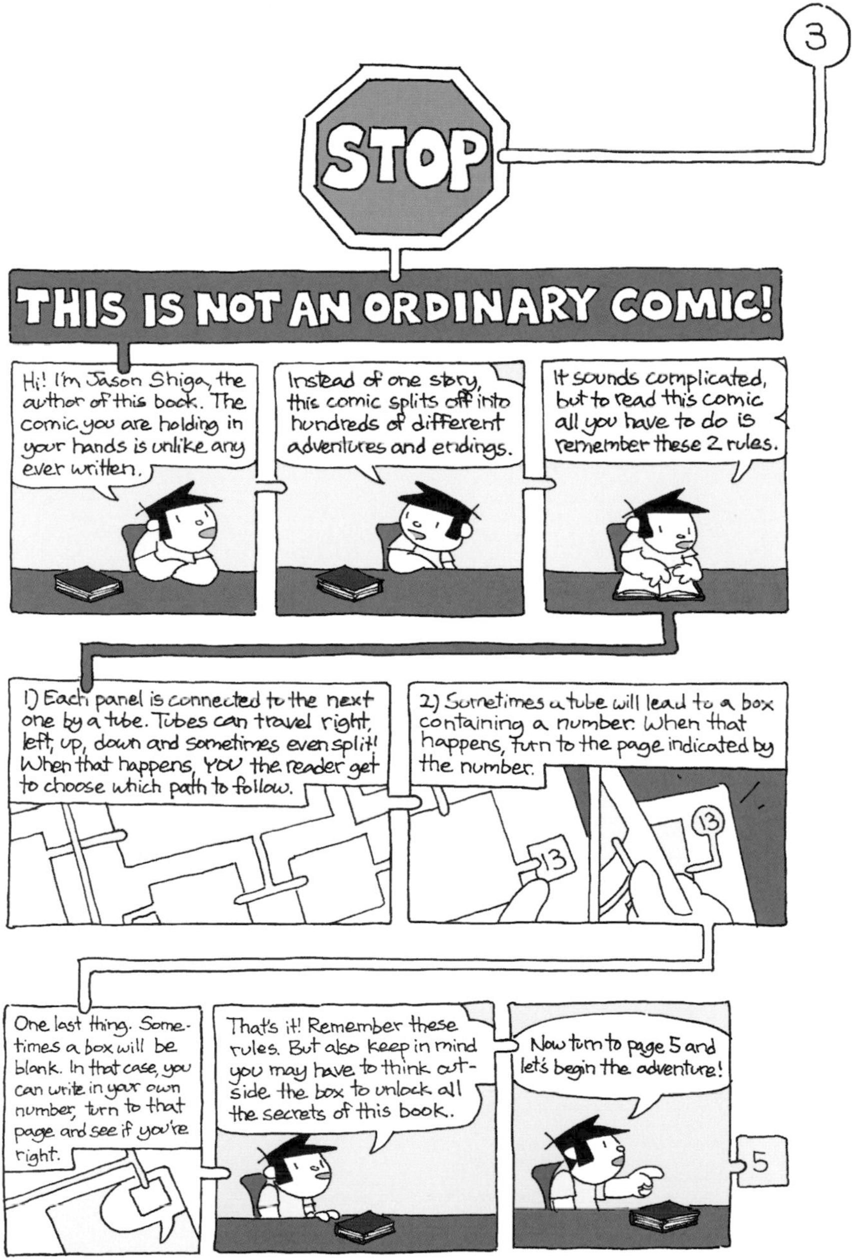

3
STOP
THIS IS NOT AN ORDINARY COMIC!
Hi! I'm Jason Shiga, the author of this book. The comic you are holding in your hands is unlike any ever written.
Instead of one story, this comic splits off into hundreds of different adventures and endings.
It sounds complicated, but to read this comic all you have to do is remember these 2 rules.
1) Each panel is connected to the next one by a tube. Tubes can travel right, left, up, down and sometimes even split! When that happens, YOU the reader get to choose which path to follow.
2) Sometimes a tube will lead to a box containing a number. When that happens, turn to the page indicated by the number.
13
13
One last thing. Sometimes a box will be blank. In that case, you can write in your own number, turn to that page and see if you're right.
That's it! Remember these rules. But also keep in mind you may have to think outside the box to unlock all the secrets of this book.
Now turn to page 5 and let's begin the adventure!
5

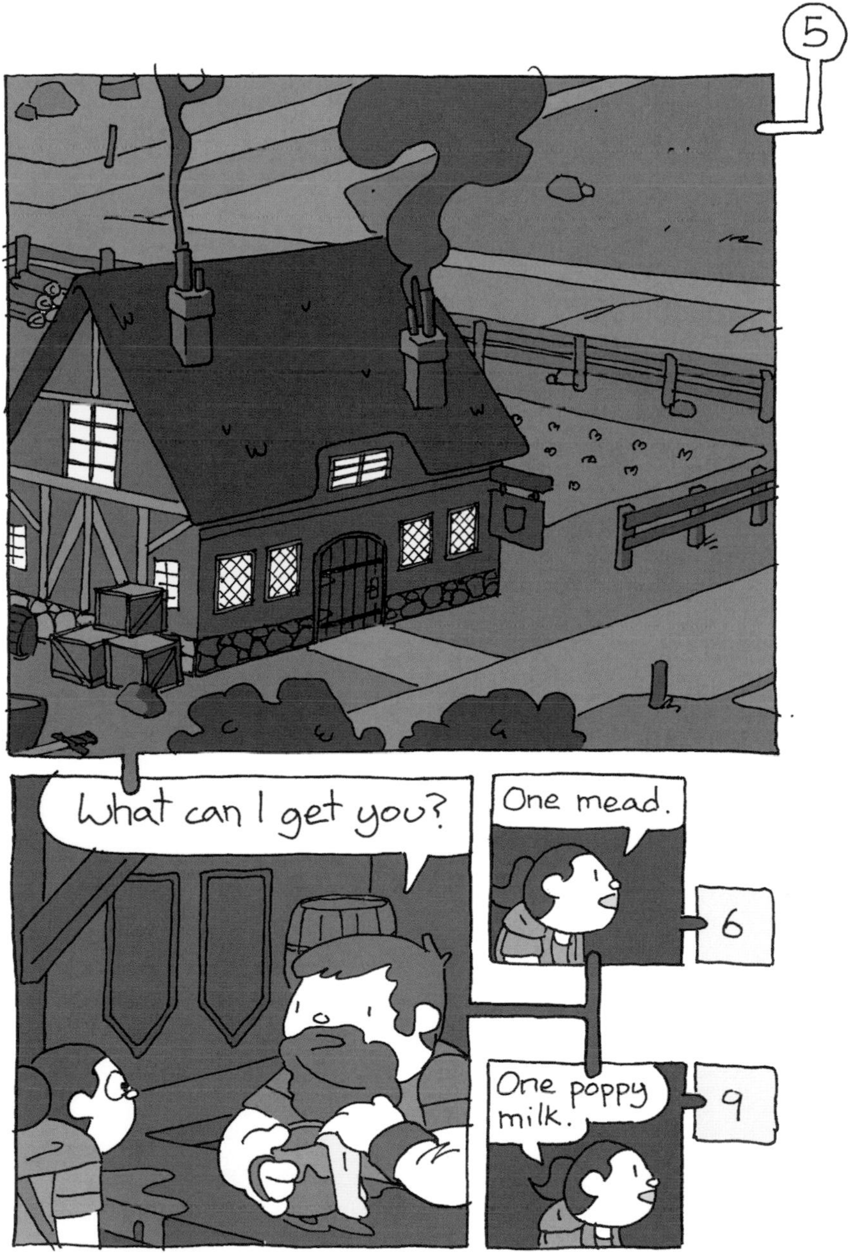
5
What can I get you?
One mead.
6
One poppy milk.
9

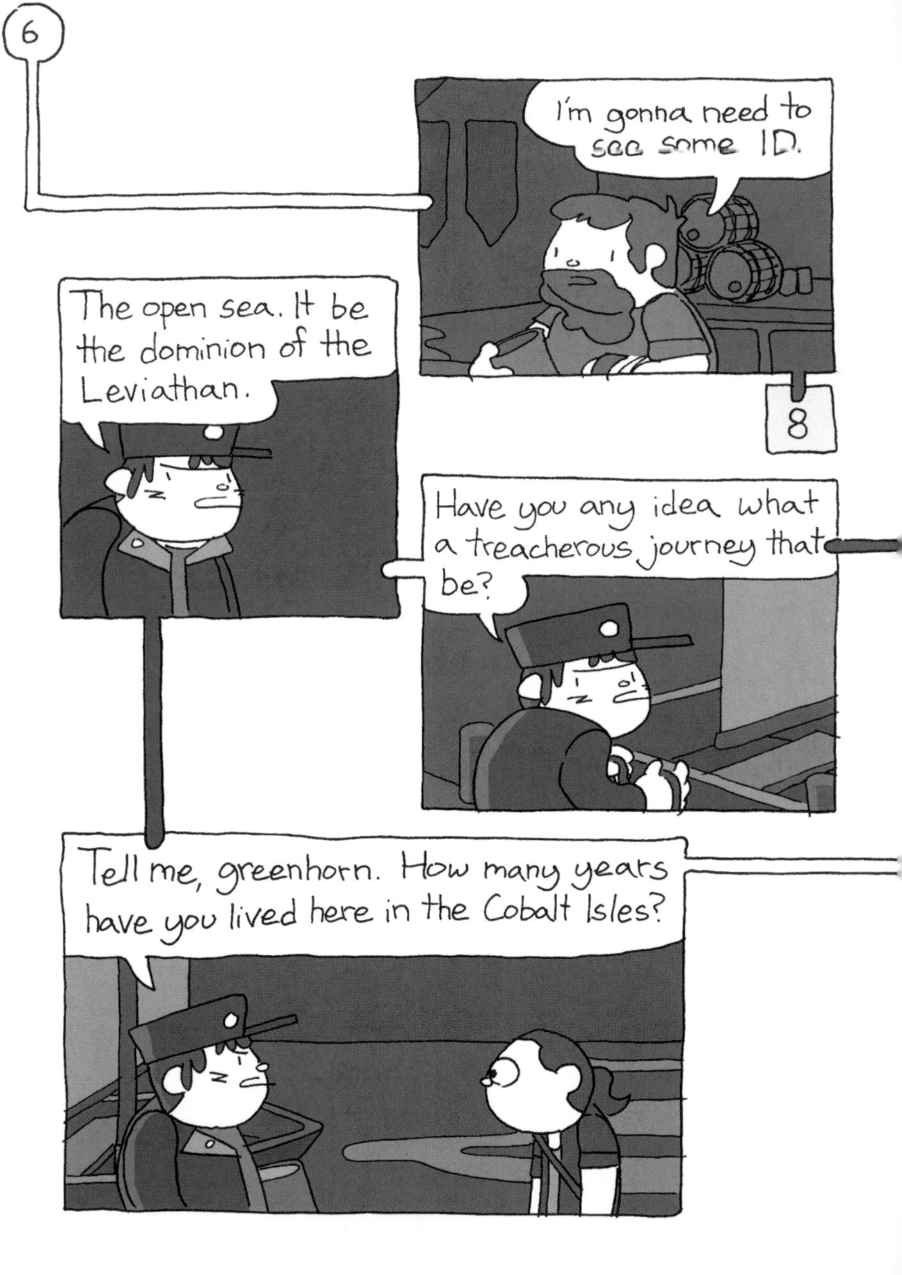
6
I'm gonna need to see some ID.
8
The open sea. It be the dominion of the Leviathan.
Have you any idea what a treacherous journey that be?
Tell me, greenhorn. How many years have you lived here in the Cobalt Isles?

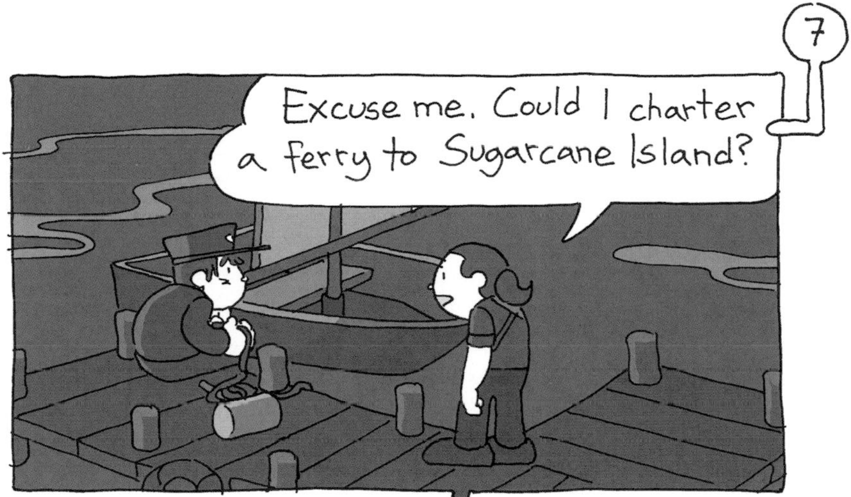
7
Excuse me. Could I charter a ferry to Sugarcane Island?

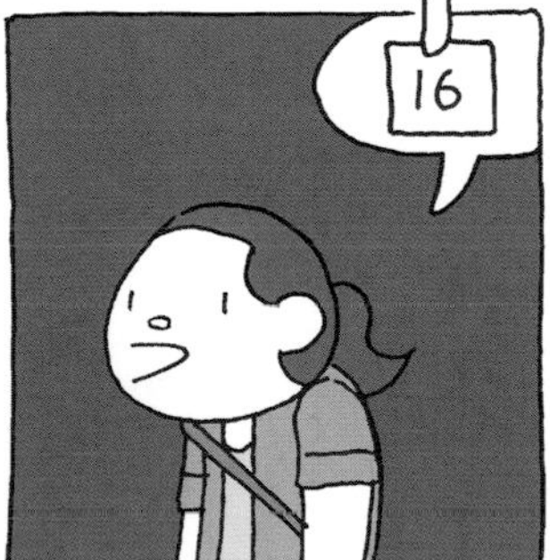
16

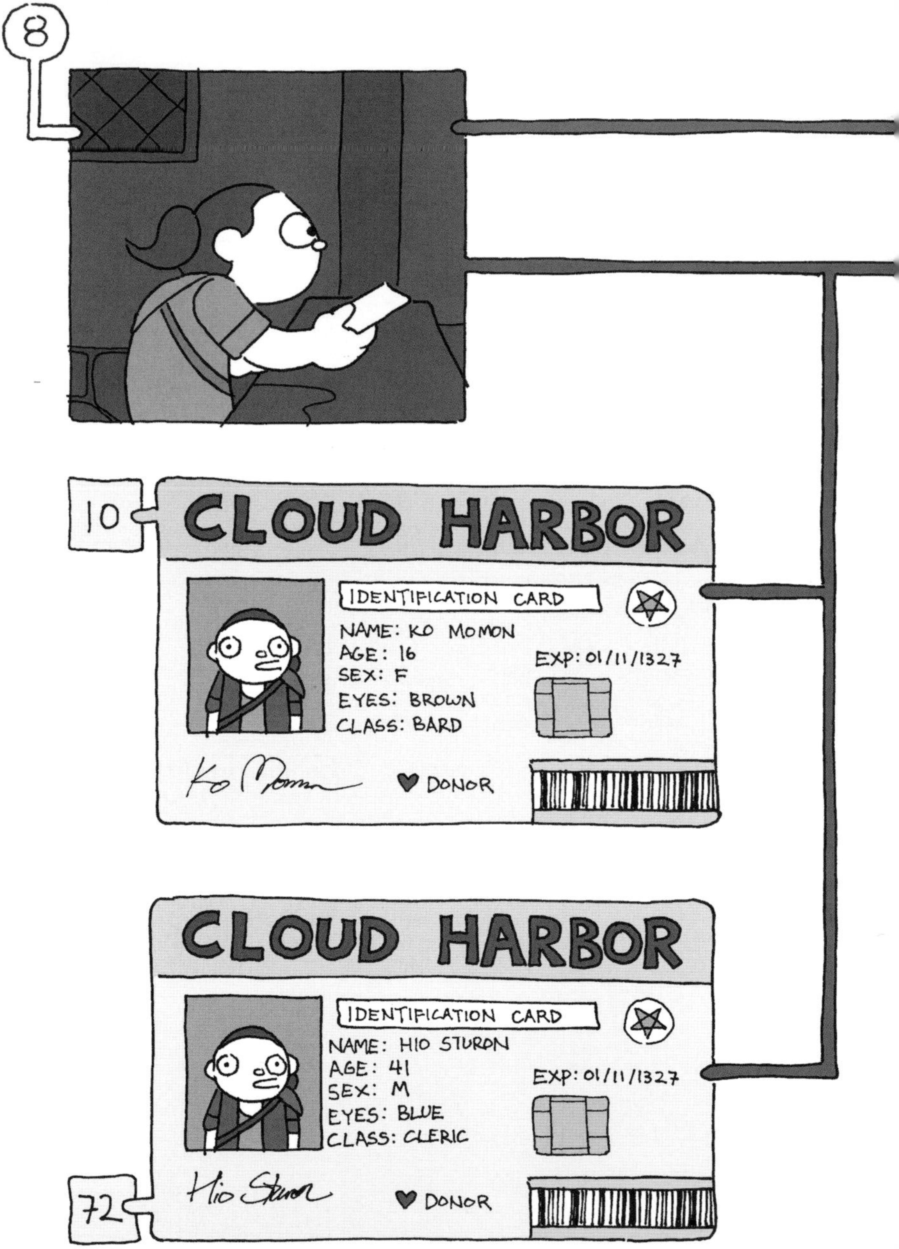
8
10
CLOUD HARBOR
IDENTIFICATION CARD
NAME: KO MOMON
AGE: 16
SEX: F
EYES: BROWN
CLASS: BARD
EXP: 01/11/1327
DONOR
CLOUD HARBOR
IDENTIFICATION CARD
NAME: HIO STURON
AGE: 41
SEX: M
EYES: BLUE
CLASS: CLERIC
EXP: 01/11/1327
DONOR
72

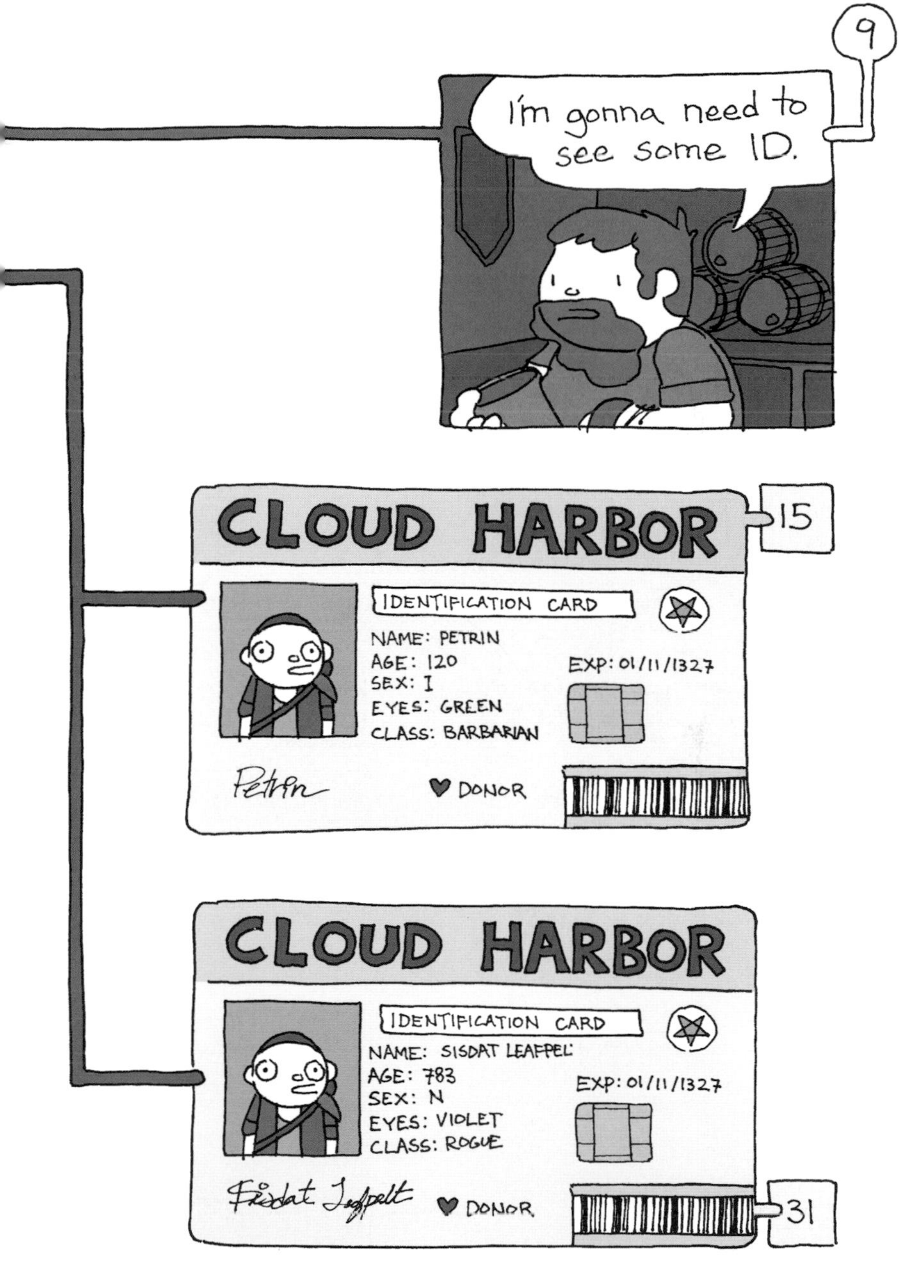
9
I'm gonna need to see some ID.
15
CLOUD HARBOR
IDENTIFICATION CARD
NAME: PETRIN
AGE: 120
SEX: I
EYES: GREEN
CLASS: BARBARIAN
EXP: 01/11/1327
Petrin
DONOR
CLOUD HARBOR
IDENTIFICATION CARD
NAME: SISDAT LEAFPEL
AGE: 783
SEX: N
EYES: VIOLET
CLASS: ROGUE
EXP: 01/11/1327
DONOR
31

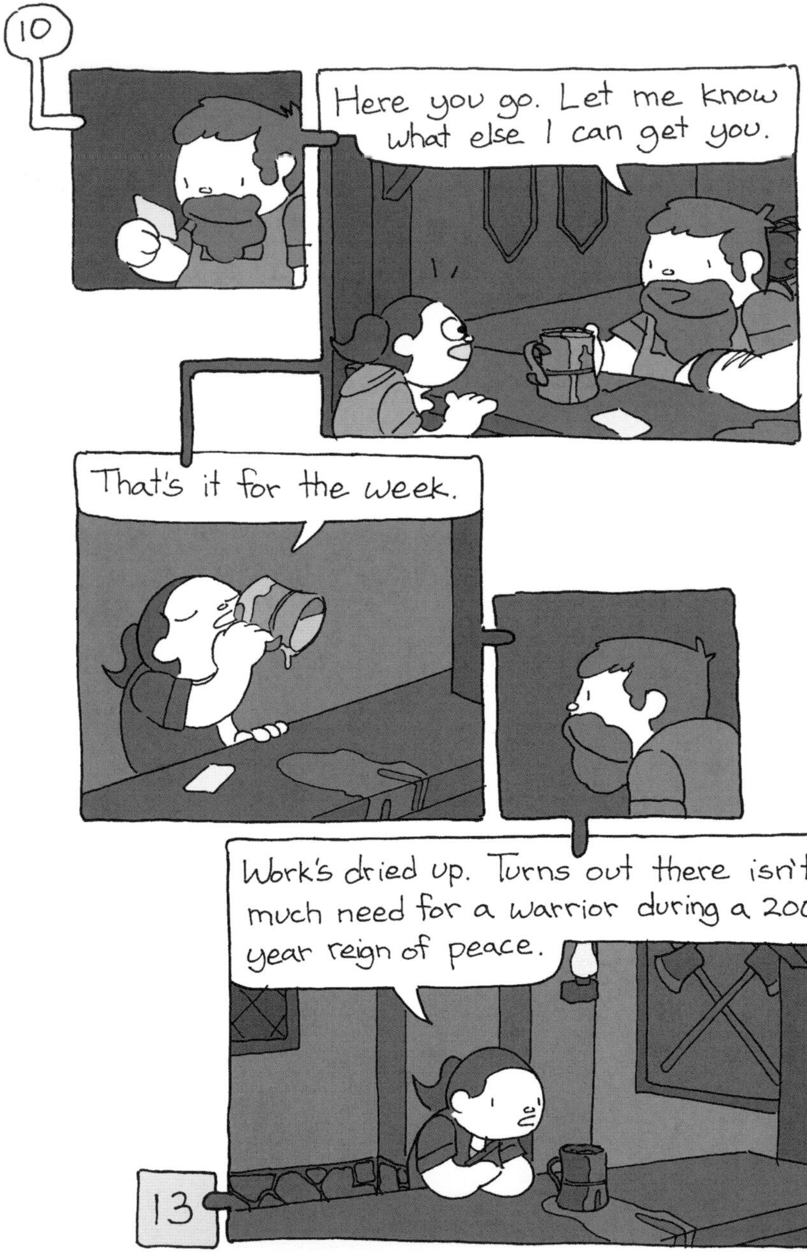
10
Here you go. Let me know what else I can get you.
That's it for the week.
Work's dried up. Turns out there isn't much need for a warrior during a 200-year reign of peace.
13

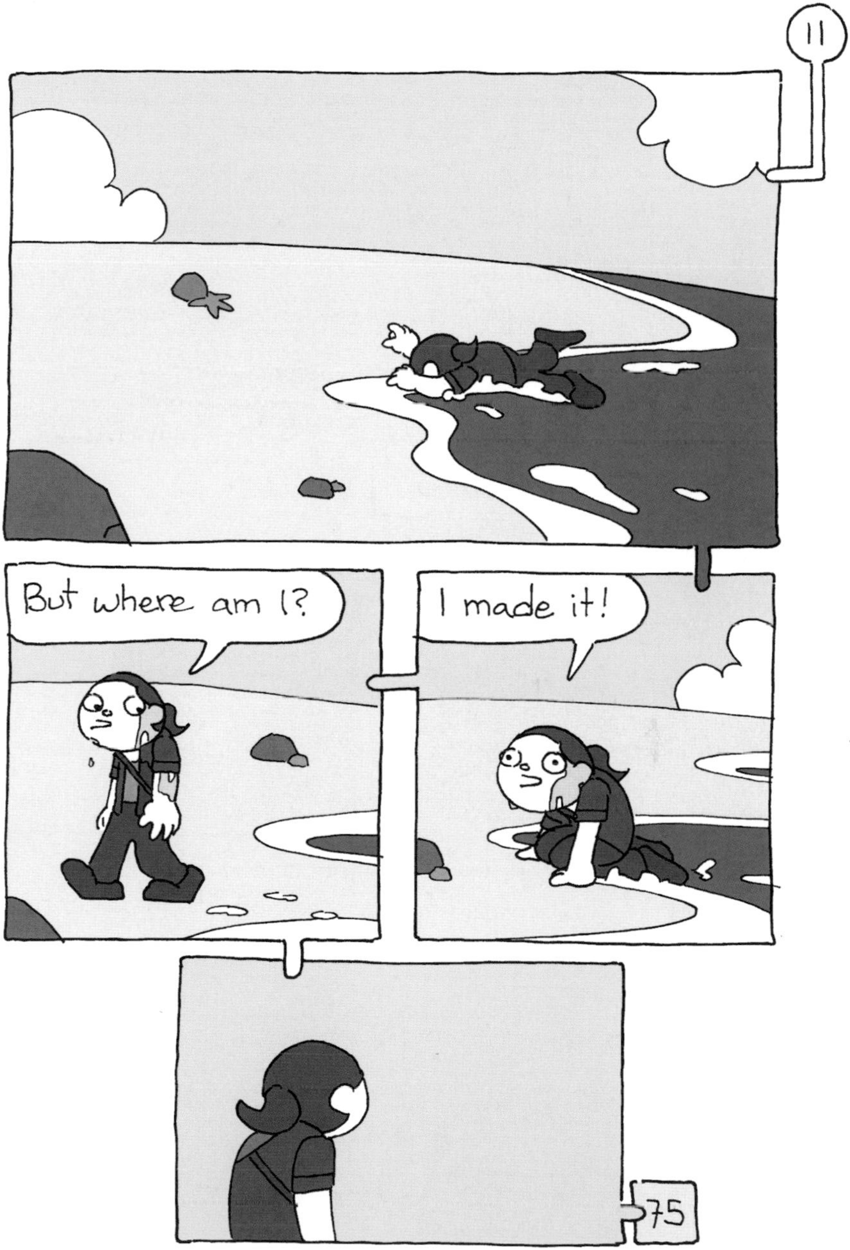
11
I made it!
But where am I?

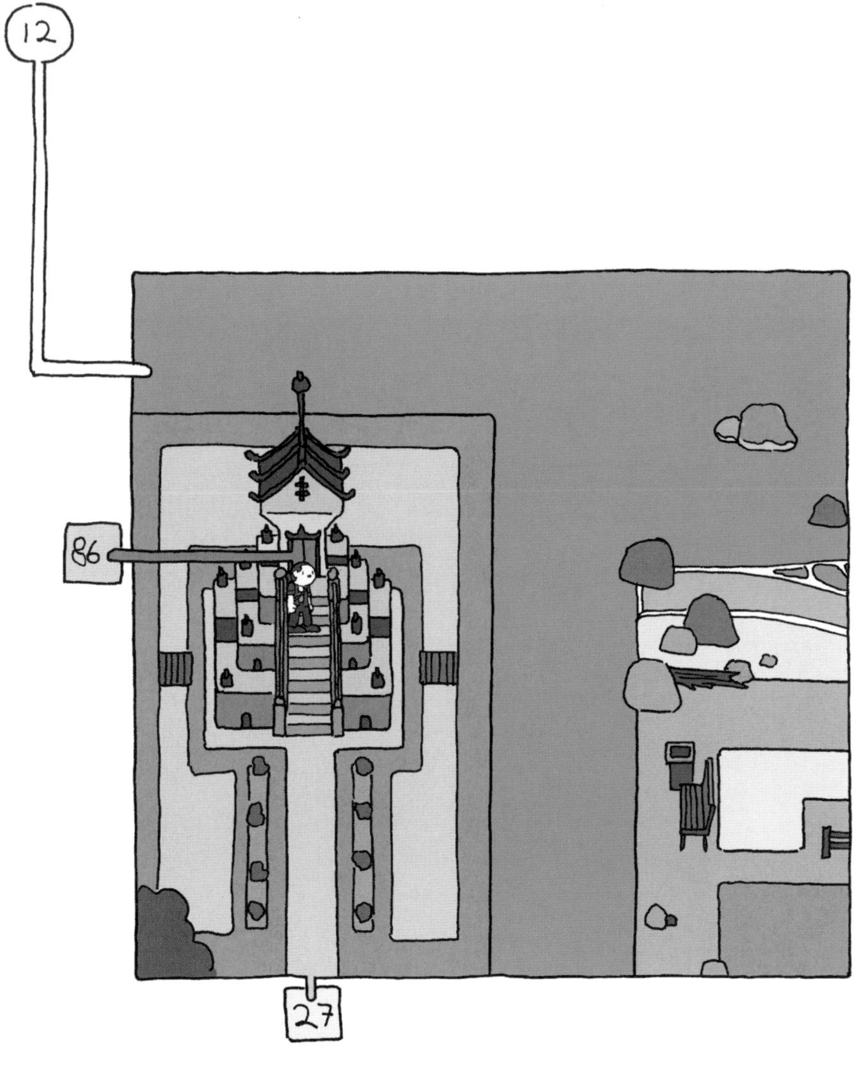
12
86
27

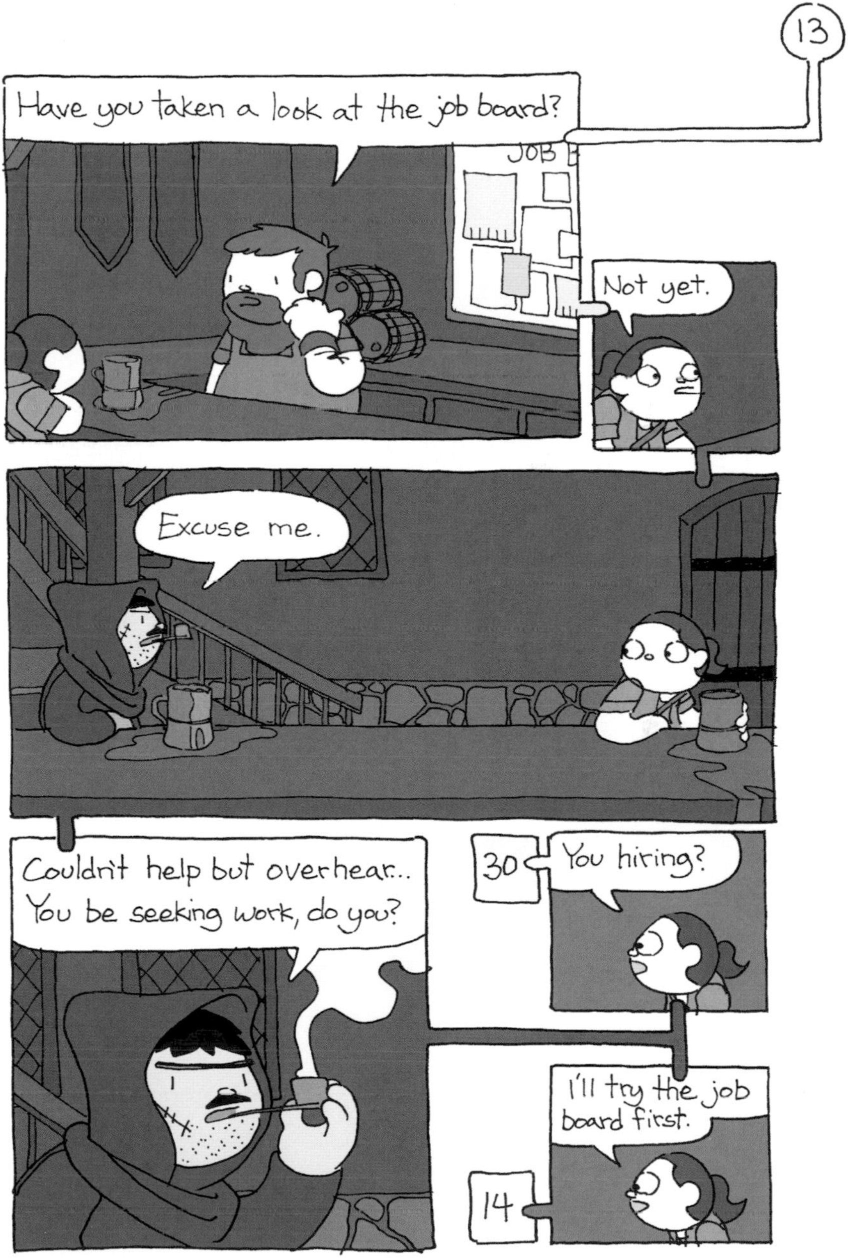
13
Have you taken a look at the job board?
JOB
Not yet.
Excuse me.
Couldn't help but overhear.. You be seeking work, do you?
30
You hiring?
I'll try the job board first.
14

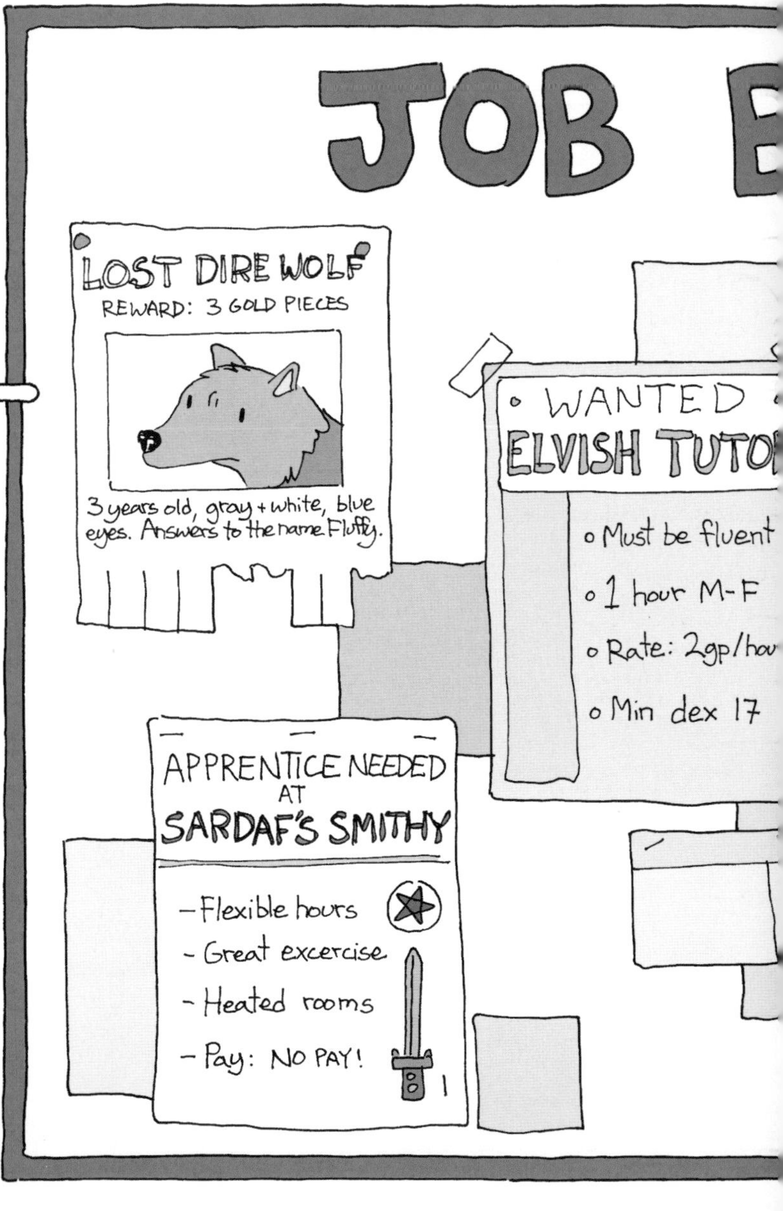
JOB B
LOST DIRE WOLF
REWARD: 3 GOLD PIECES
3 years old, gray + white, blue eyes. Answers to the name Fluffy.
• WANTED •
ELVISH TUTO
• Must be fluent
• 1 hour M-F
• Rate: 2gp/hou
• Min dex 17
APPRENTICE NEEDED AT
SARDAF'S SMITHY
– Flexible hours
– Great excercise
– Heated rooms
– Pay: NO PAY!

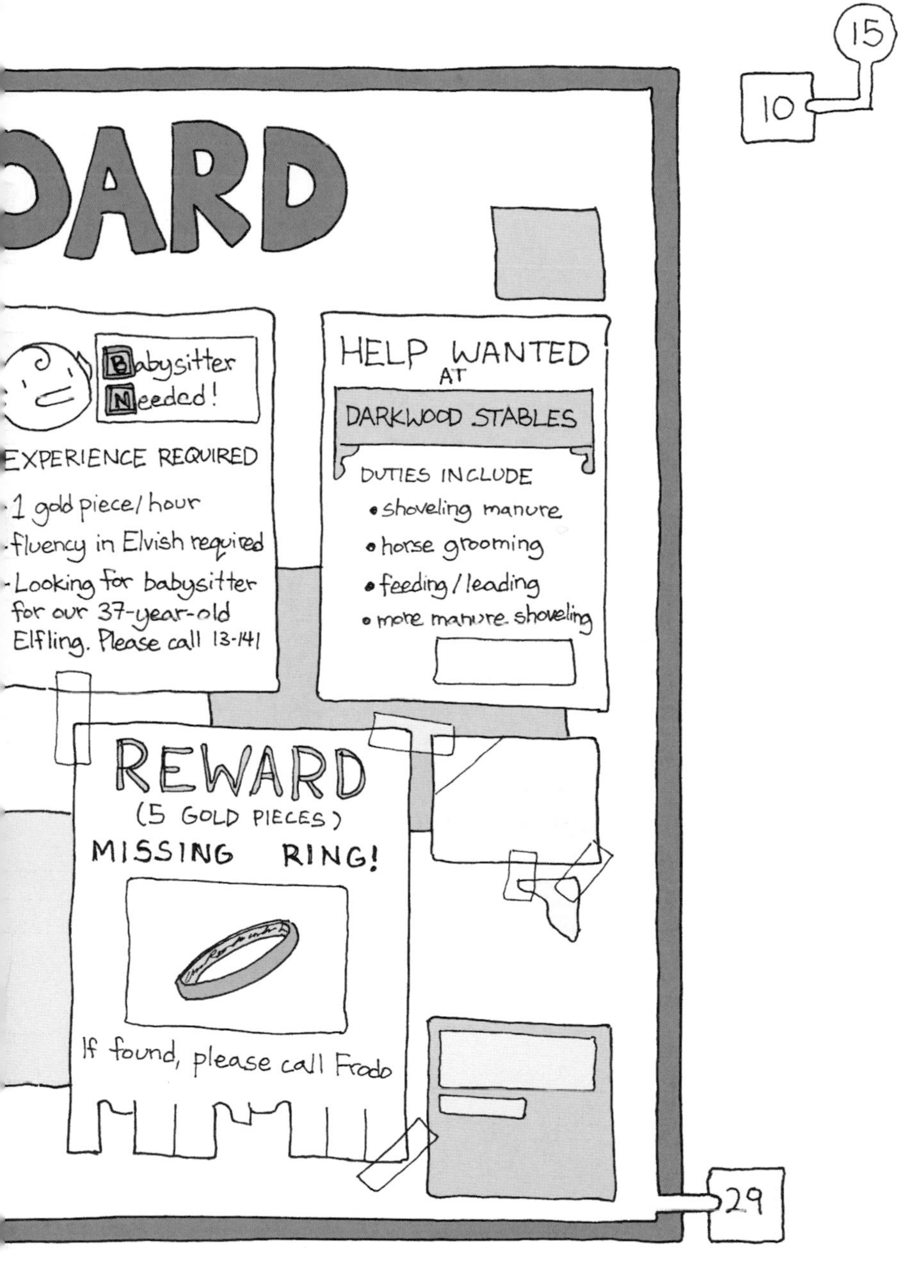
15
10
OARD
Babysitter Needed!
EXPERIENCE REQUIRED
·1 gold piece/hour
·fluency in Elvish required
·Looking for babysitter for our 37-year-old Elfling. Please call 13-141
HELP WANTED AT
DARKWOOD STABLES
DUTIES INCLUDE
• shoveling manure
• horse grooming
• feeding/leading
• more manure shoveling
REWARD
(5 GOLD PIECES)
MISSING RING!
If found, please call Frodo
29

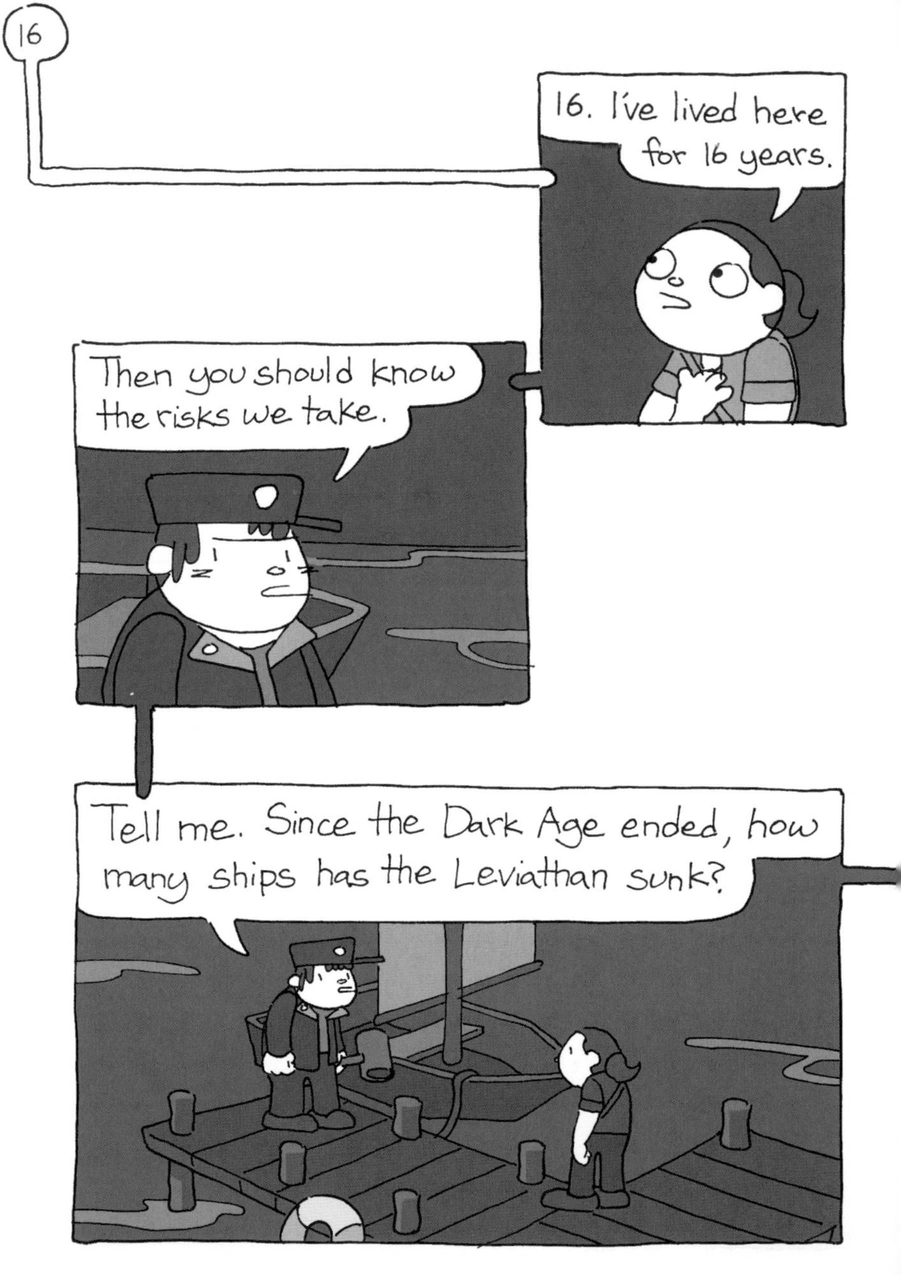
16
16. I've lived here for 16 years.
Then you should know the risks we take.
Tell me. Since the Dark Age ended, how many ships has the Leviathan sunk?

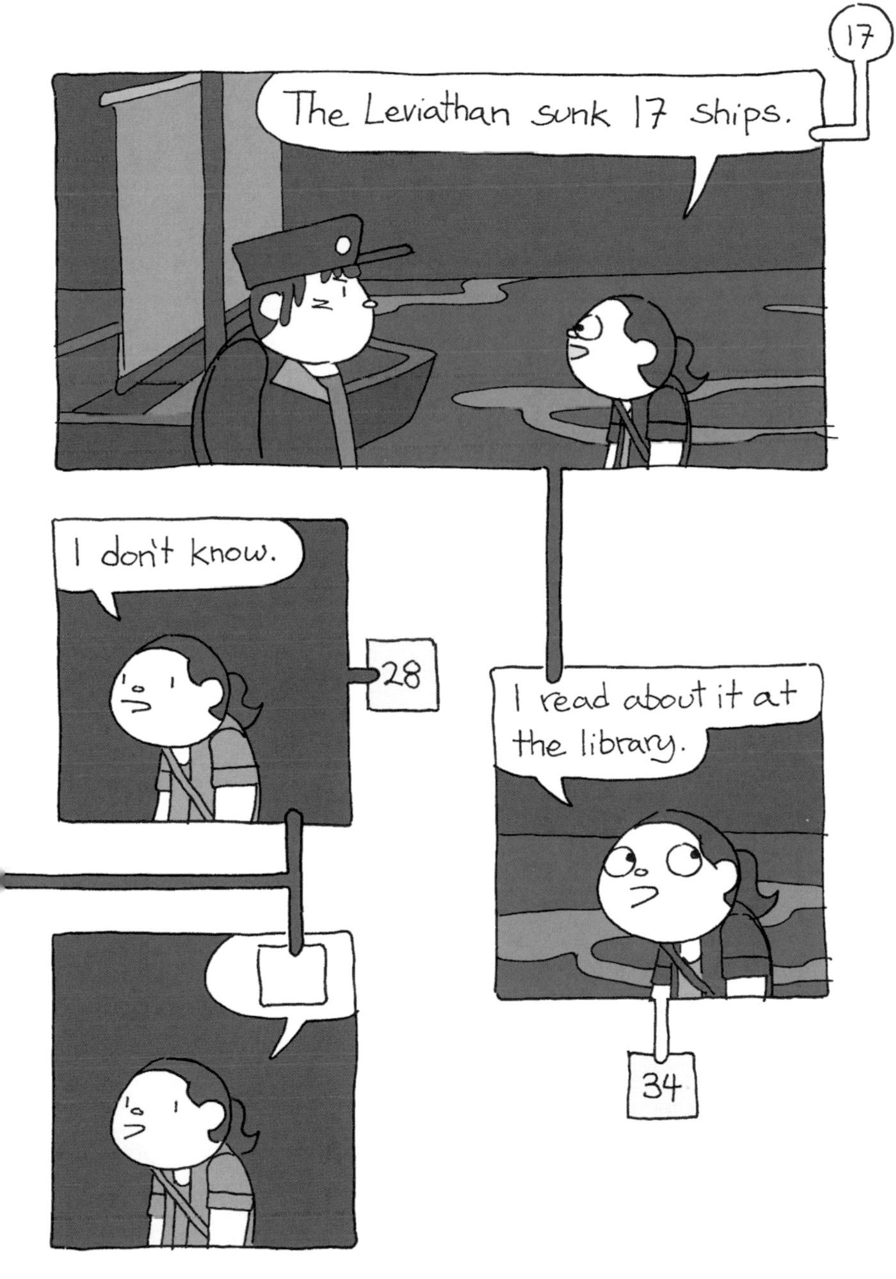
17
The Leviathan sunk 17 ships.
I don't know.
28
I read about it at the library.
34

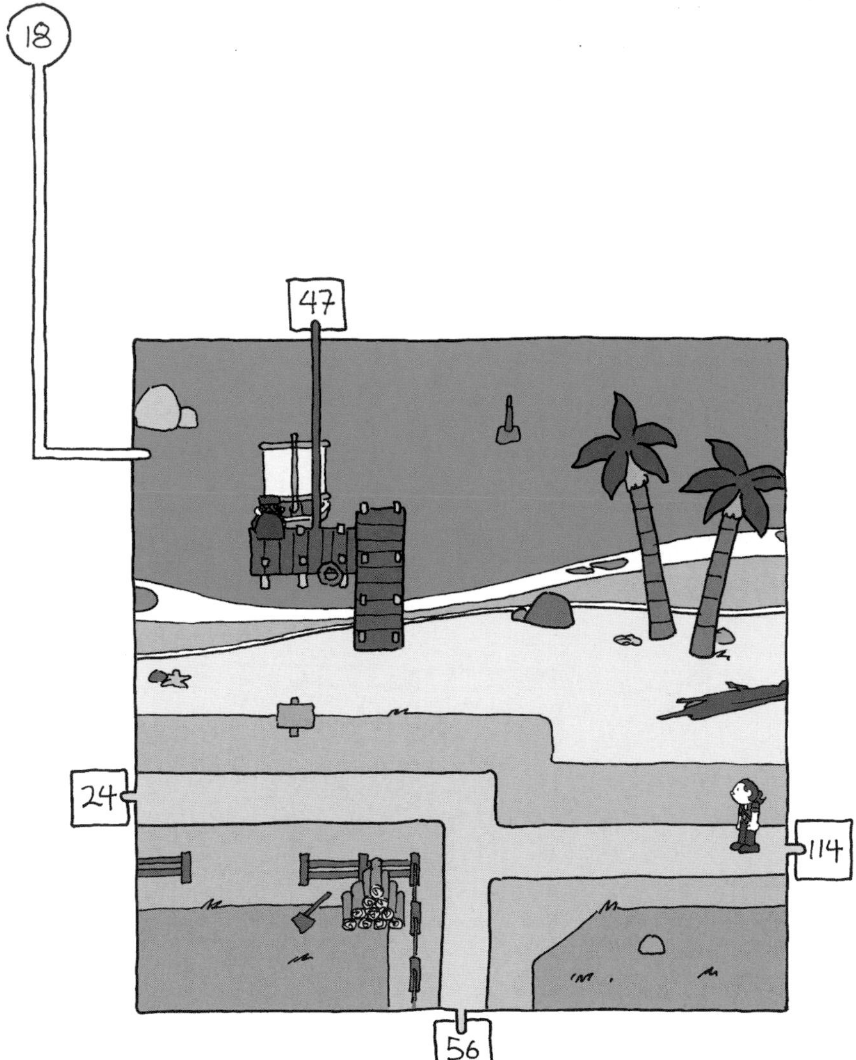
18
47
24
114
56

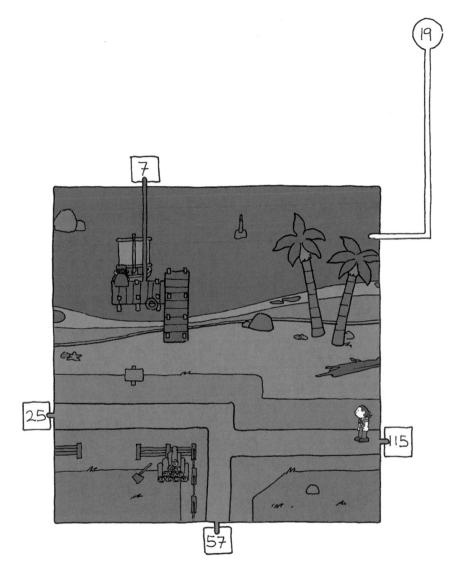

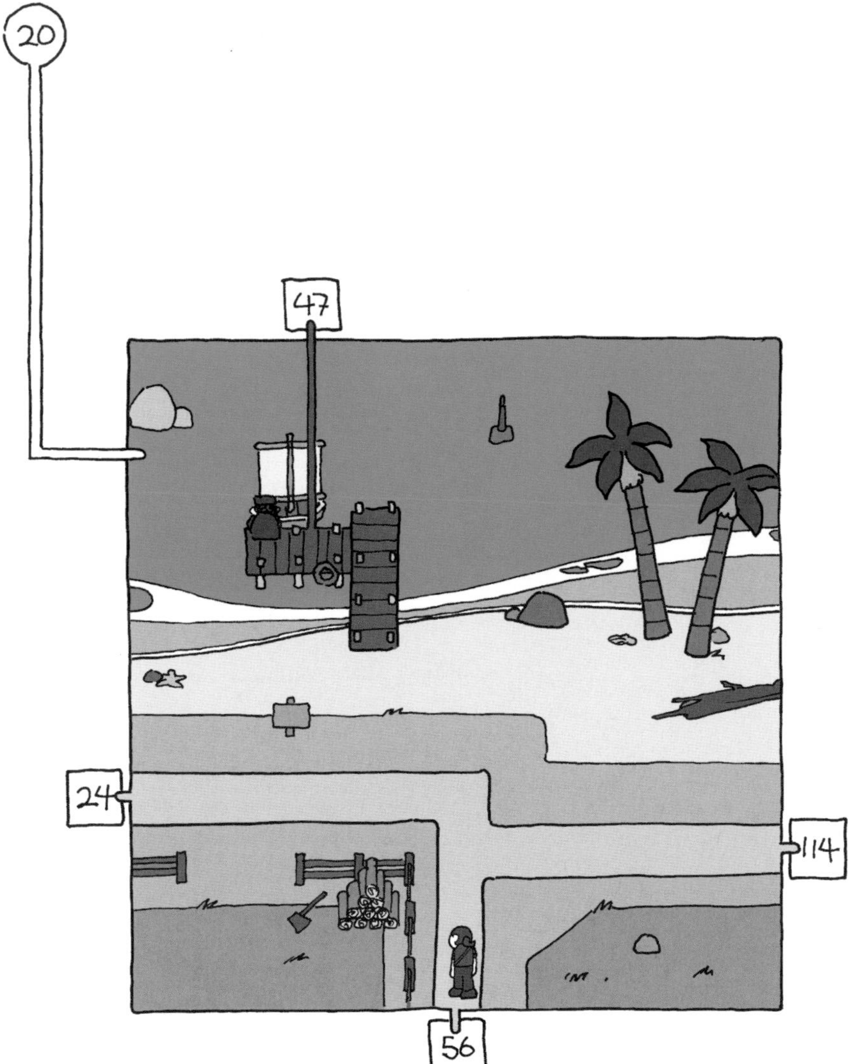
20
47
24
114
56

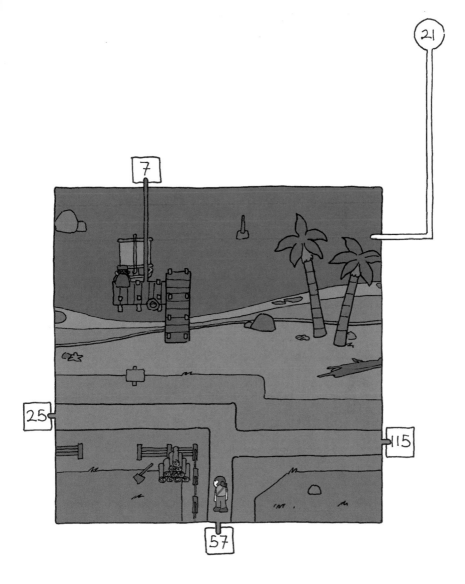

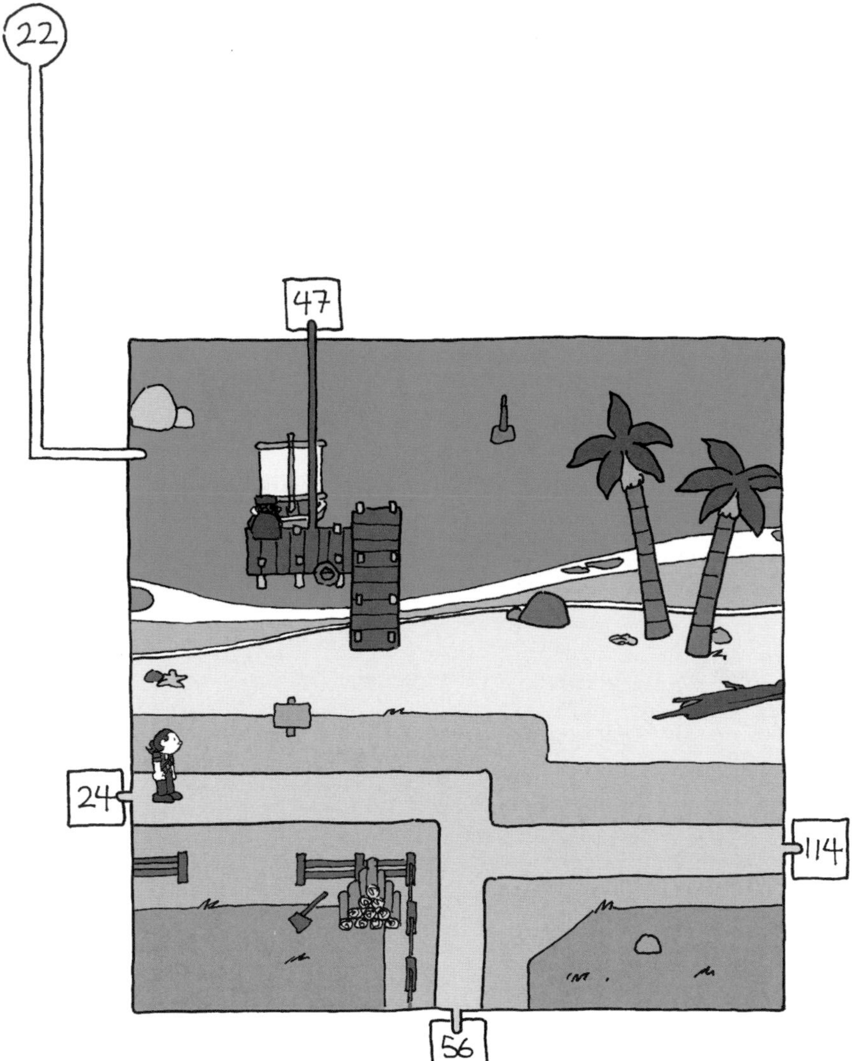
22
47
24
114
56

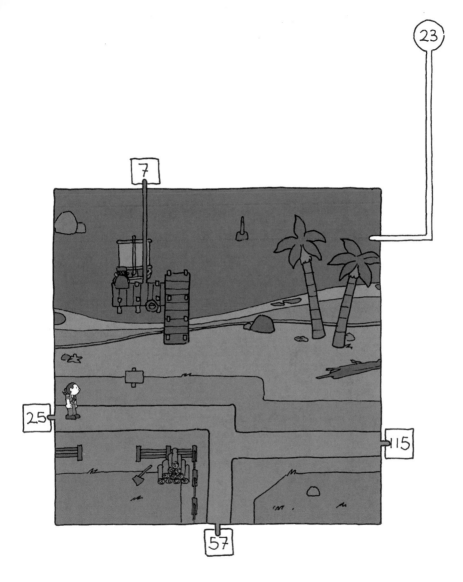

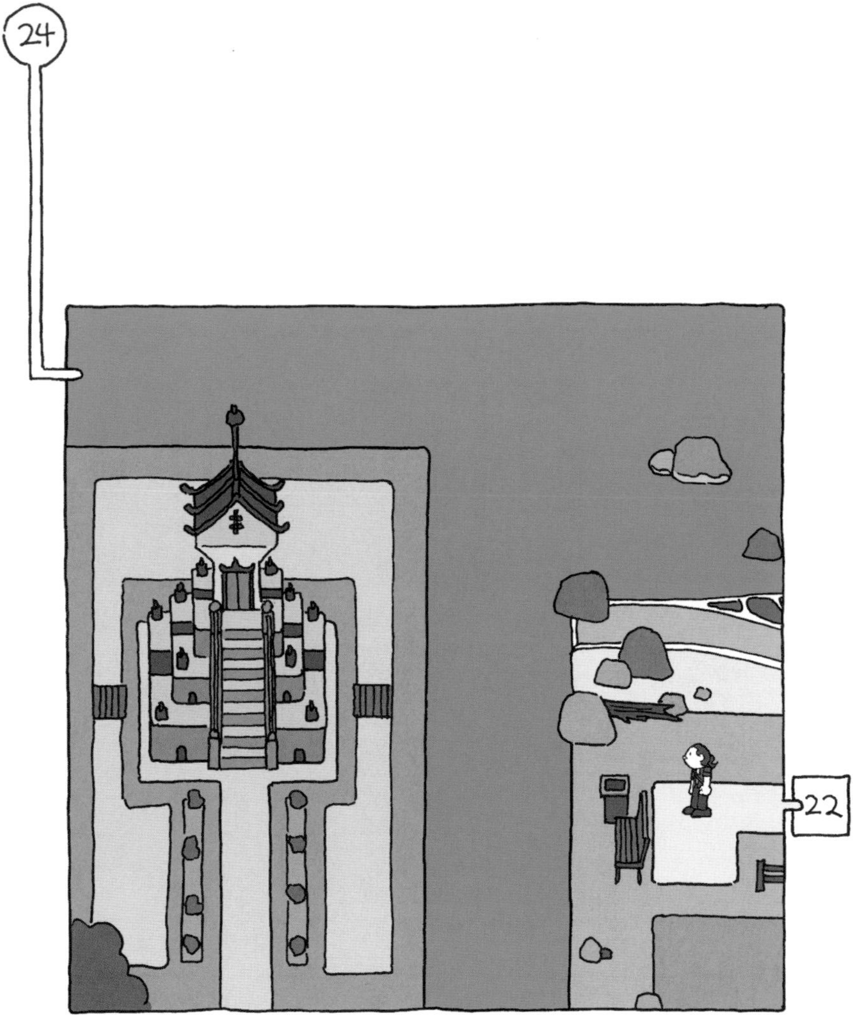
24
22

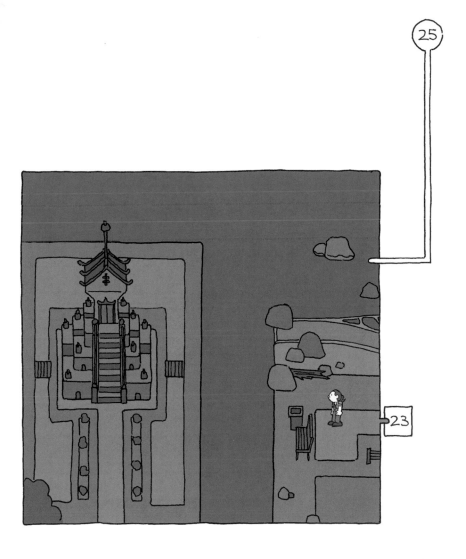

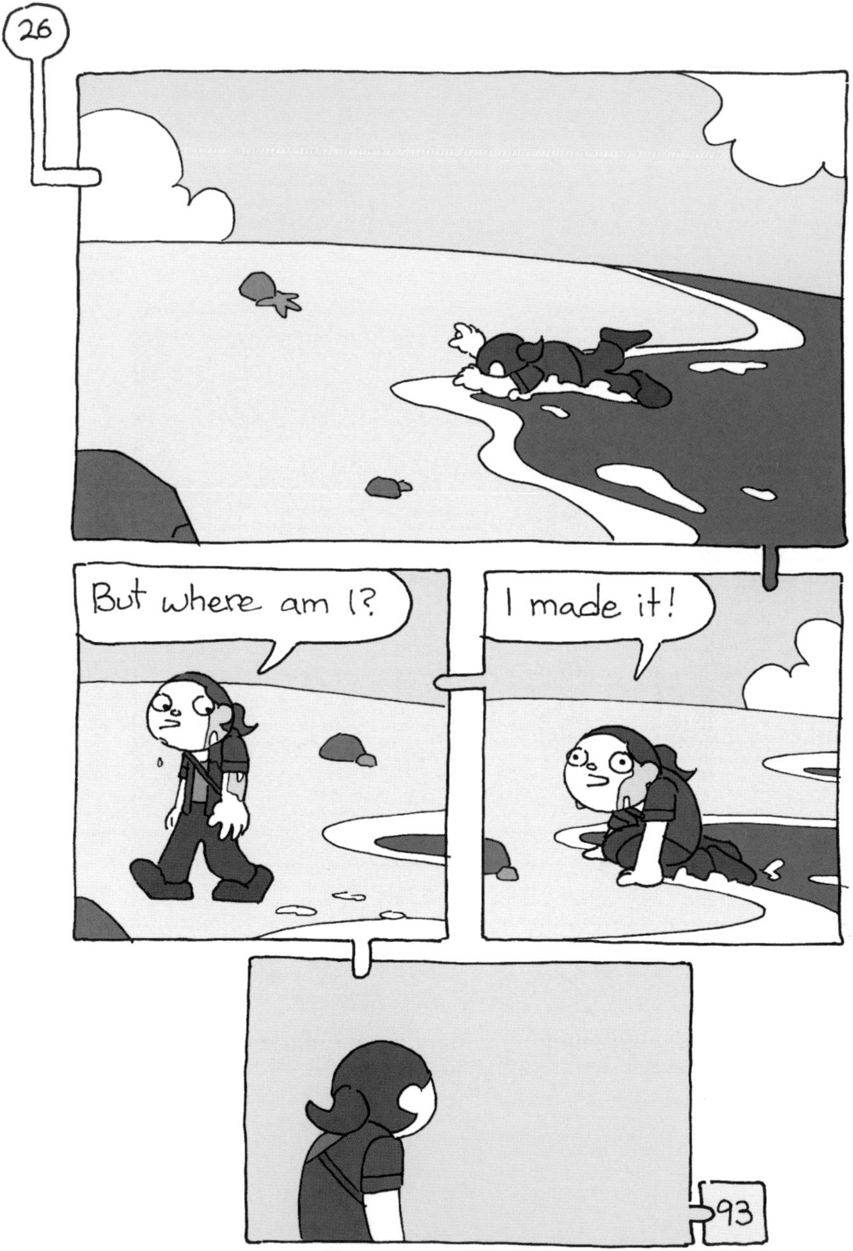
26
I made it!
But where am I?
93

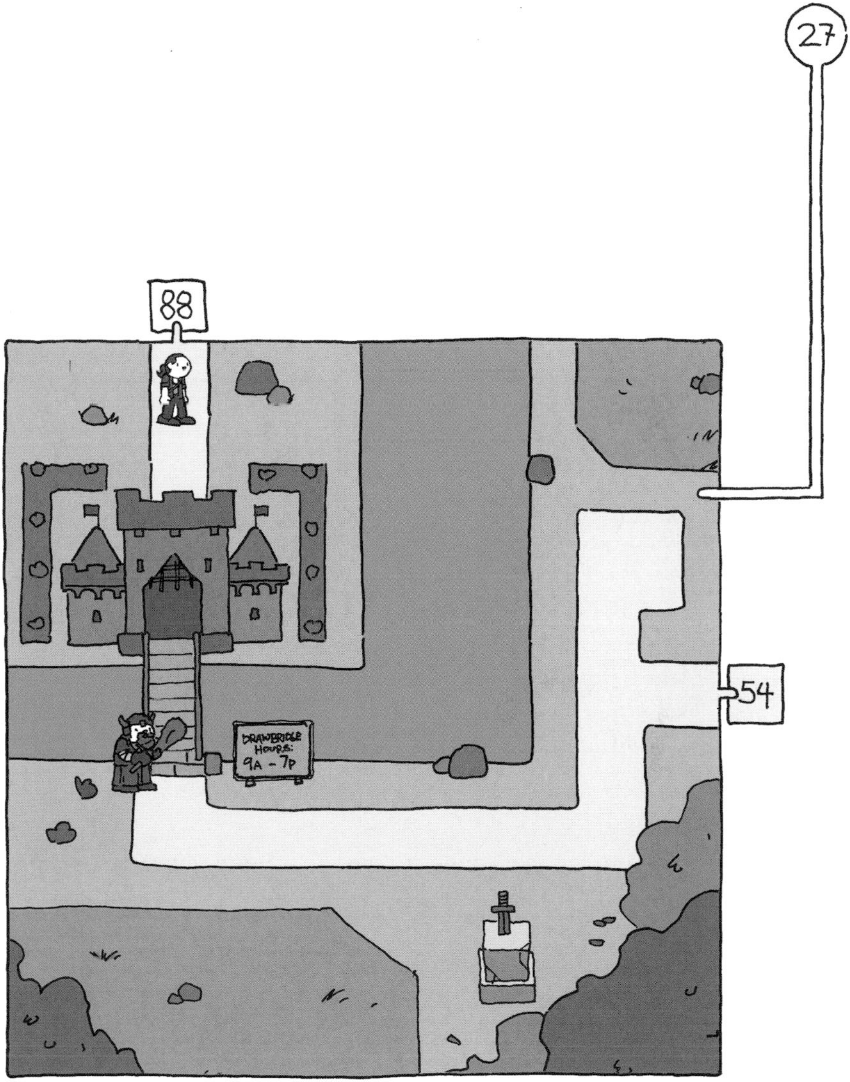
27
88
54
DRAWBRIDGE HOURS:
9A - 7P

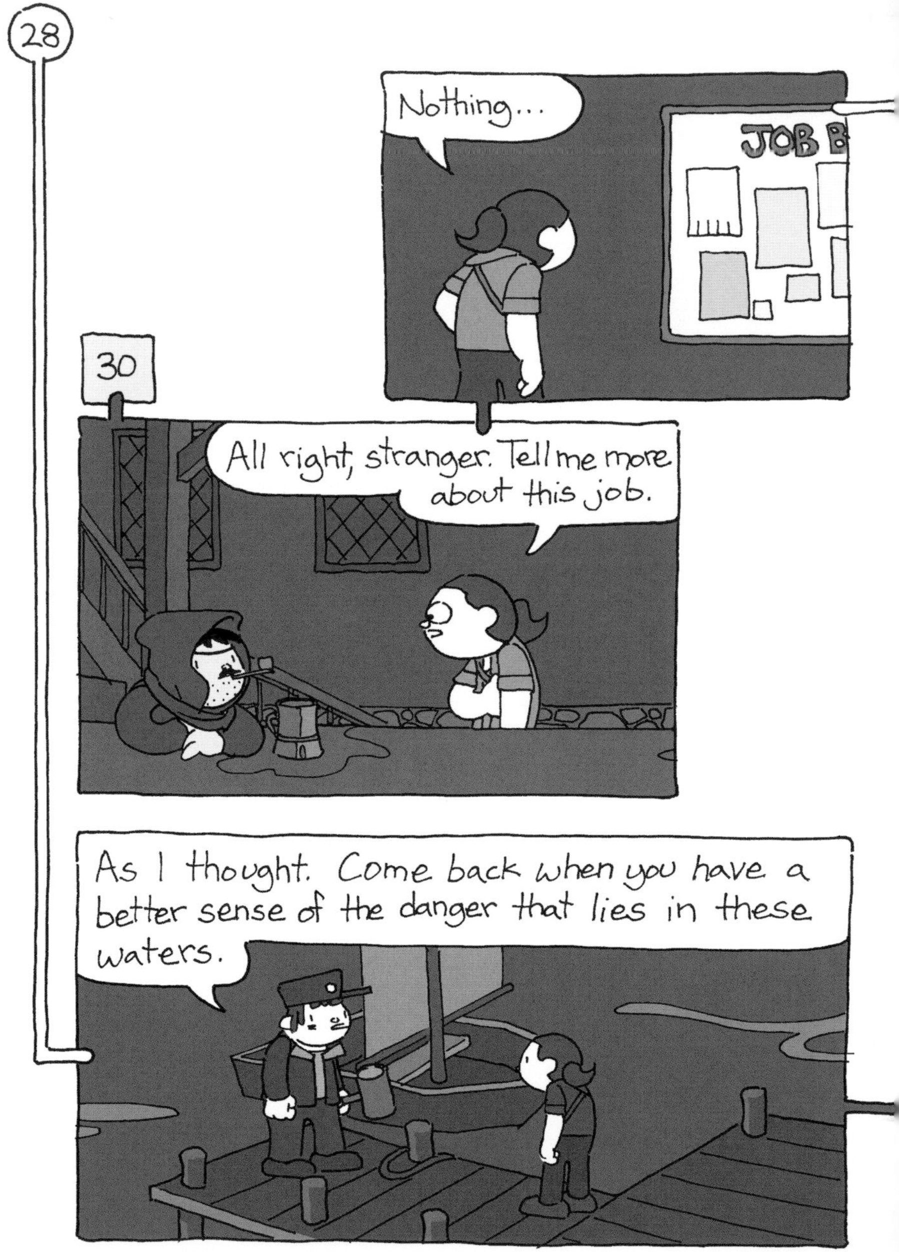
28
Nothing...
JOB B
30
All right, stranger. Tell me more about this job.
As I thought. Come back when you have a better sense of the danger that lies in these waters.

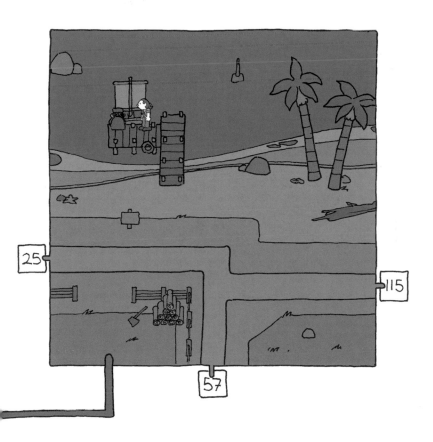

25

115

57

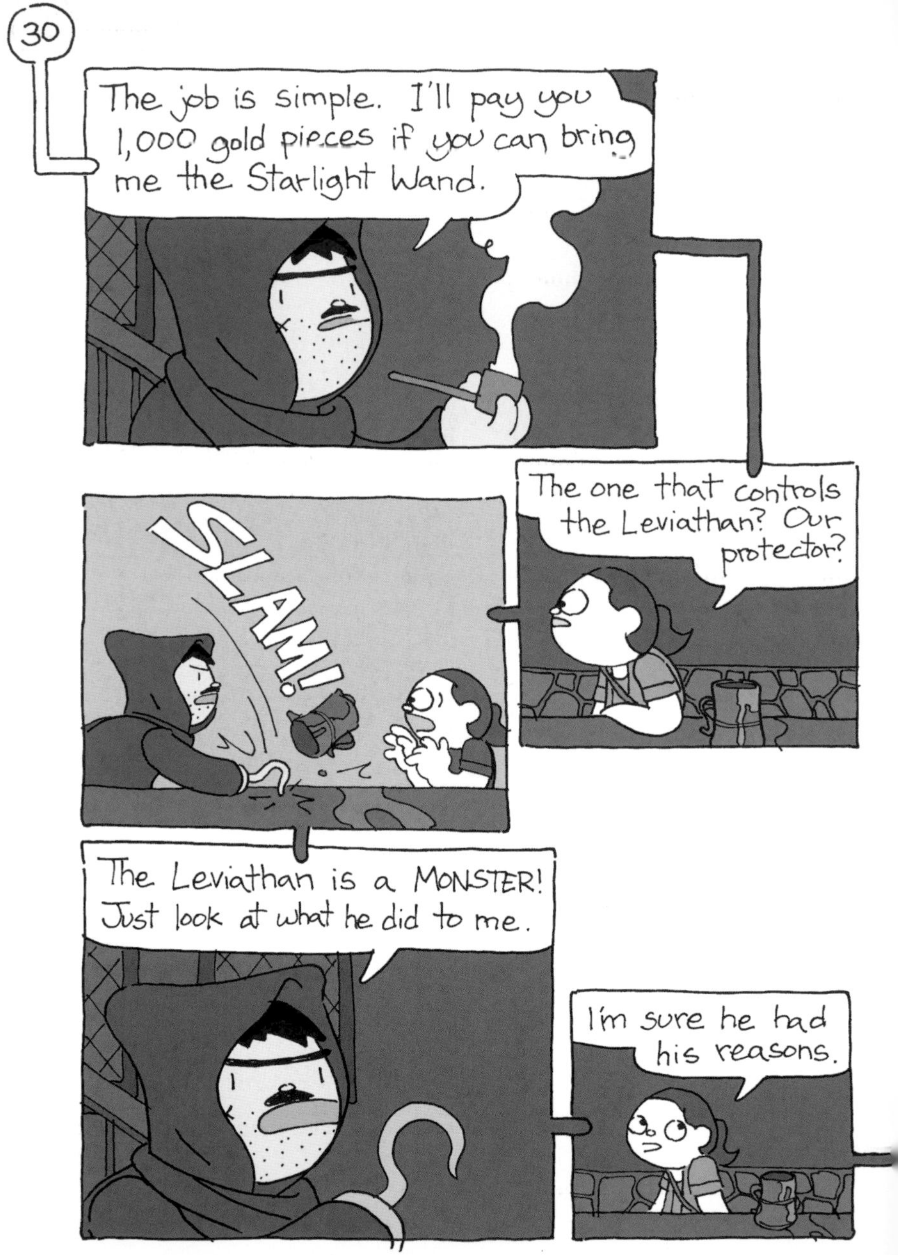
The job is simple. I'll pay you 1,000 gold pieces if you can bring me the Starlight Wand.
The one that controls the Leviathan? Our protector?
SLAM!
The Leviathan is a MONSTER! Just look at what he did to me.
I'm sure he had his reasons.

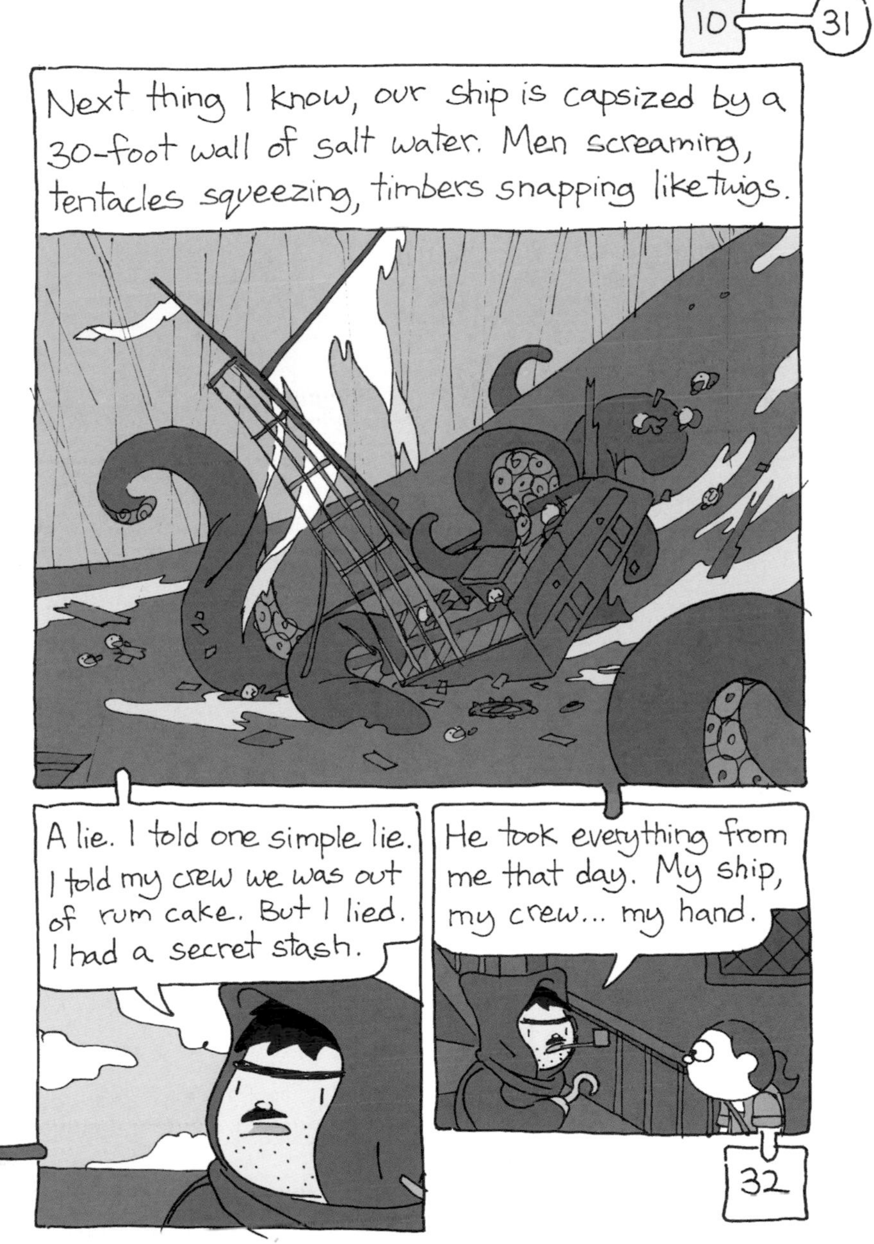
10
31
Next thing I know, our ship is capsized by a 30-foot wall of salt water. Men screaming, tentacles squeezing, timbers snapping like twigs.
A lie. I told one simple lie. I told my crew we was out of rum cake. But I lied. I had a secret stash.
He took everything from me that day. My ship, my crew... my hand.
32

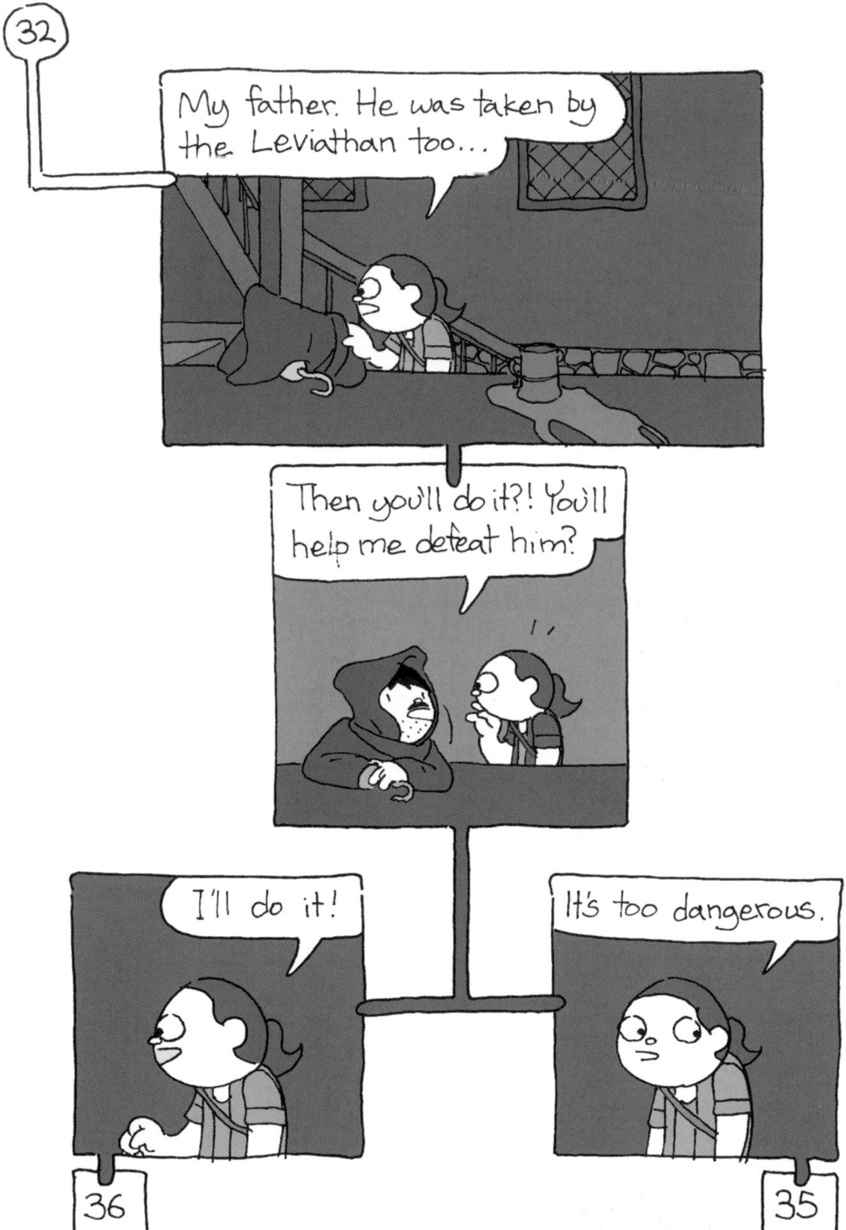
32
My father. He was taken by the Leviathan too...
Then you'll do it?! You'll help me defeat him?
I'll do it!
It's too dangerous.
36
35

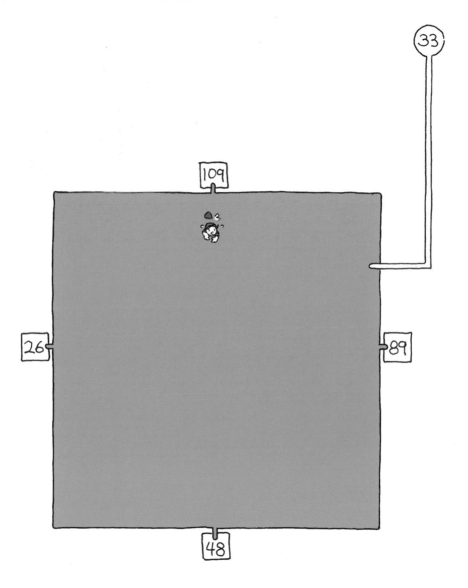

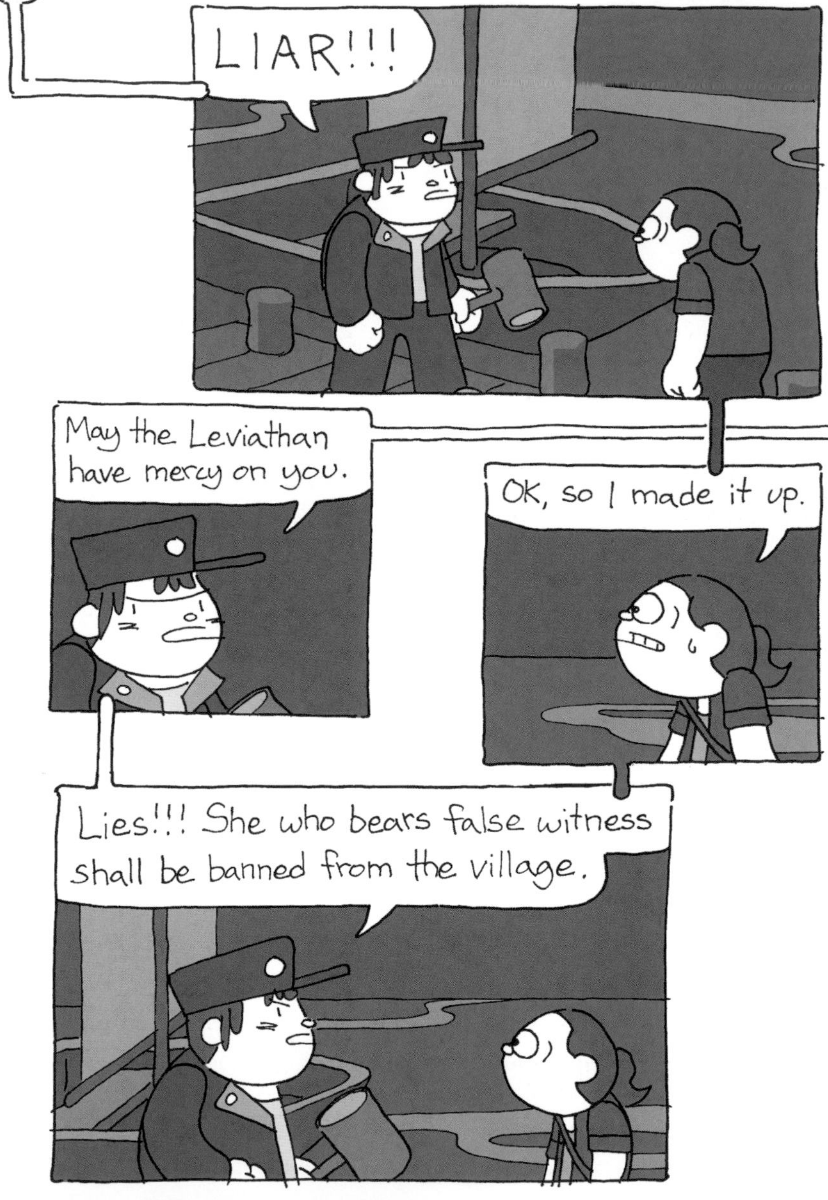
LIAR!!!
May the Leviathan have mercy on you.
OK, so I made it up.
Lies!!! She who bears false witness shall be banned from the village.

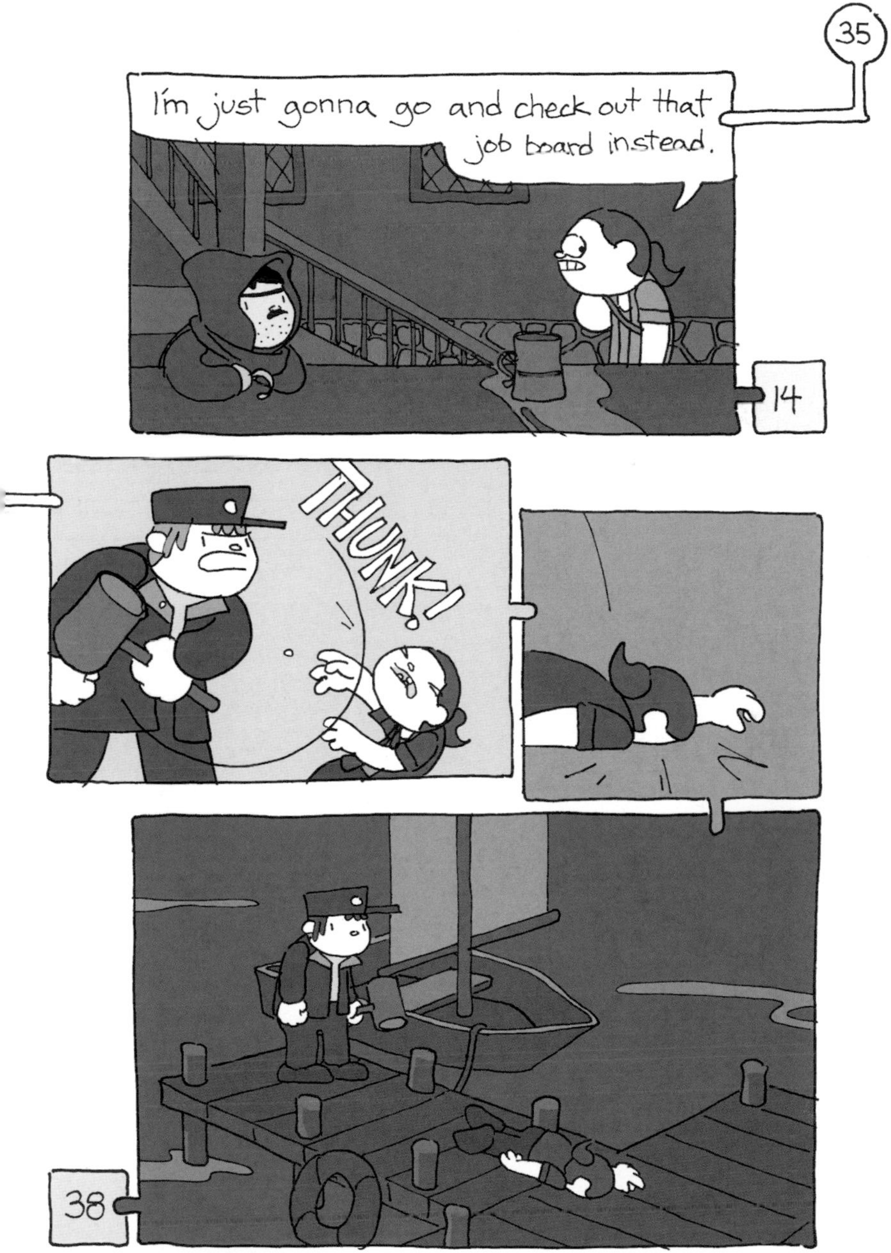
35
I'm just gonna go and check out that job board instead.
14
THUNK!
38

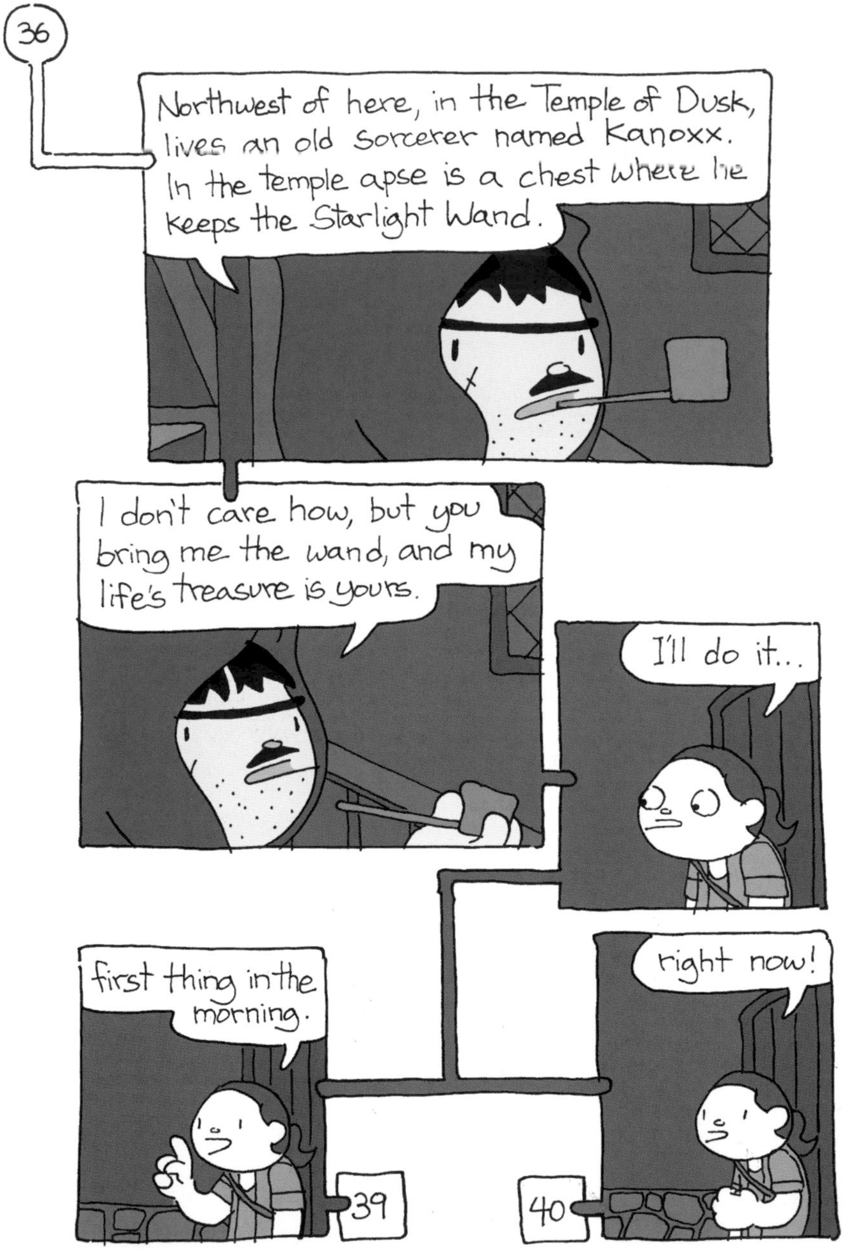
36
Northwest of here, in the Temple of Dusk, lives an old sorcerer named Kanoxx. In the temple apse is a chest where he keeps the Starlight Wand.
I don't care how, but you bring me the wand, and my life's treasure is yours.
I'll do it...
first thing in the morning.
39
right now!
40

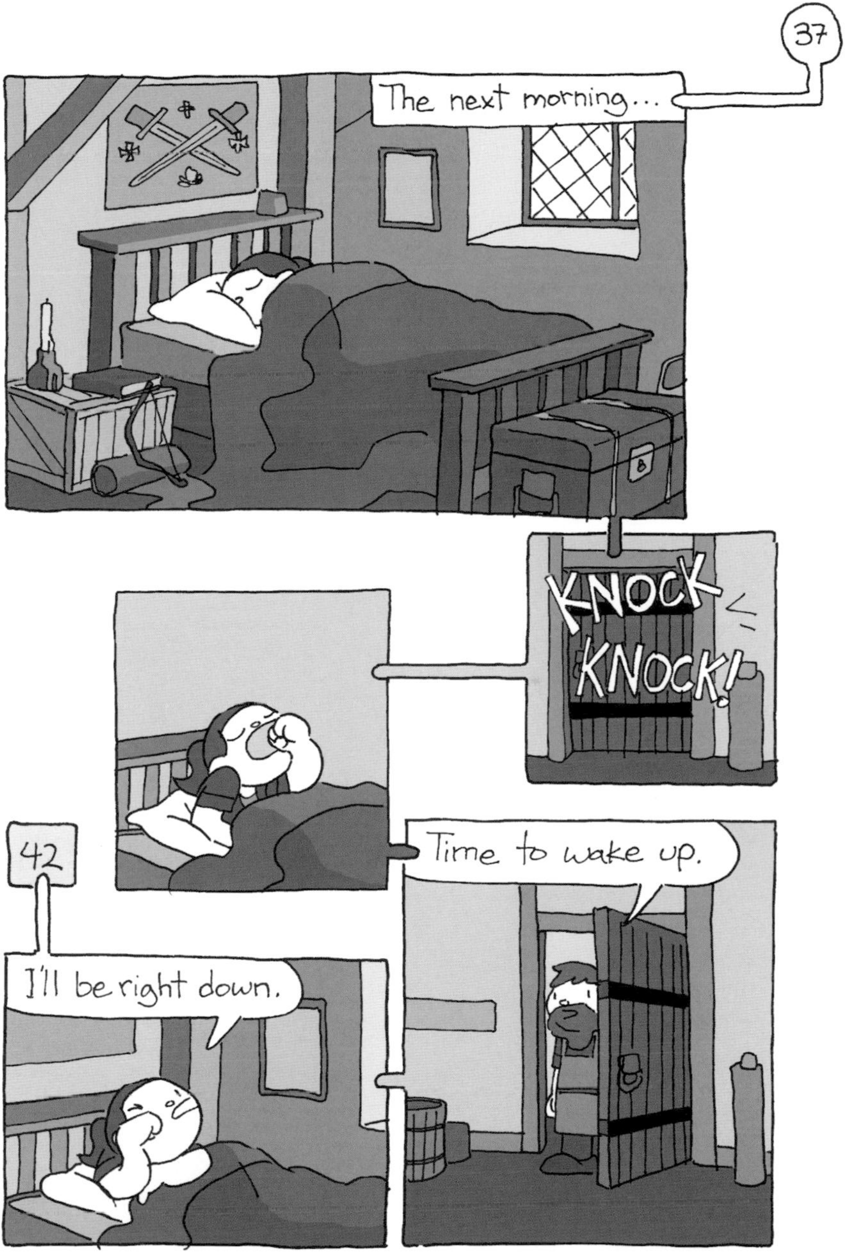
37
The next morning...
KNOCK
KNOCK!
Time to wake up.
42
I'll be right down.

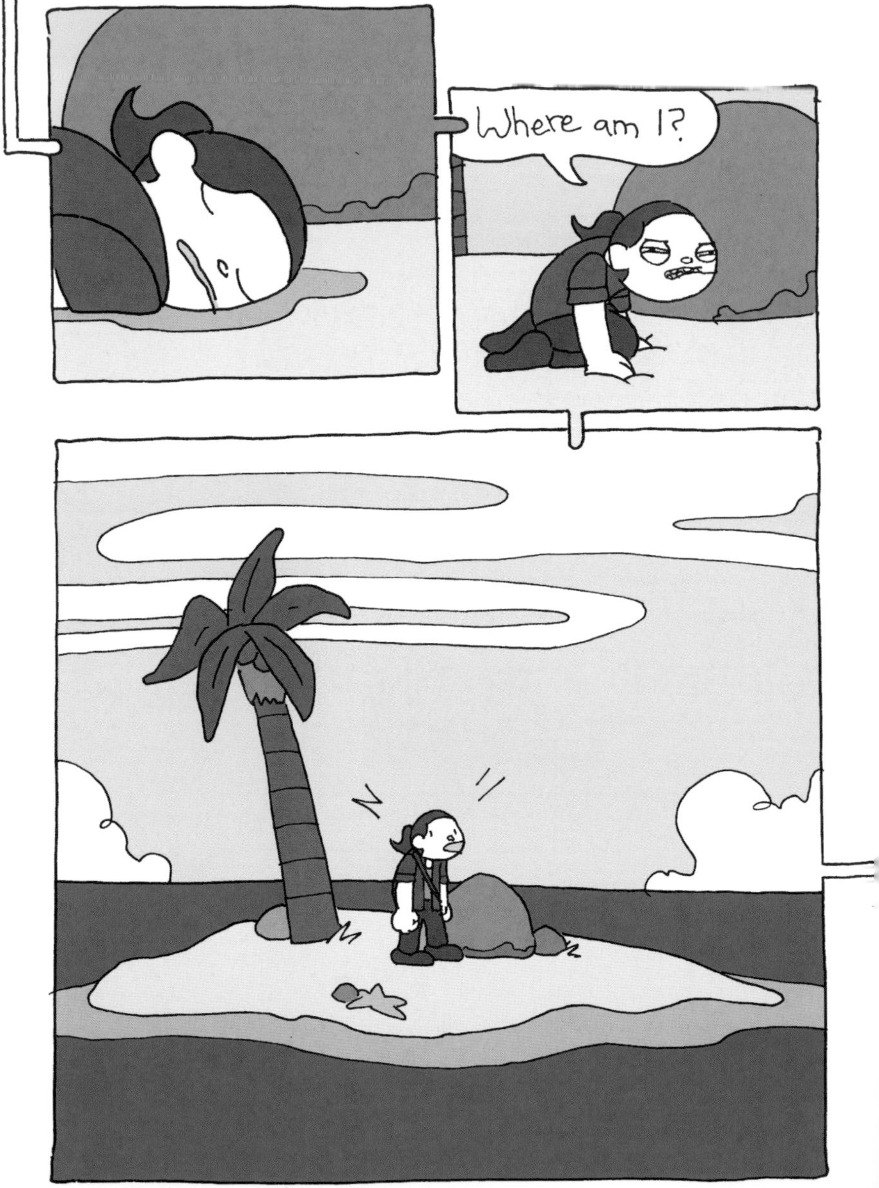
Where am I?

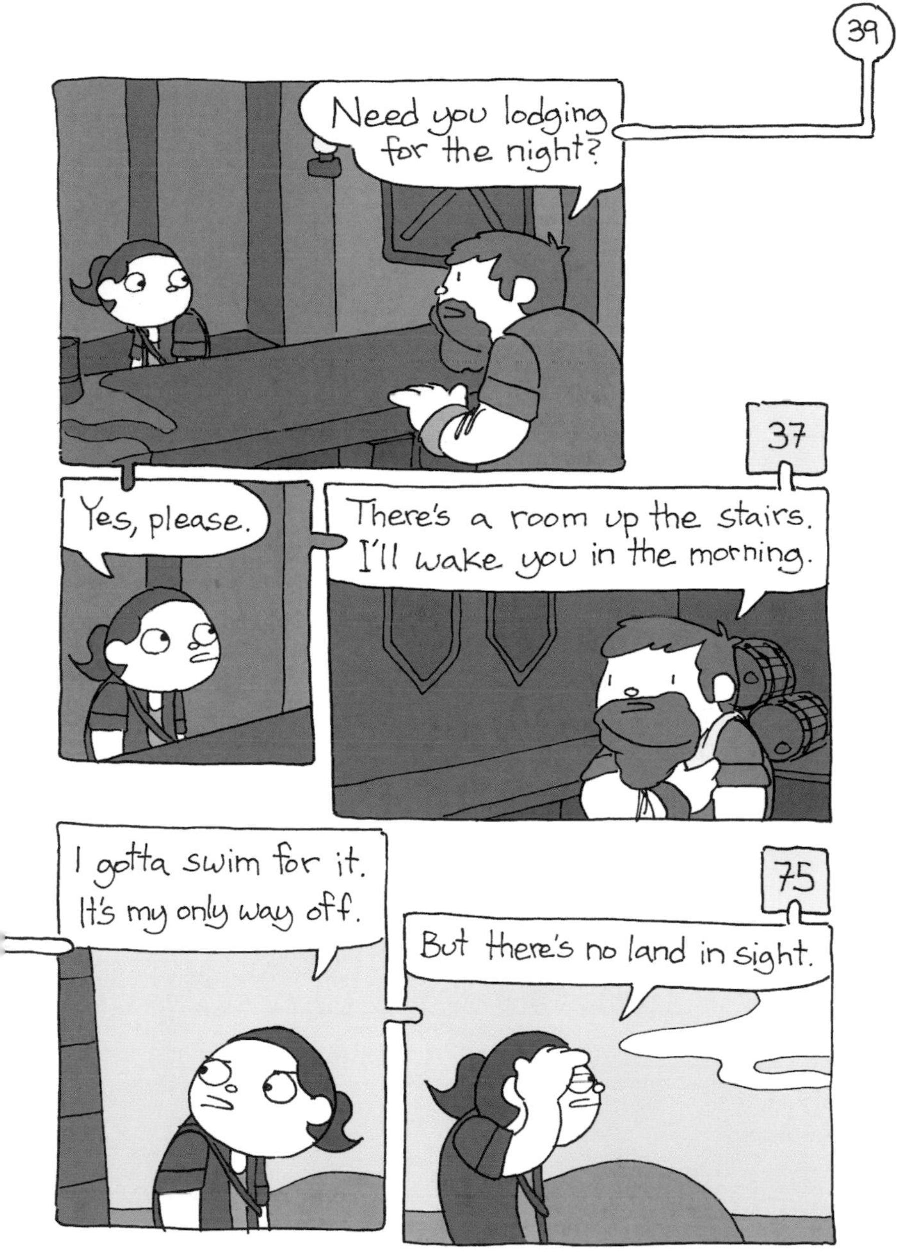
39
Need you lodging for the night?
Yes, please.
37
There's a room up the stairs. I'll wake you in the morning.
I gotta swim for it. It's my only way off.
75
But there's no land in sight.

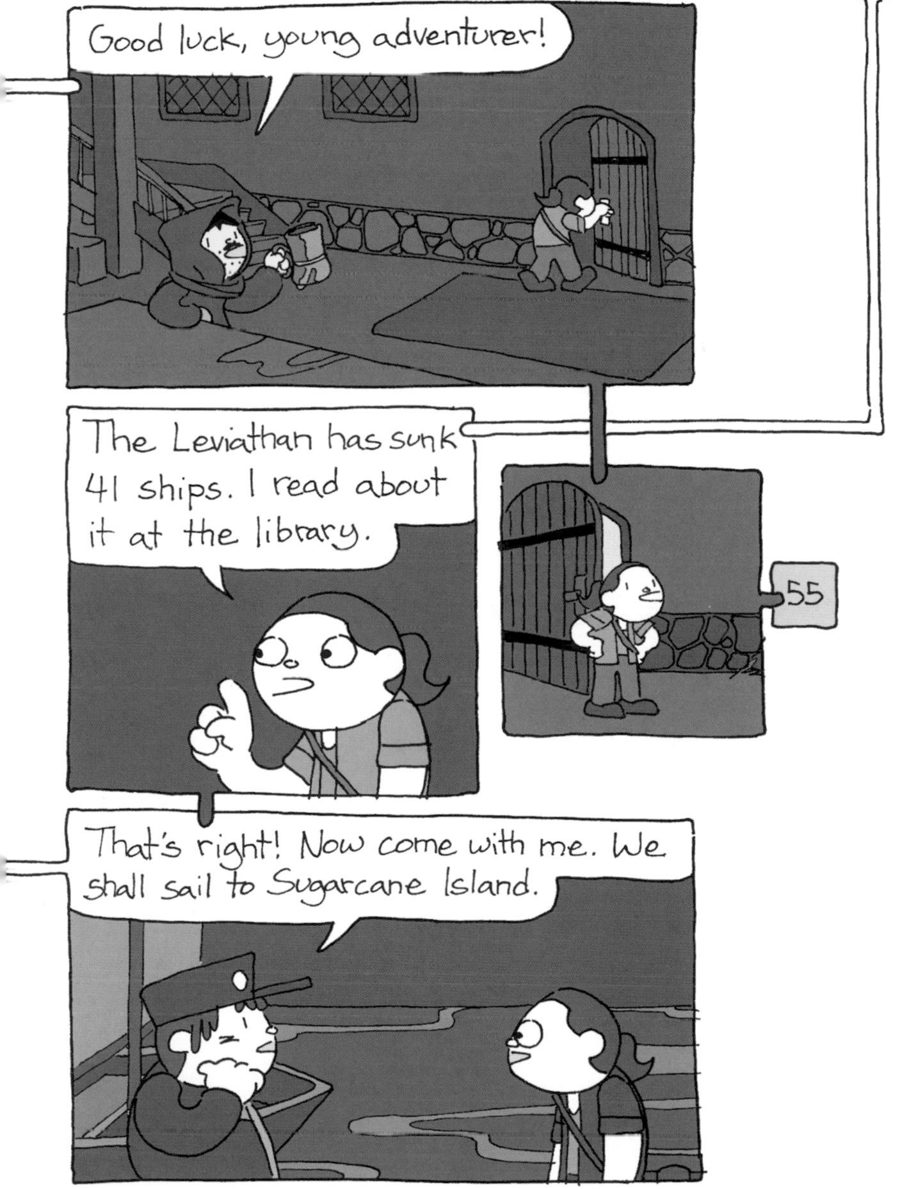
Good luck, young adventurer!
The Leviathan has sunk 41 ships. I read about it at the library.
55
That's right! Now come with me. We shall sail to Sugarcane Island.

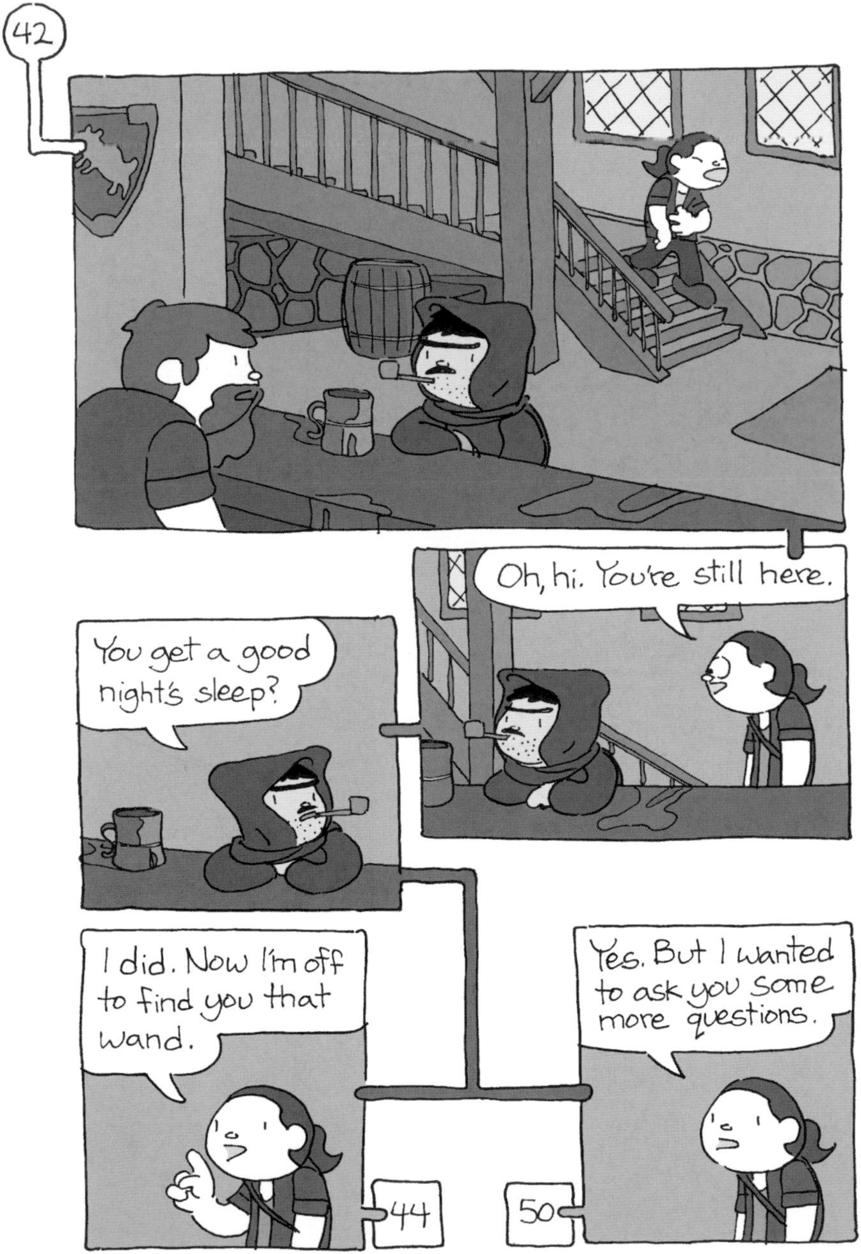
42
Oh, hi. You're still here.
You get a good night's sleep?
I did. Now I'm off to find you that wand.
44
Yes. But I wanted to ask you some more questions.
50

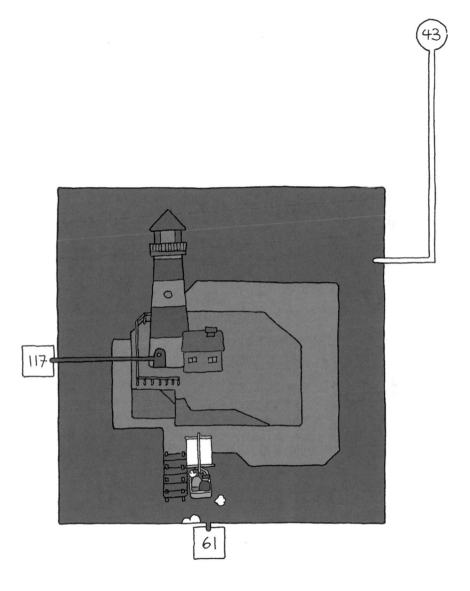

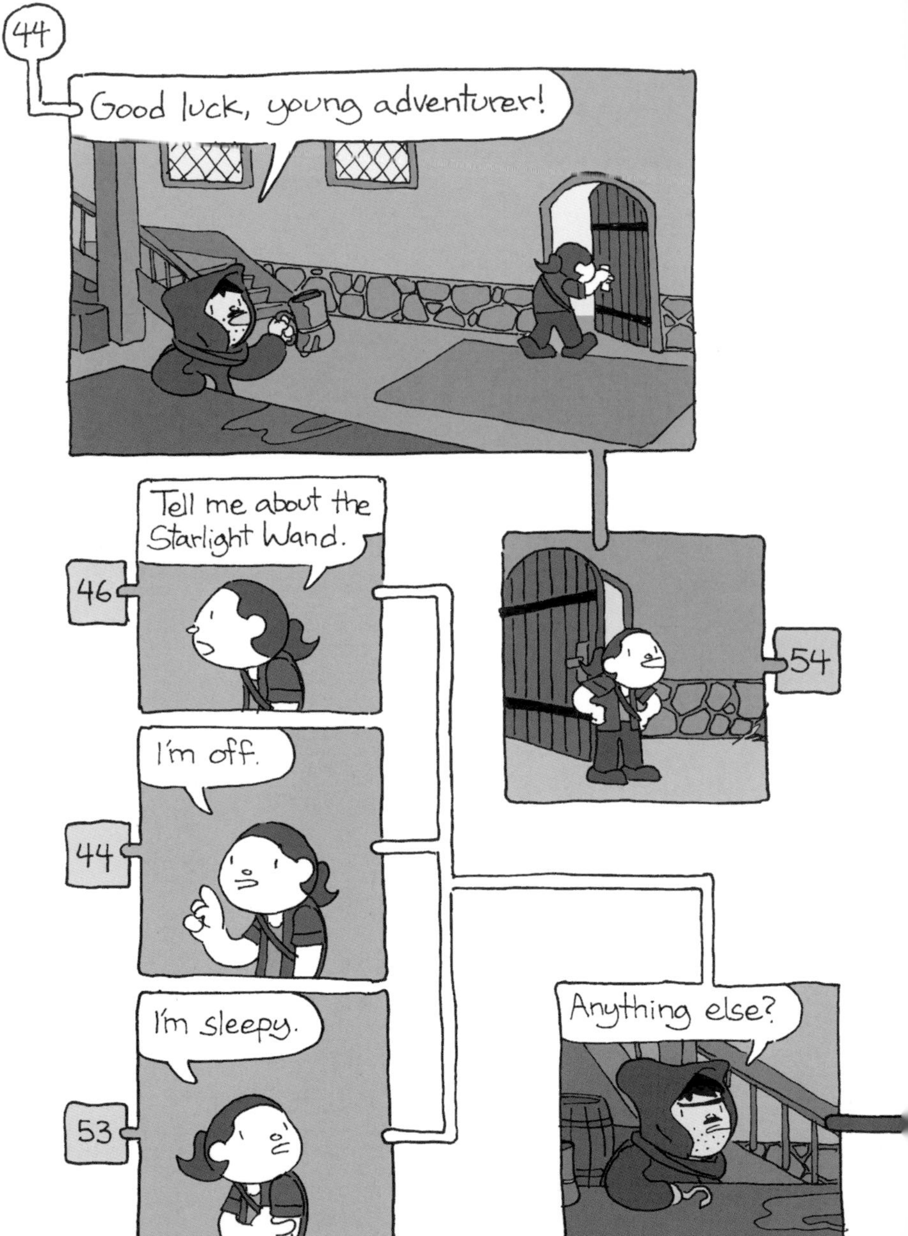
44
Good luck, young adventurer!
54
Tell me about the Starlight Wand.
46
I'm off.
44
I'm sleepy.
53
Anything else?

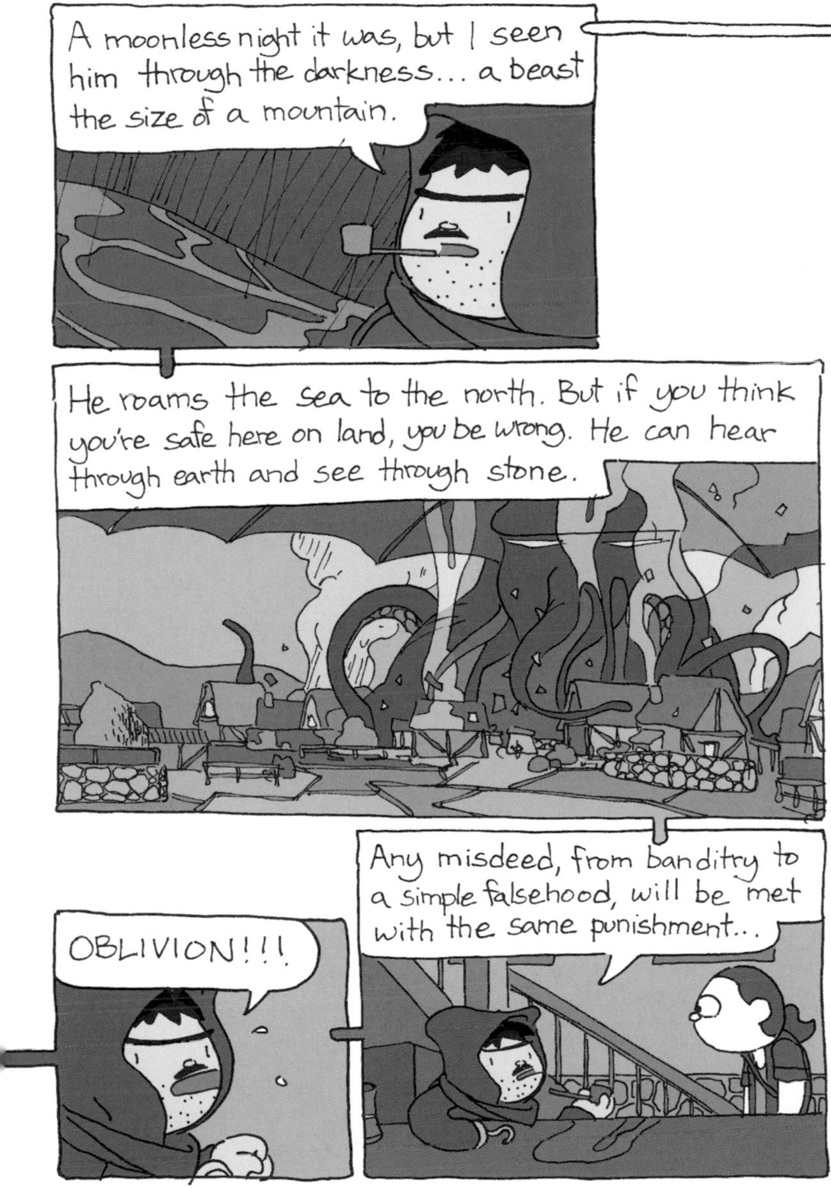
A moonless night it was, but I seen him through the darkness... a beast the size of a mountain.
He roams the sea to the north. But if you think you're safe here on land, you be wrong. He can hear through earth and see through stone.
Any misdeed, from banditry to a simple falsehood, will be met with the same punishment...
OBLIVION!!!

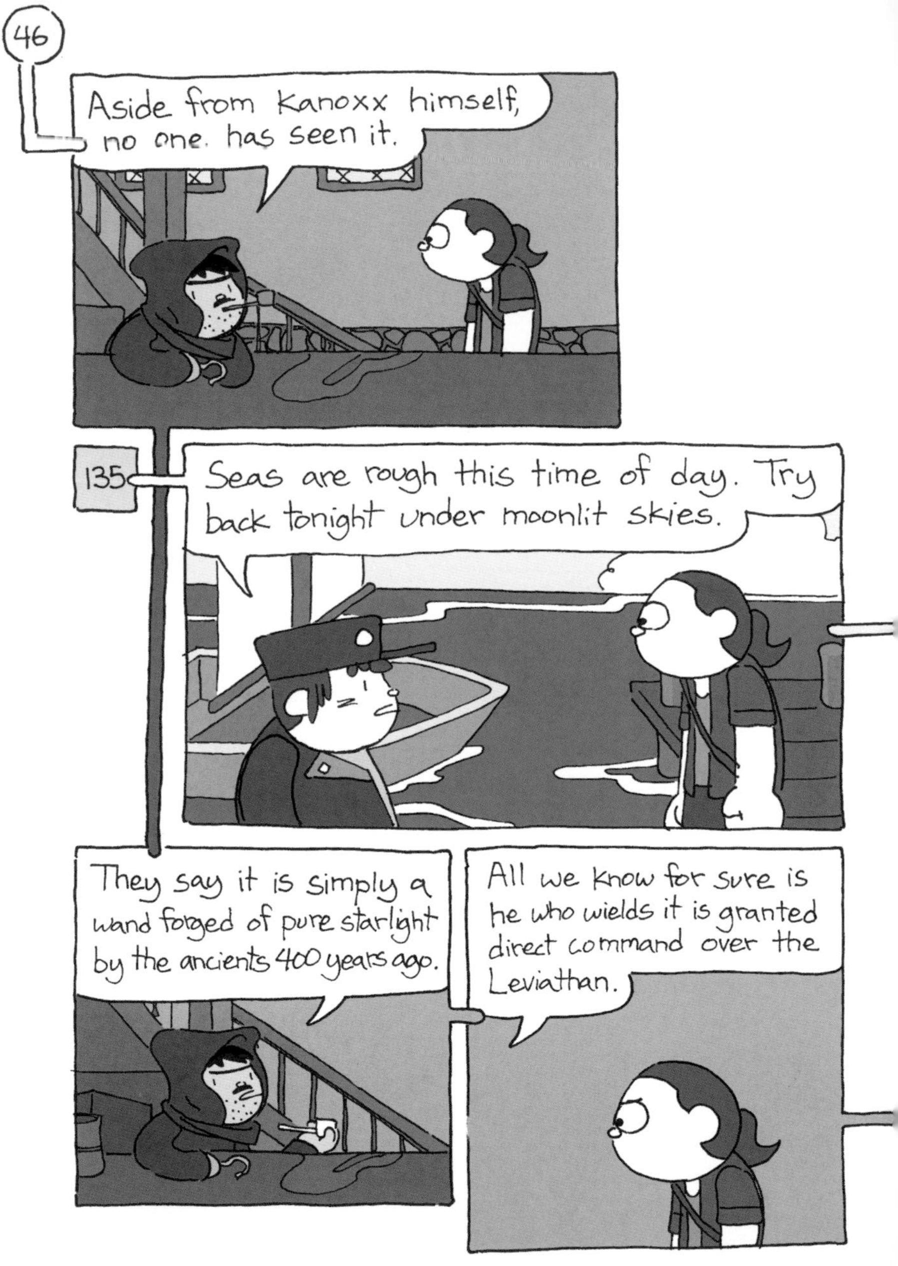
46
Aside from Kanoxx himself, no one has seen it.
135
Seas are rough this time of day. Try back tonight under moonlit skies.
They say it is simply a wand forged of pure starlight by the ancients 400 years ago.
All we know for sure is he who wields it is granted direct command over the Leviathan.

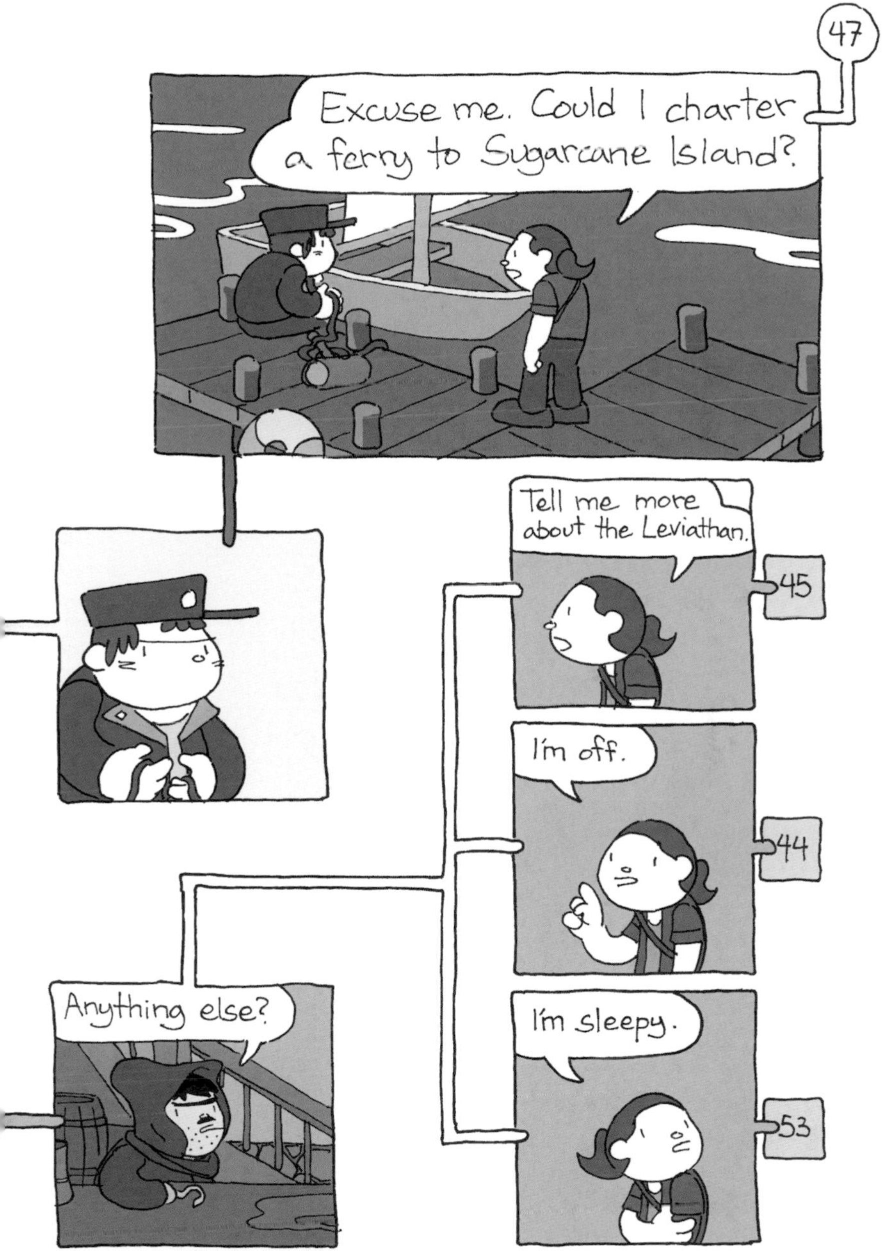
47
Excuse me. Could I charter a ferry to Sugarcane Island?
Anything else?
Tell me more about the Leviathan.
45
I'm off.
44
I'm sleepy.
53

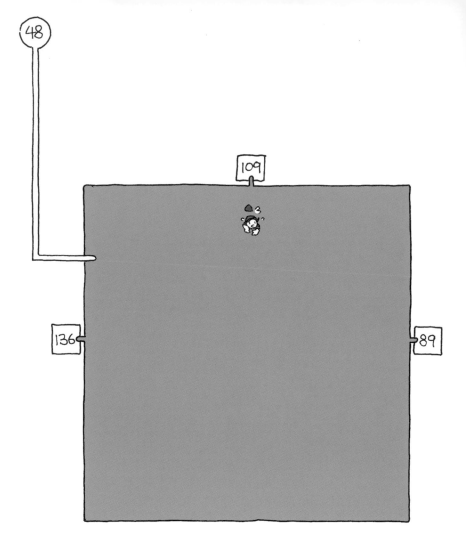

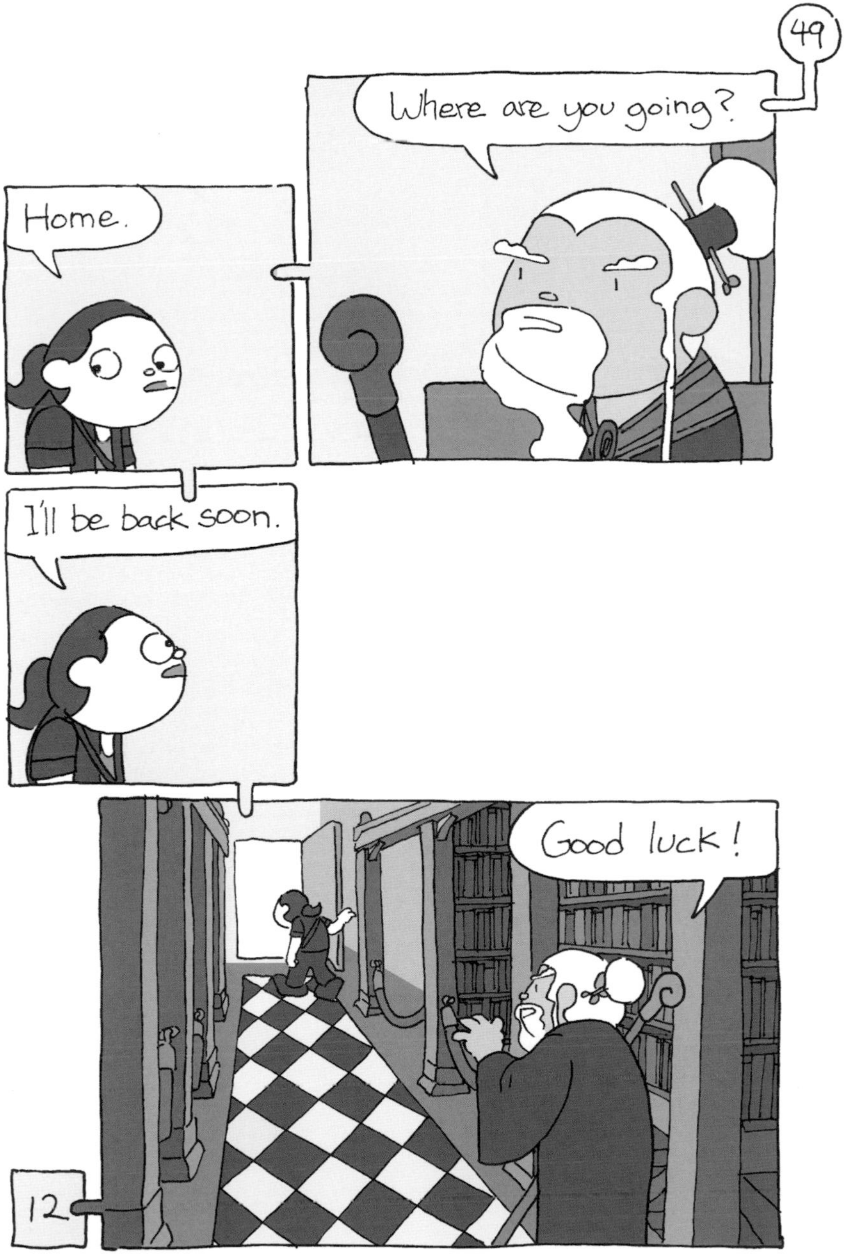
49
Where are you going?
Home.
I'll be back soon.
Good luck!
12

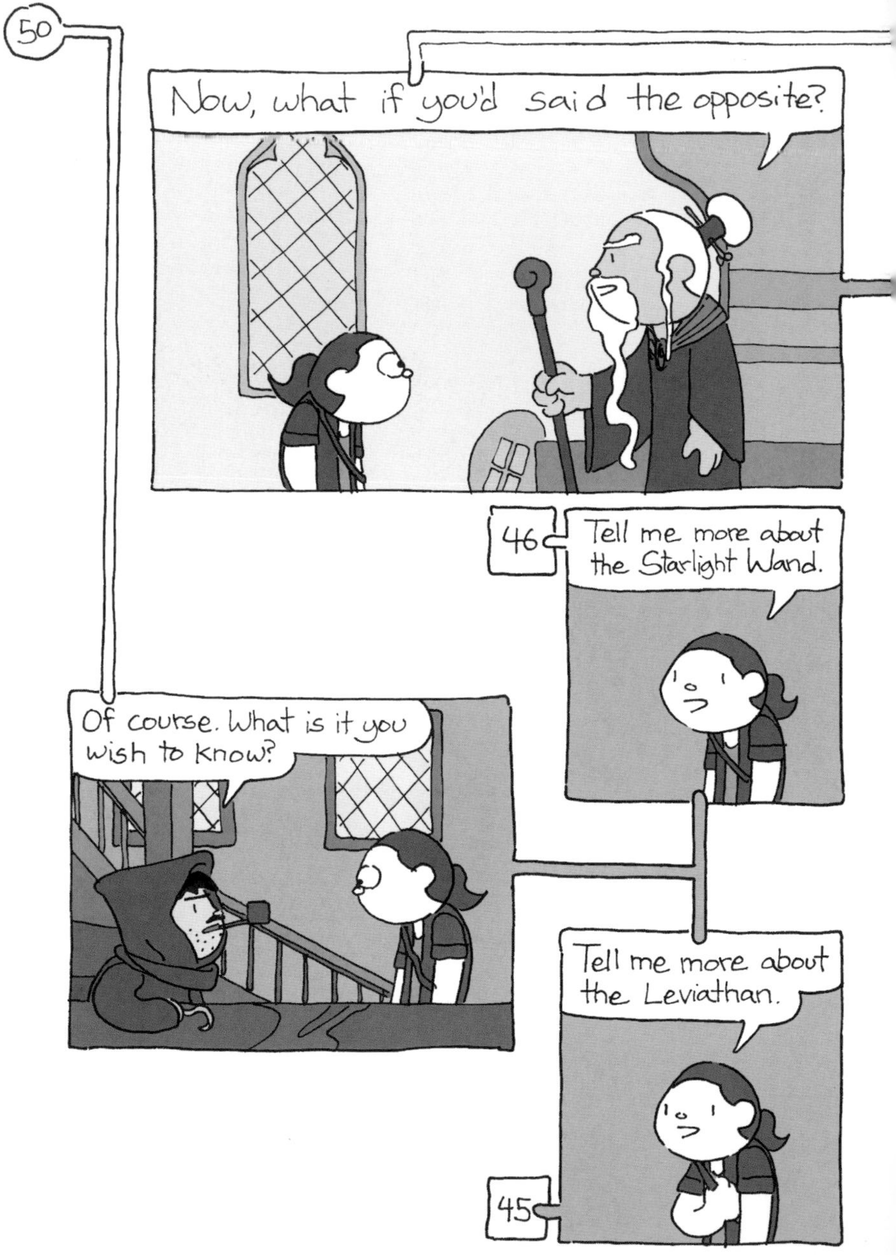
50
Now, what if you'd said the opposite?
46
Tell me more about the Starlight Wand.
Of course. What is it you wish to know?
Tell me more about the Leviathan.
45

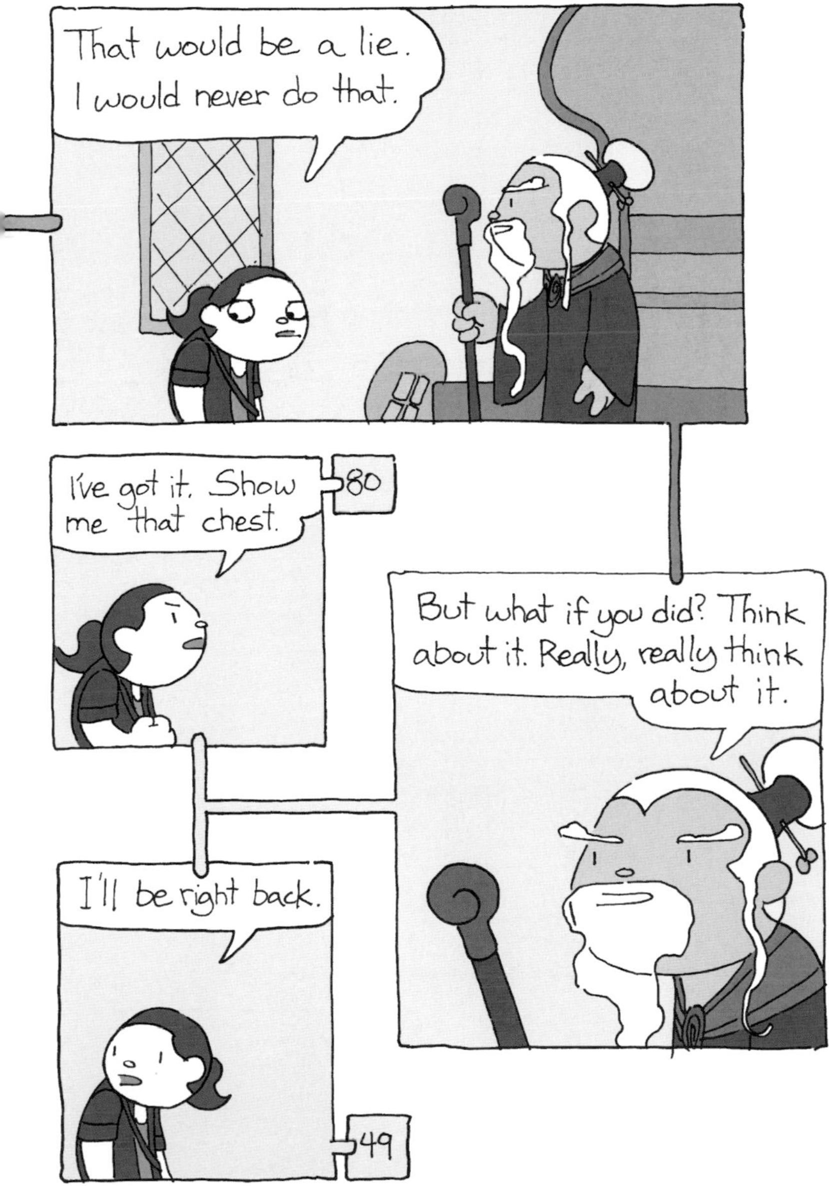
That would be a lie. I would never do that.
But what if you did? Think about it. Really, really think about it.
I've got it. Show me that chest.
80
I'll be right back.
49

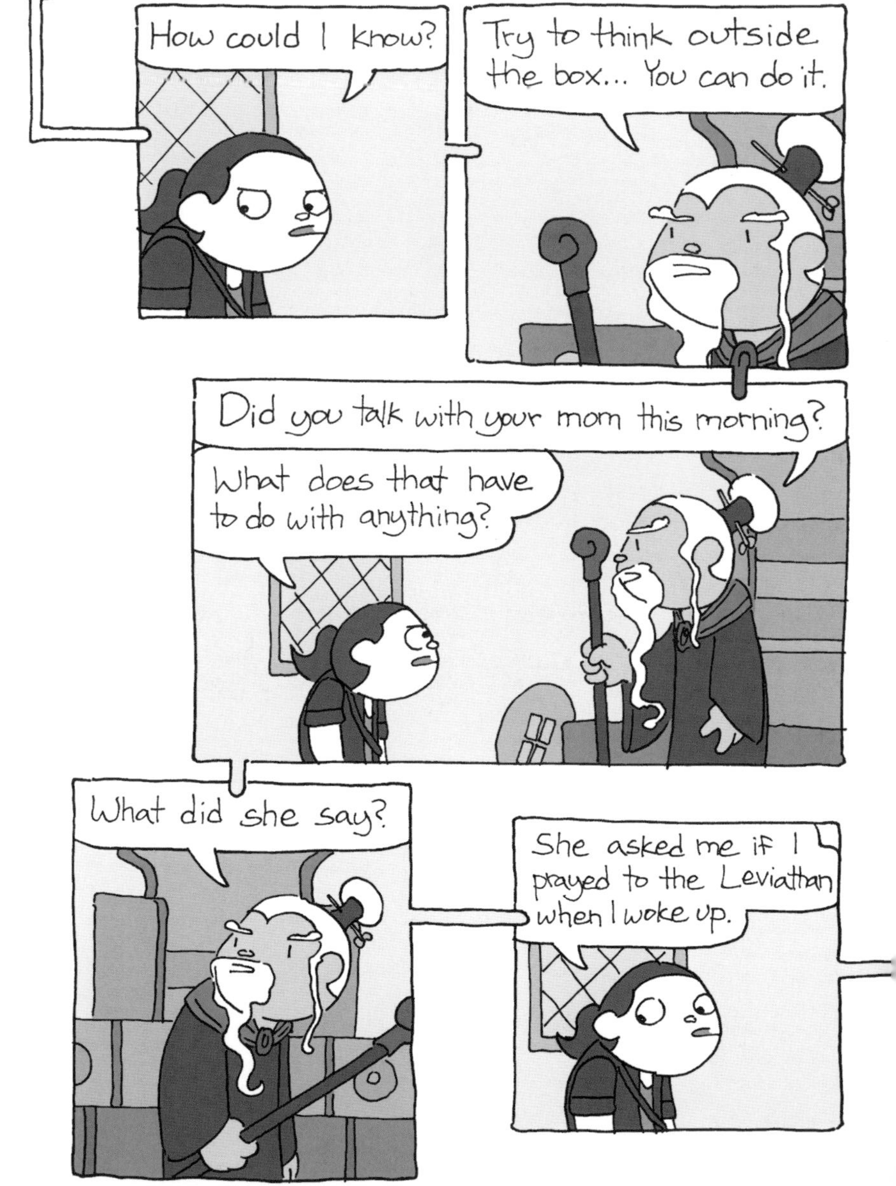
How could I know?
Try to think outside the box... You can do it.
Did you talk with your mom this morning?
What does that have to do with anything?
What did she say?
She asked me if I prayed to the Leviathan when I woke up.

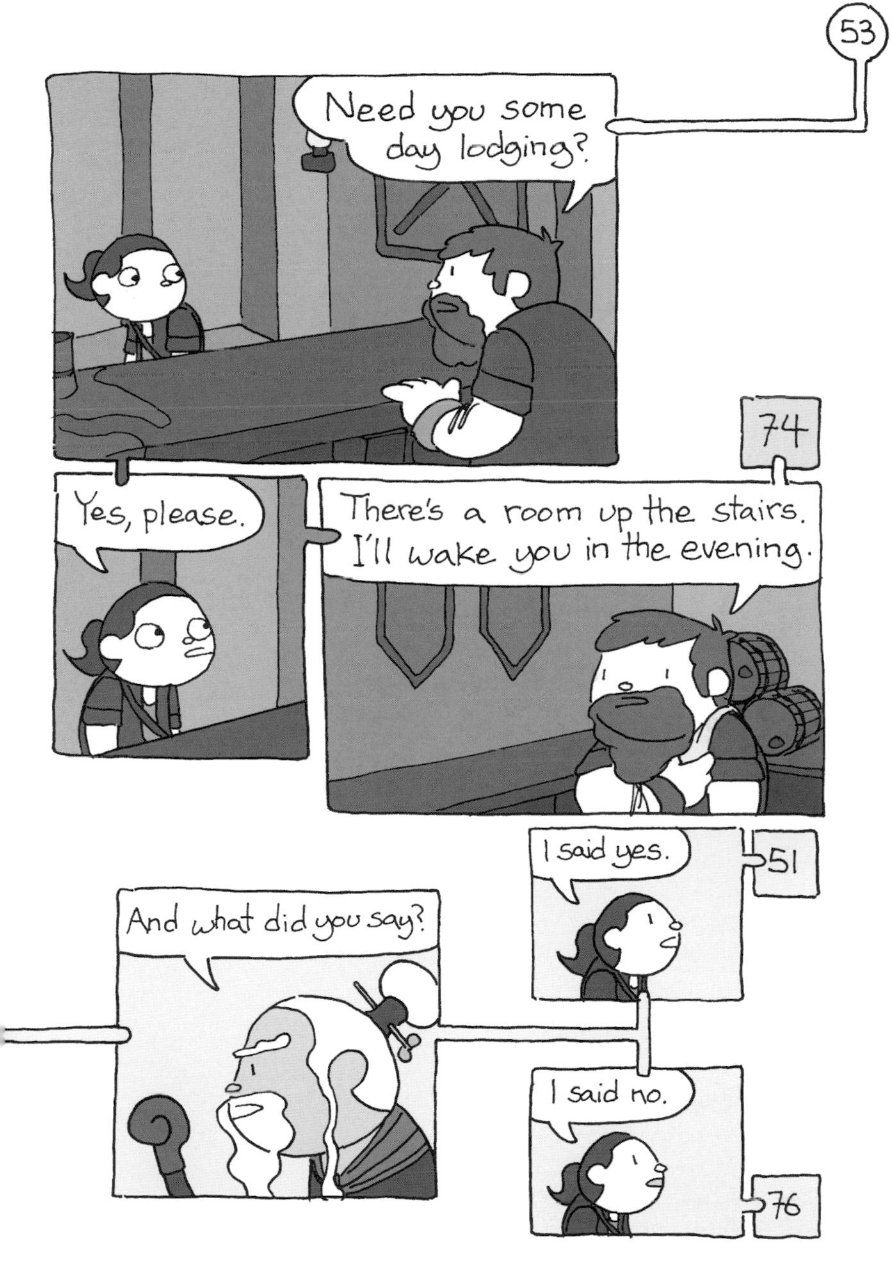

53
Need you some day lodging?
74
Yes, please.
There's a room up the stairs. I'll wake you in the evening.
And what did you say?
I said yes.
51
I said no.
76

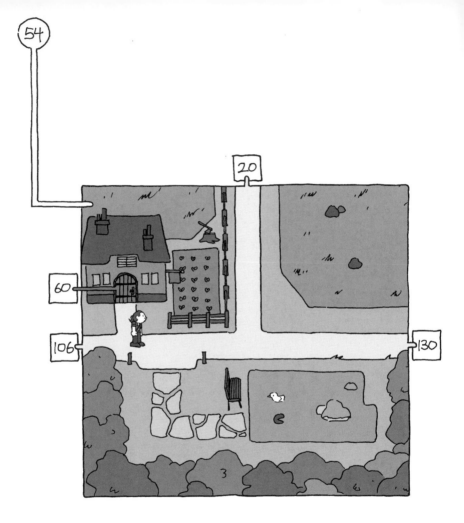

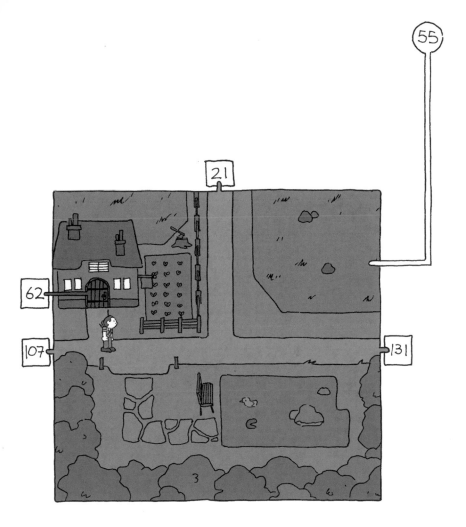

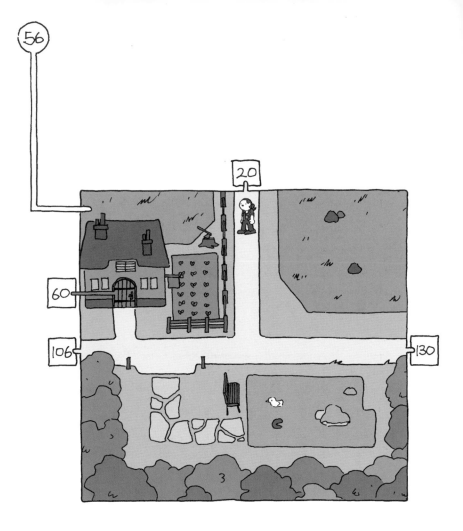

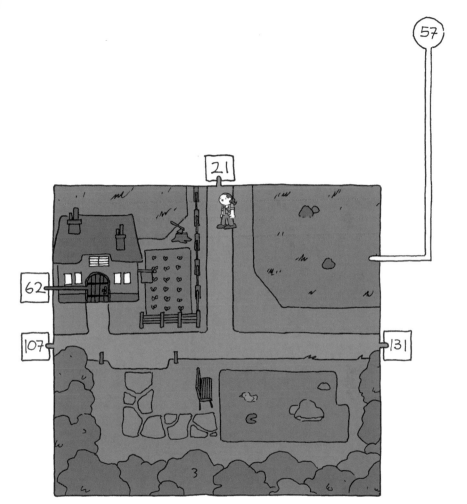

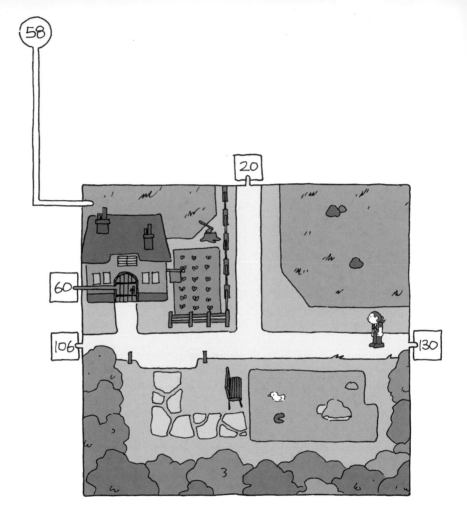

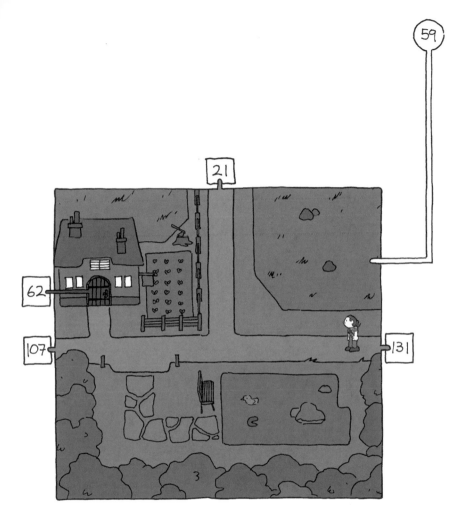

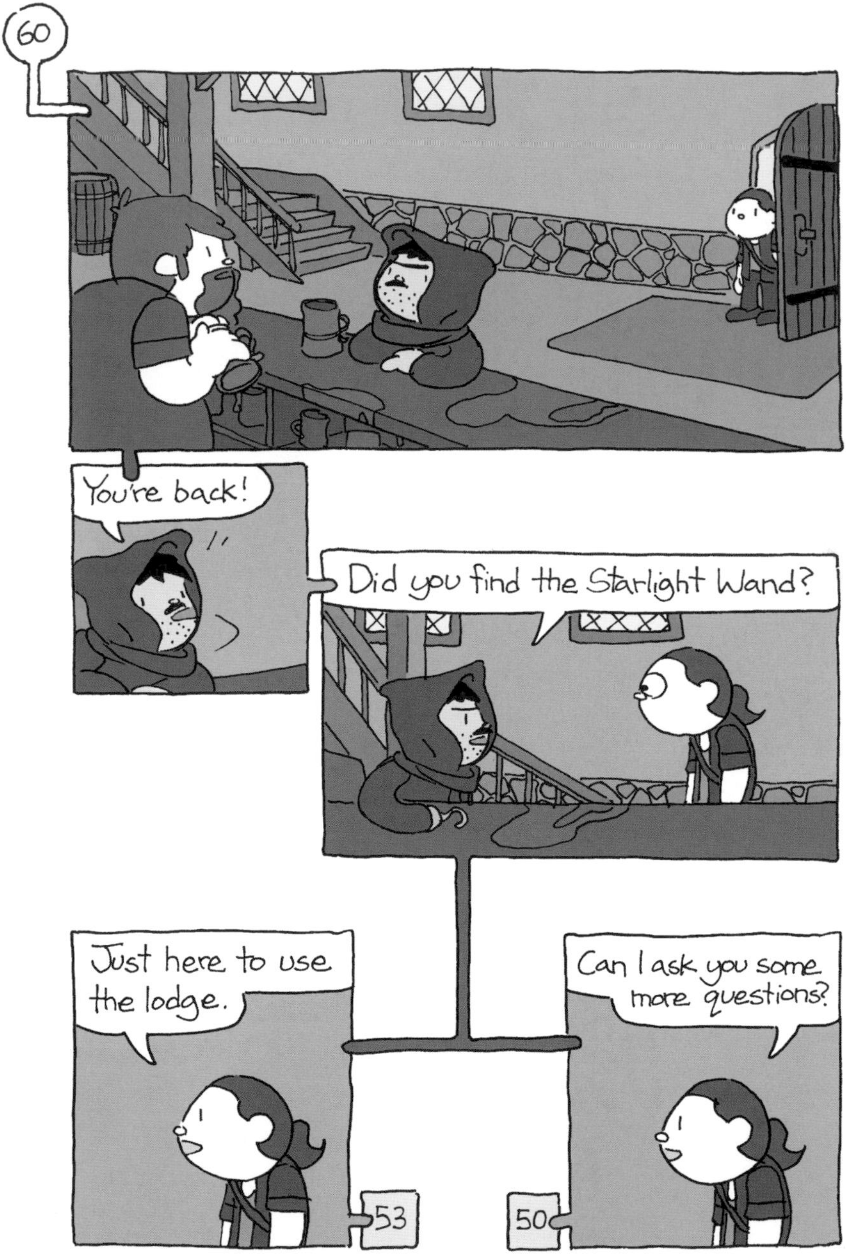
60
You're back!
Did you find the Starlight Wand?
Just here to use the lodge.
53
Can I ask you some more questions?
50

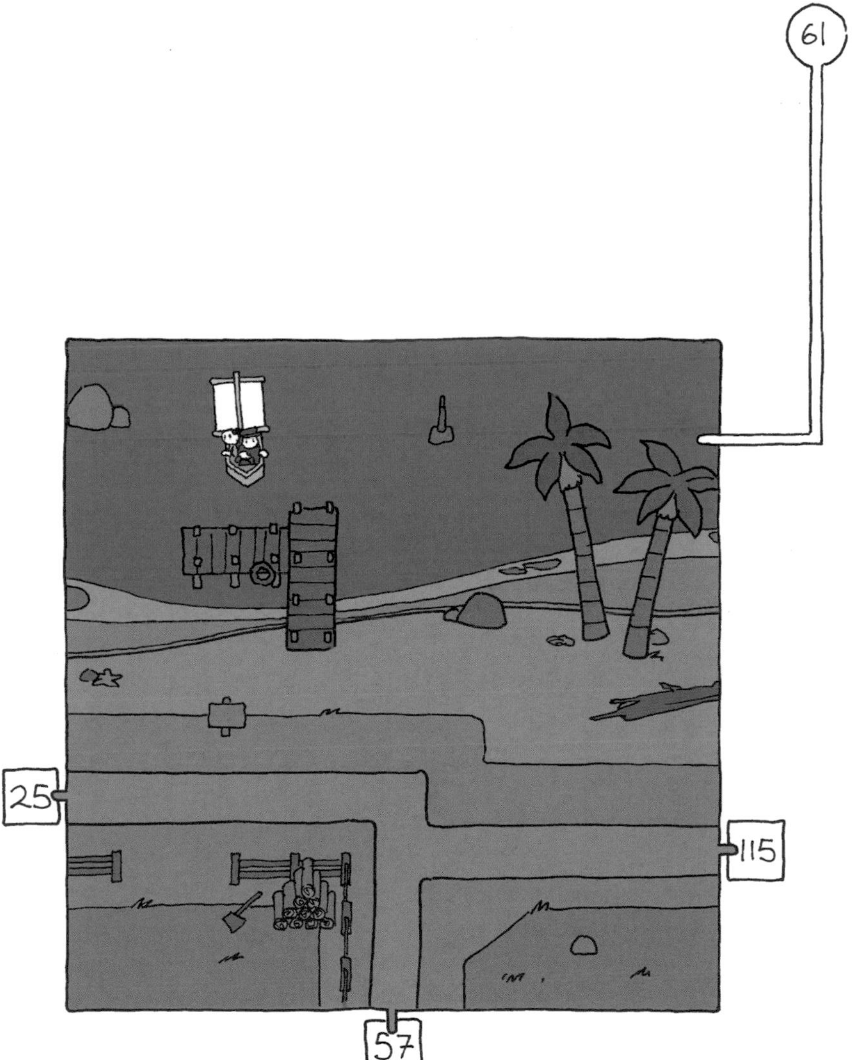
61
25
115
57

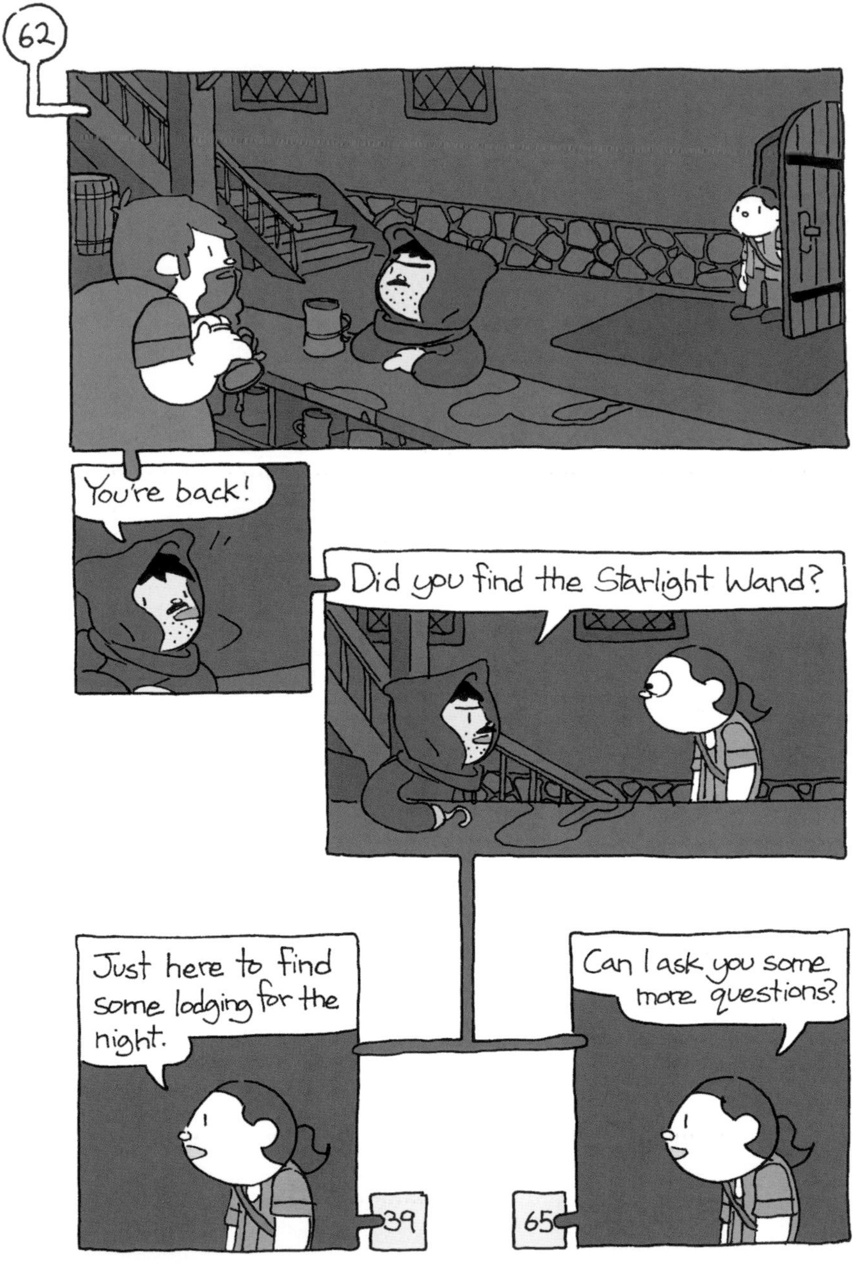
62
You're back!
Did you find the Starlight Wand?
Just here to find some lodging for the night.
39
Can I ask you some more questions?
65

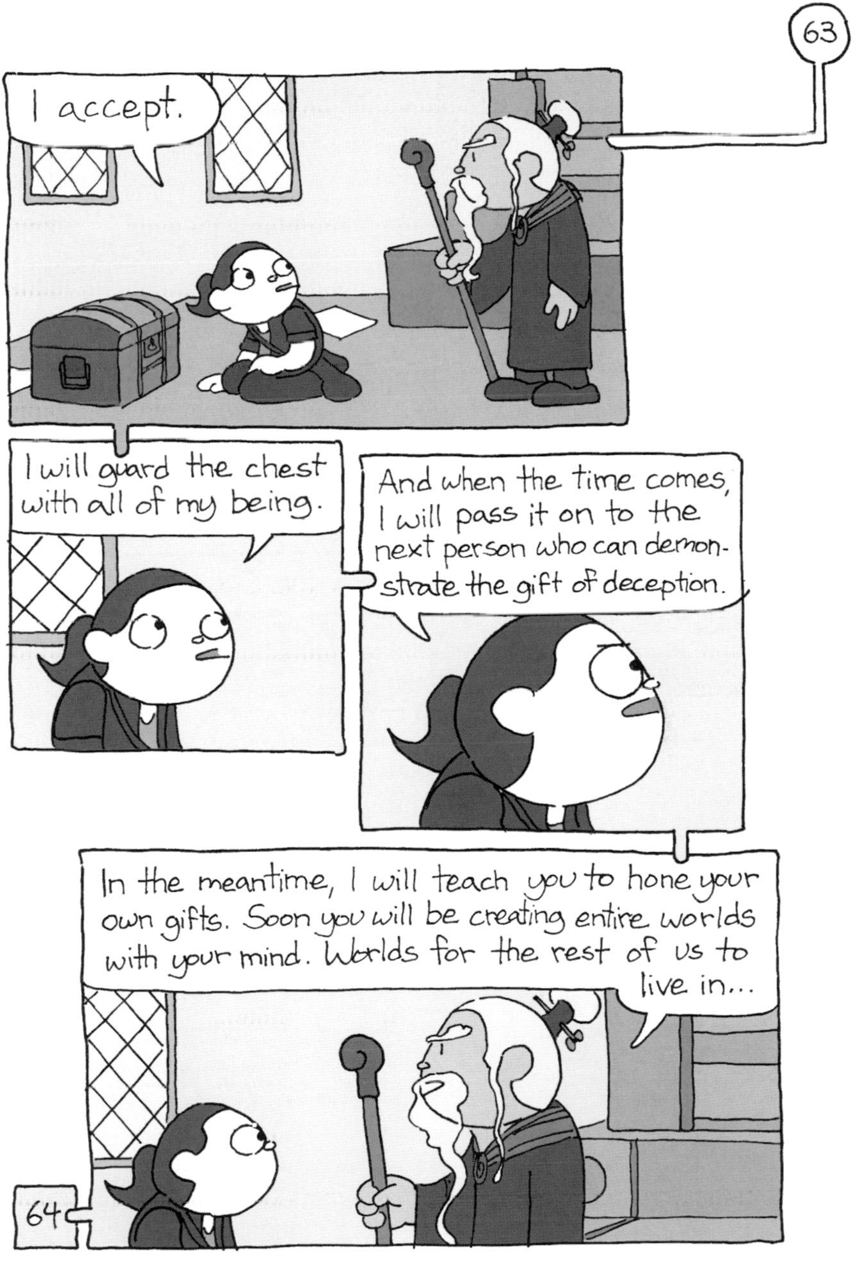
63
I accept.
I will guard the chest with all of my being.
And when the time comes, I will pass it on to the next person who can demonstrate the gift of deception.
In the meantime, I will teach you to hone your own gifts. Soon you will be creating entire worlds with your mind. Worlds for the rest of us to live in...
64

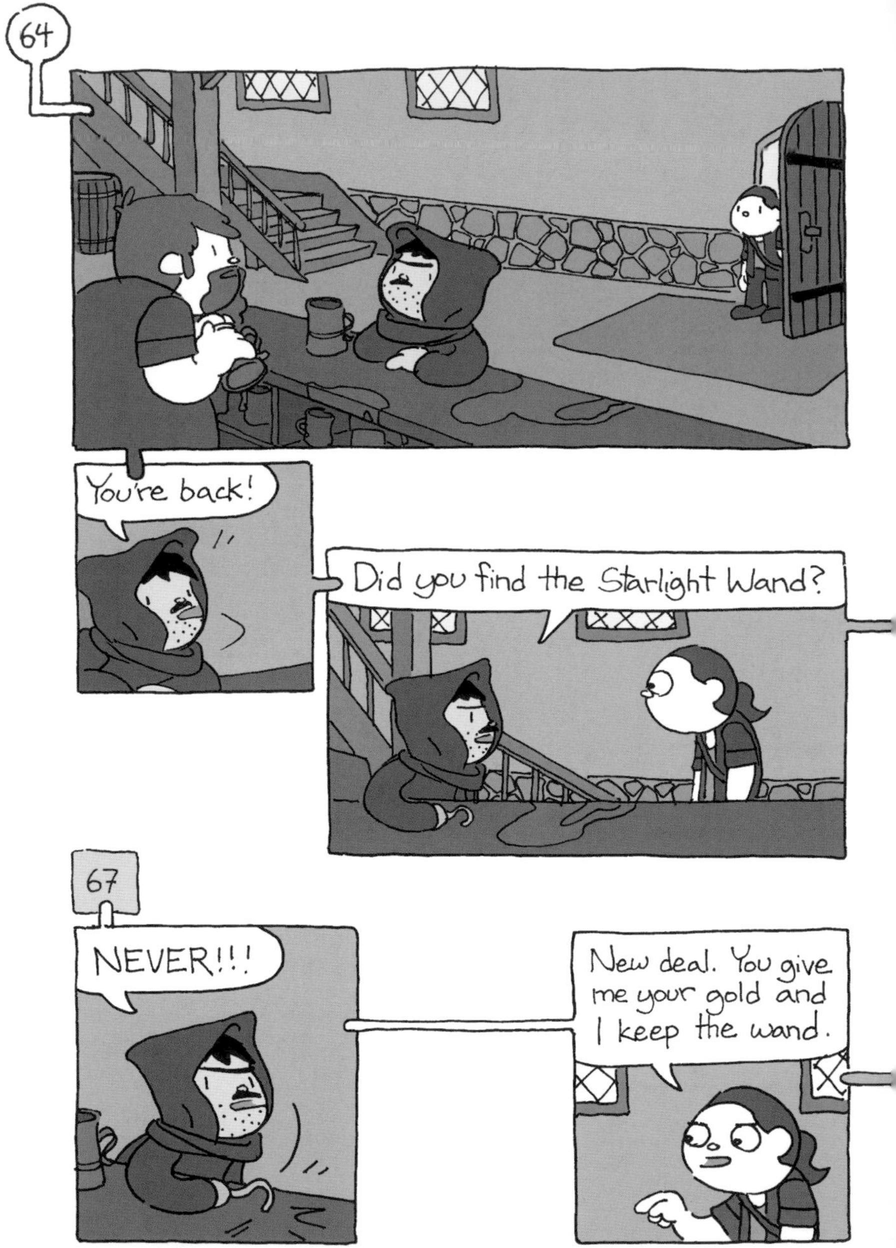
64
You're back!
Did you find the Starlight Wand?
67
NEVER!!!
New deal. You give me your gold and I keep the wand.

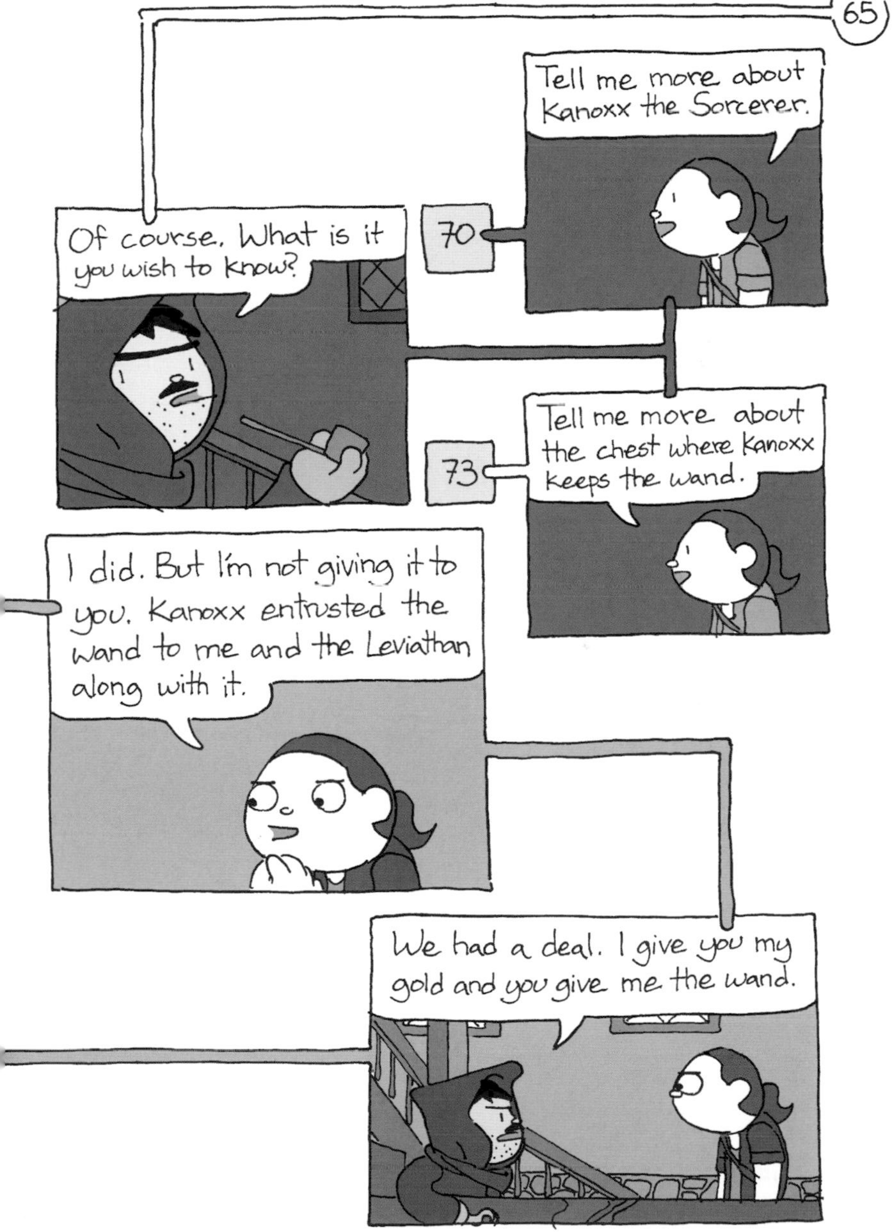
Of course. What is it you wish to know?
Tell me more about Kanoxx the Sorcerer.
70
Tell me more about the chest where Kanoxx keeps the wand.
73
I did. But I'm not giving it to you. Kanoxx entrusted the wand to me and the Leviathan along with it.
We had a deal. I give you my gold and you give me the wand.

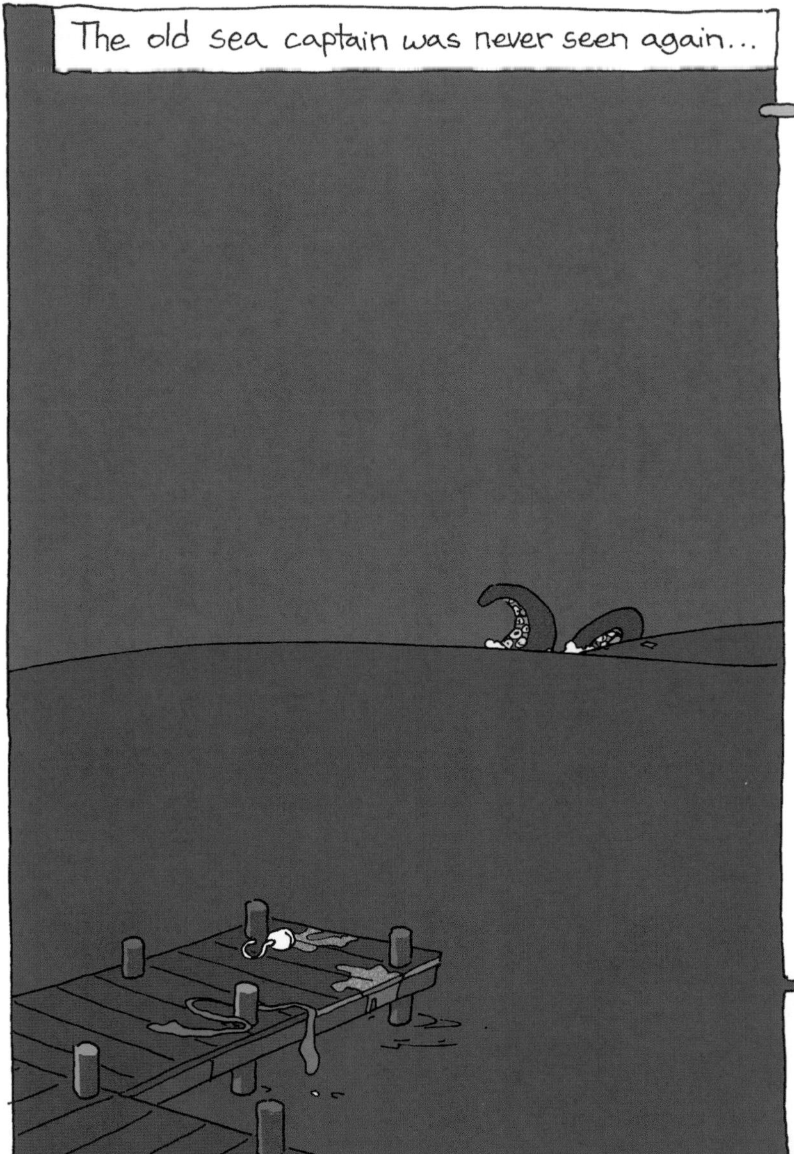
The old sea captain was never seen again...

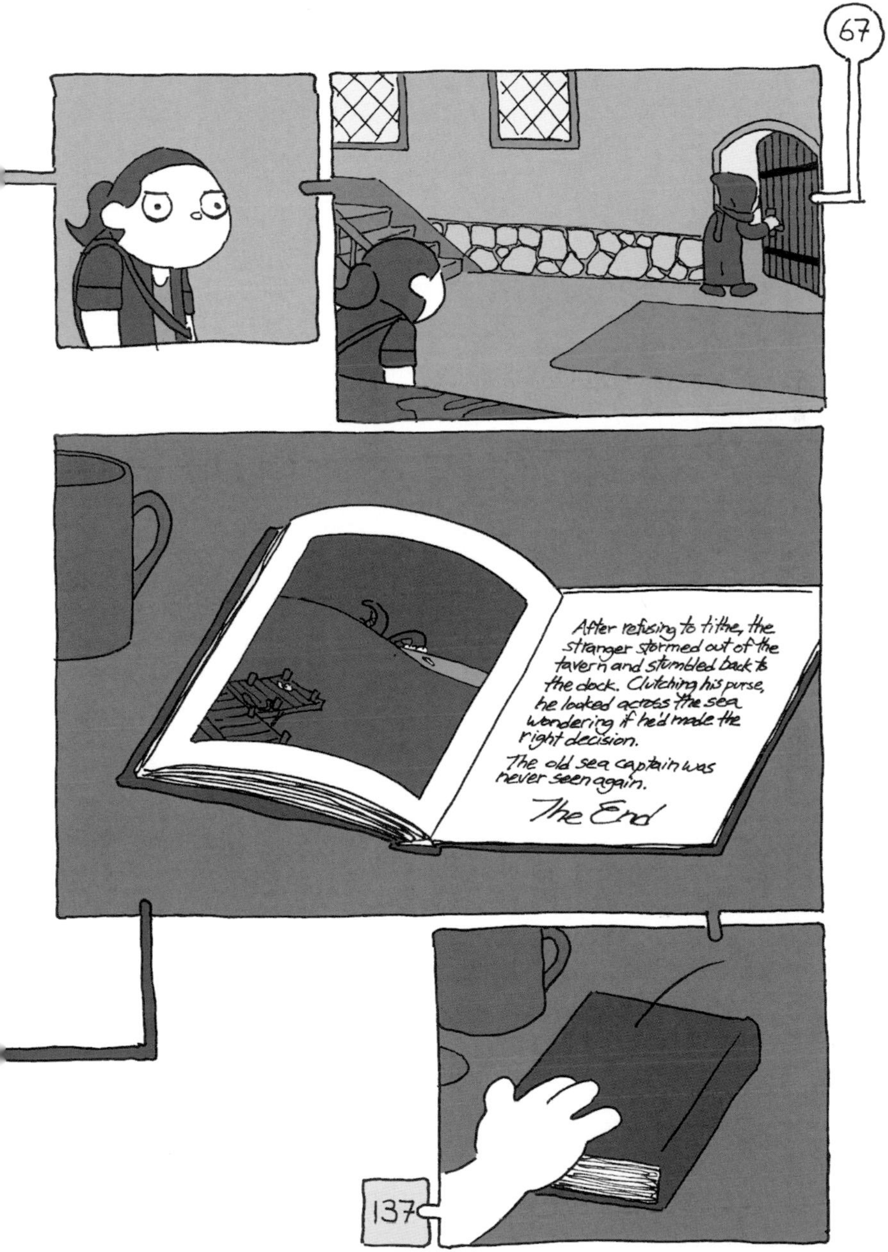
67
After refusing to tithe, the stranger stormed out of the tavern and stumbled back to the dock. Clutching his purse, he looked across the sea wondering if he'd made the right decision.
The old sea captain was never seen again.
The End
137

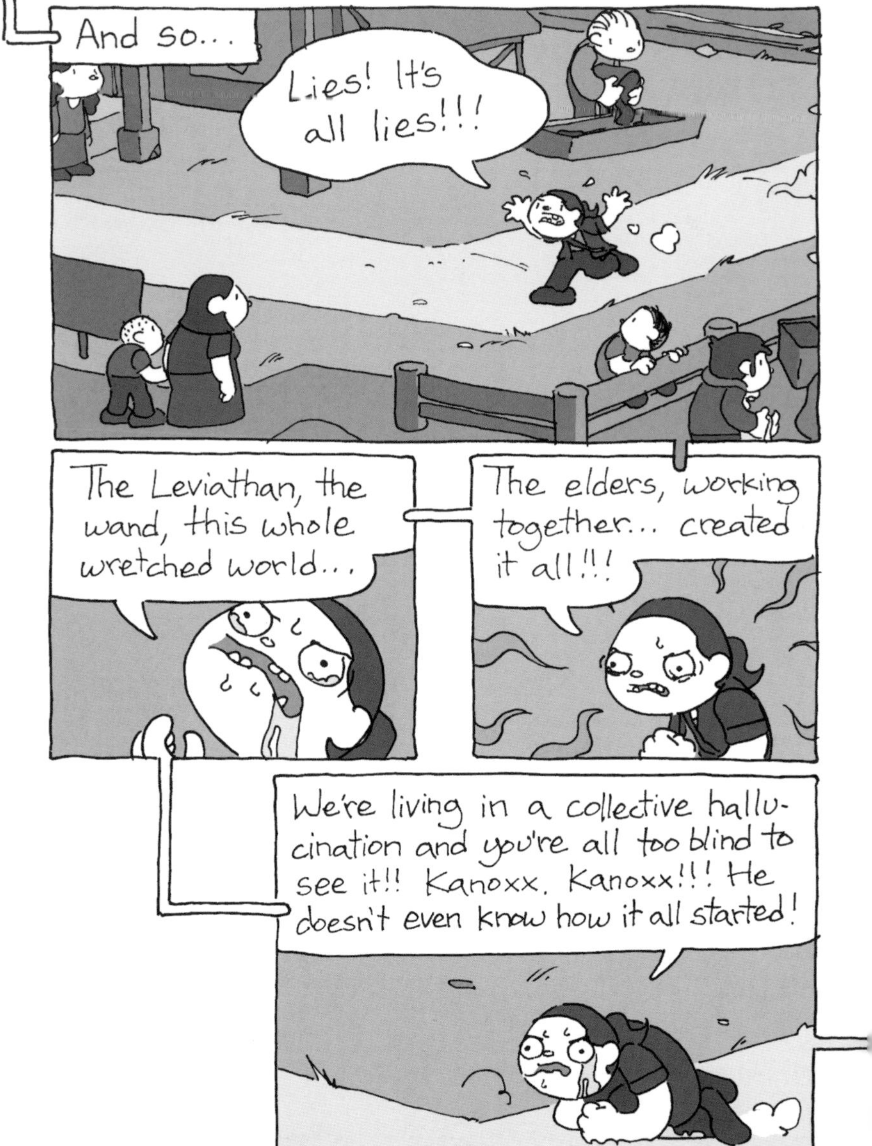
And so...
Lies! It's all lies!!!
The Leviathan, the wand, this whole wretched world...
The elders, working together... created it all!!!
We're living in a collective hallucination and you're all too blind to see it!! Kanoxx. Kanoxx!!! He doesn't even know how it all started!

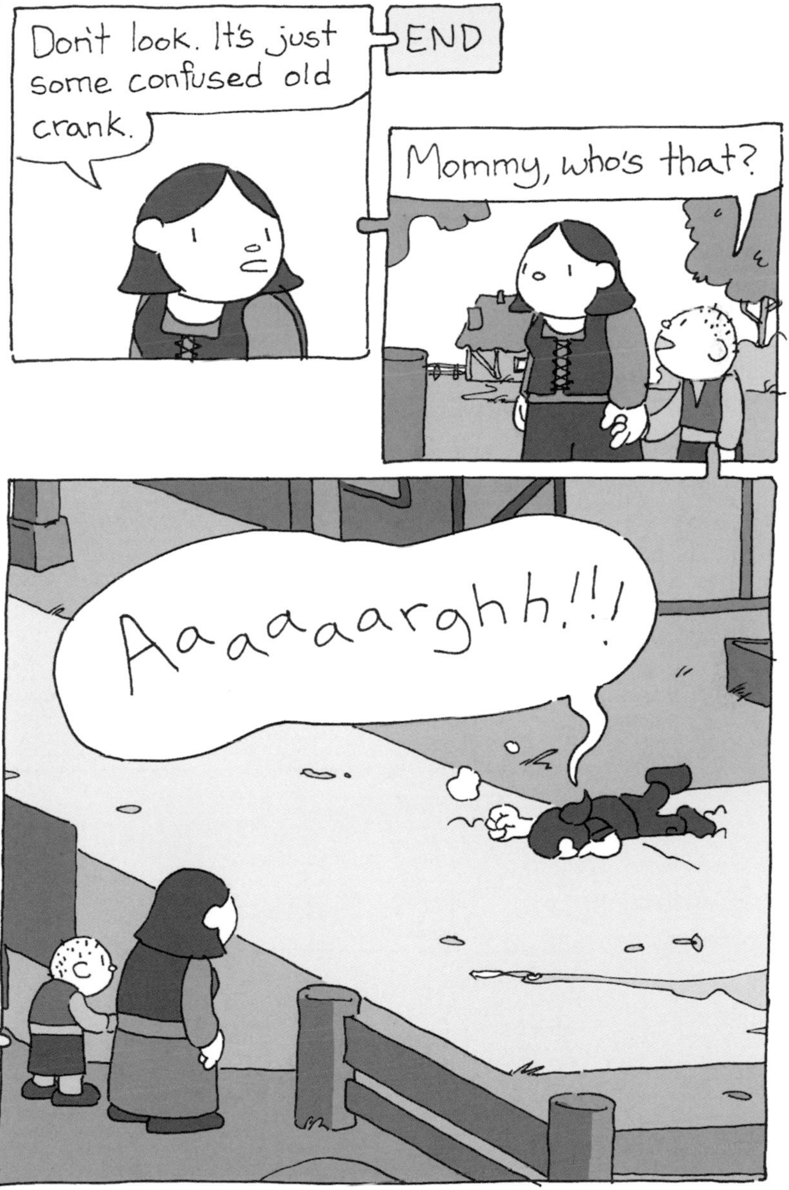
Aaaaaarghh!!!
Mommy, who's that?
Don't look. It's just some confused old crank.
END

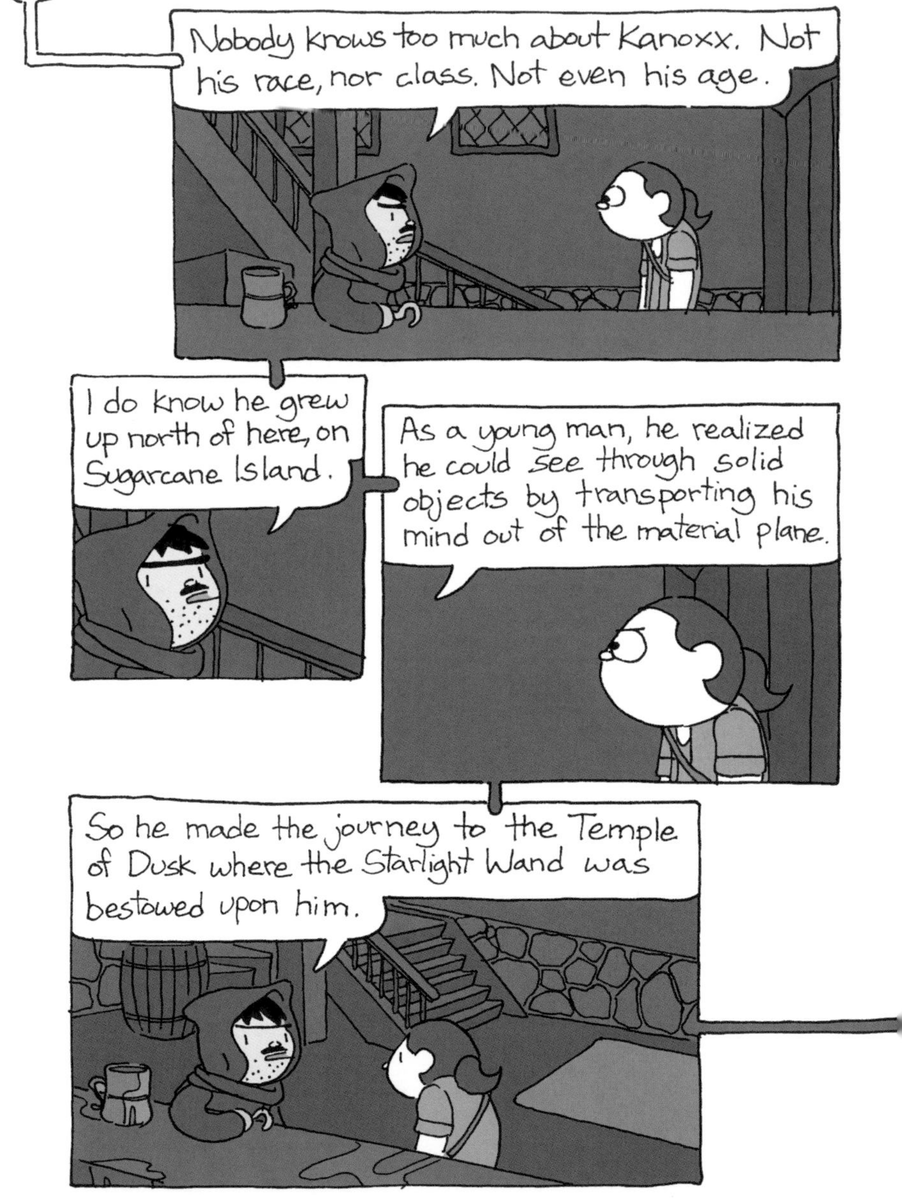
Nobody knows too much about Kanoxx. Not his race, nor class. Not even his age.
I do know he grew up north of here, on Sugarcane Island.
As a young man, he realized he could see through solid objects by transporting his mind out of the material plane.
So he made the journey to the Temple of Dusk where the Starlight Wand was bestowed upon him.

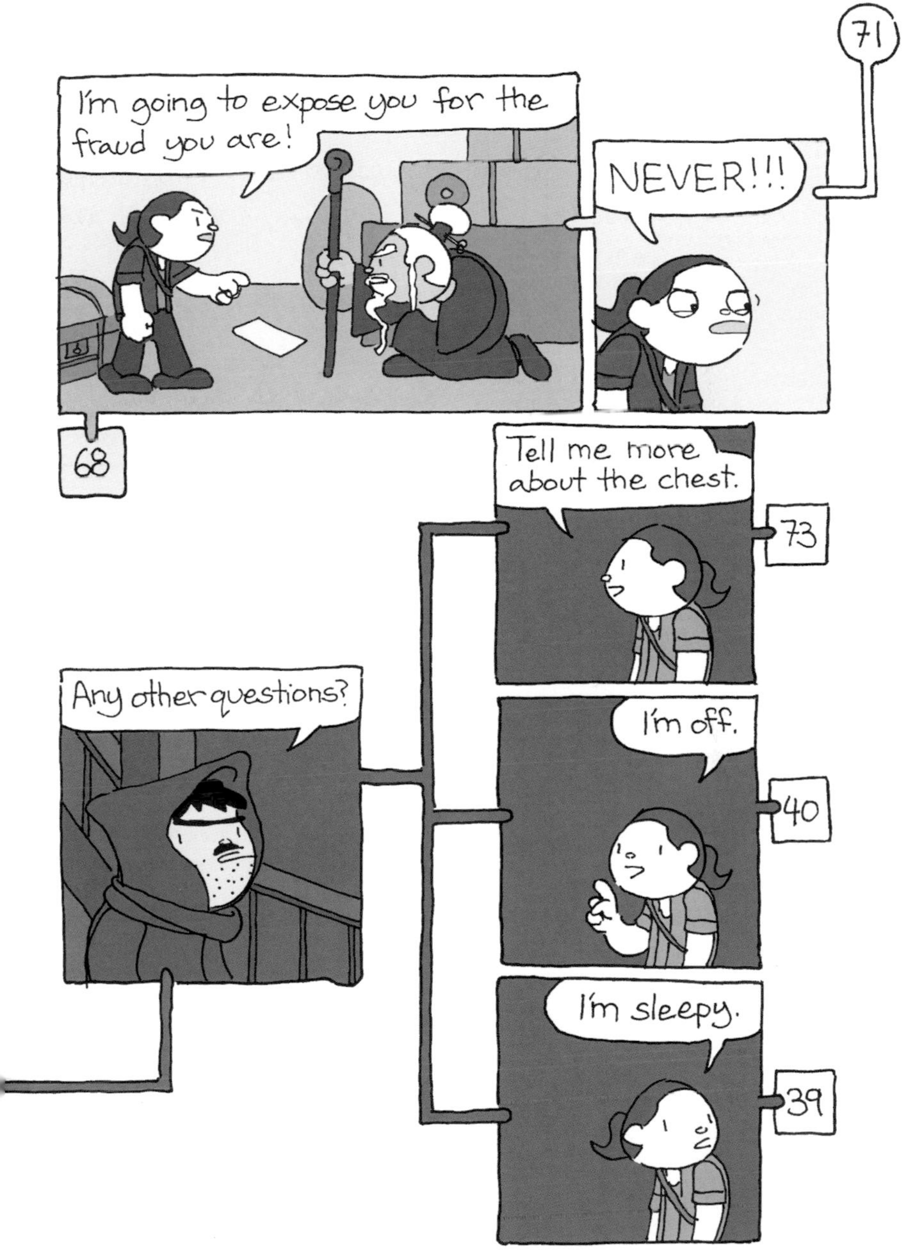
71
I'm going to expose you for the fraud you are!
68
NEVER!!!
Tell me more about the chest.
73
Any other questions?
I'm off.
40
I'm sleepy.
39

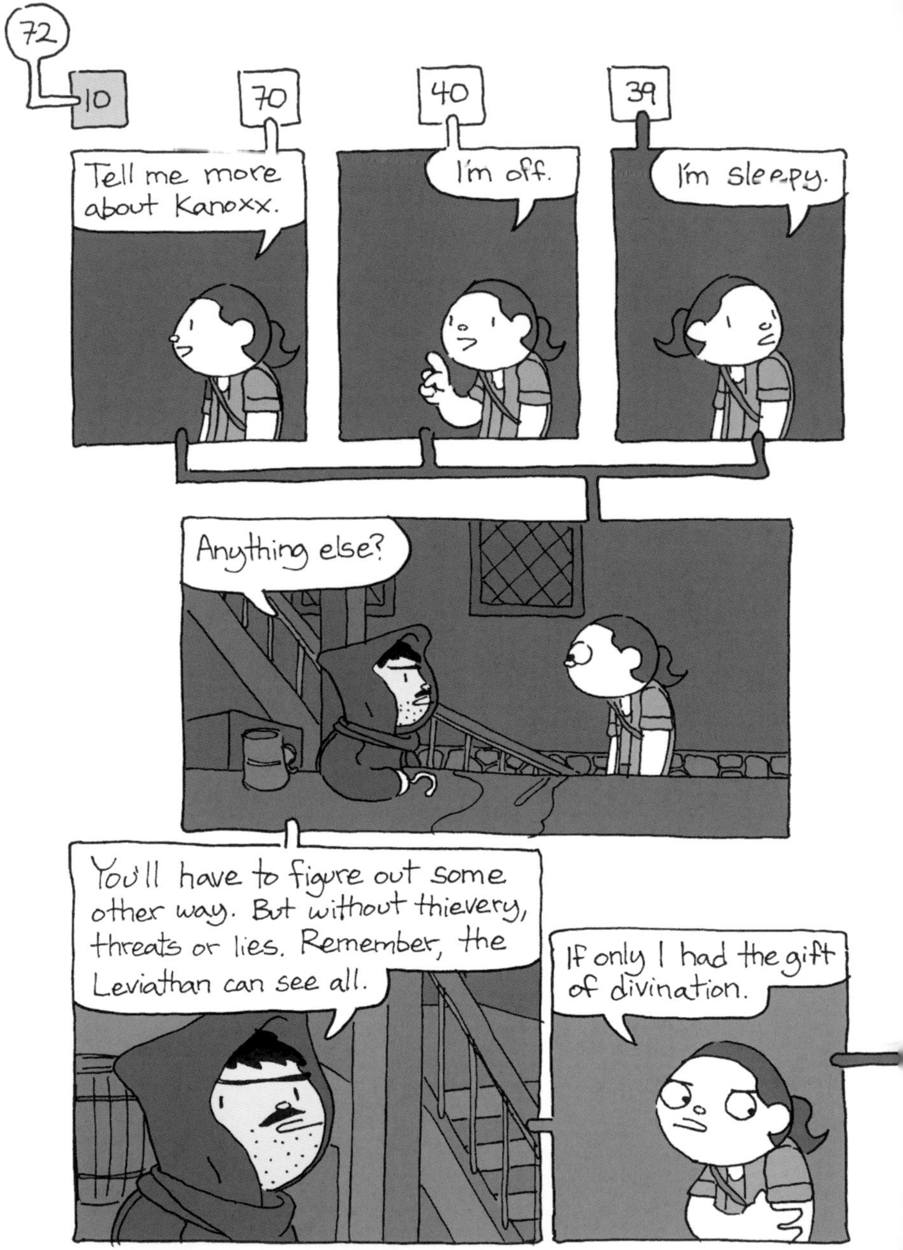
72
10
70
40
39
Tell me more about Kanoxx.
I'm off.
I'm sleepy.
Anything else?
You'll have to figure out some other way. But without thievery, threats or lies. Remember, the Leviathan can see all.
If only I had the gift of divination.

Ah, the chest. They say Kanoxx has it on full display in the temple apse.

'Tis made of solid oak. No holes or cracks. The only entry is behind a locked hasp on the lid.

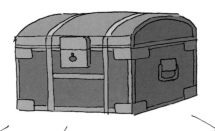

According to legend, Kanoxx will open the chest for anyone who can describe the wand contained inside.

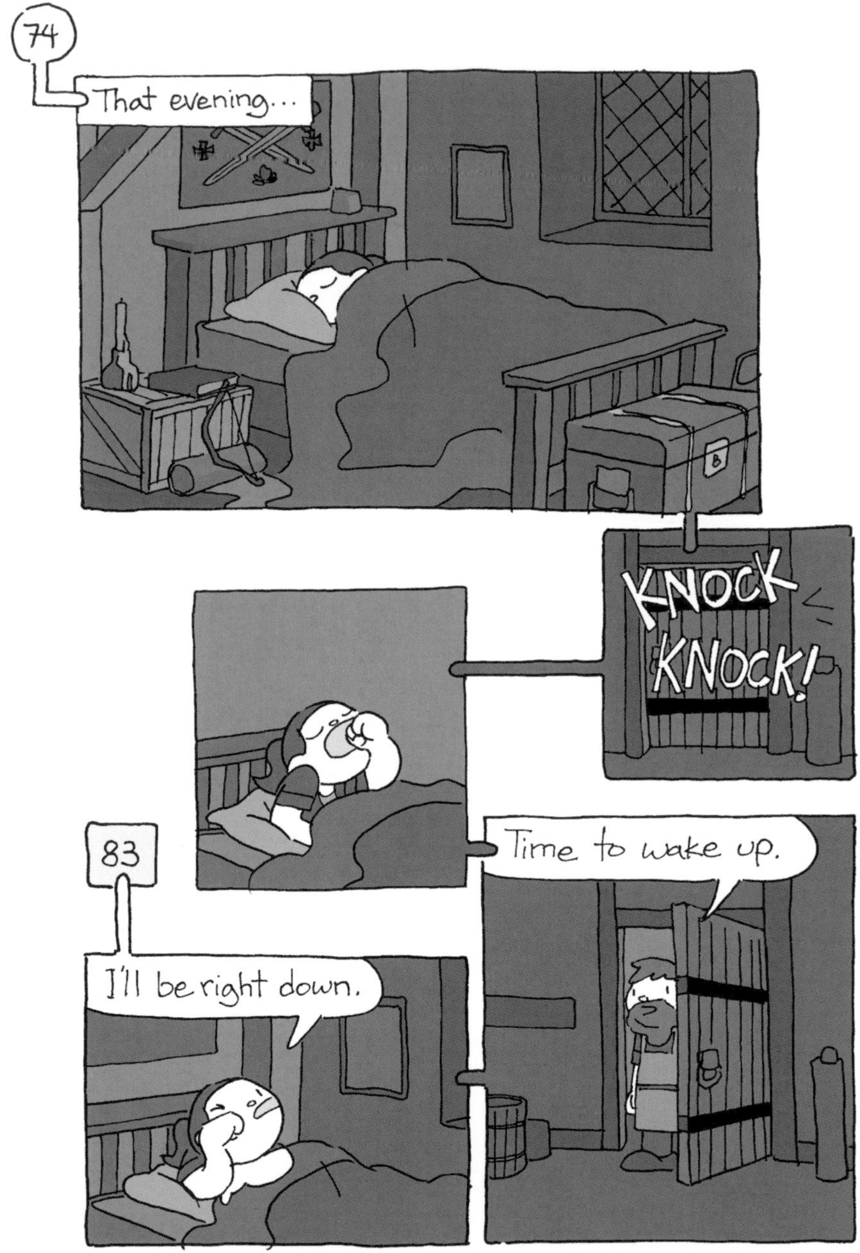

74
That evening...
KNOCK
KNOCK!
Time to wake up.
83
I'll be right down.

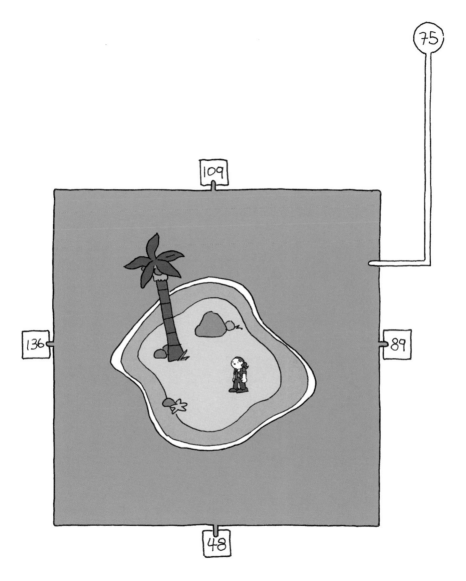

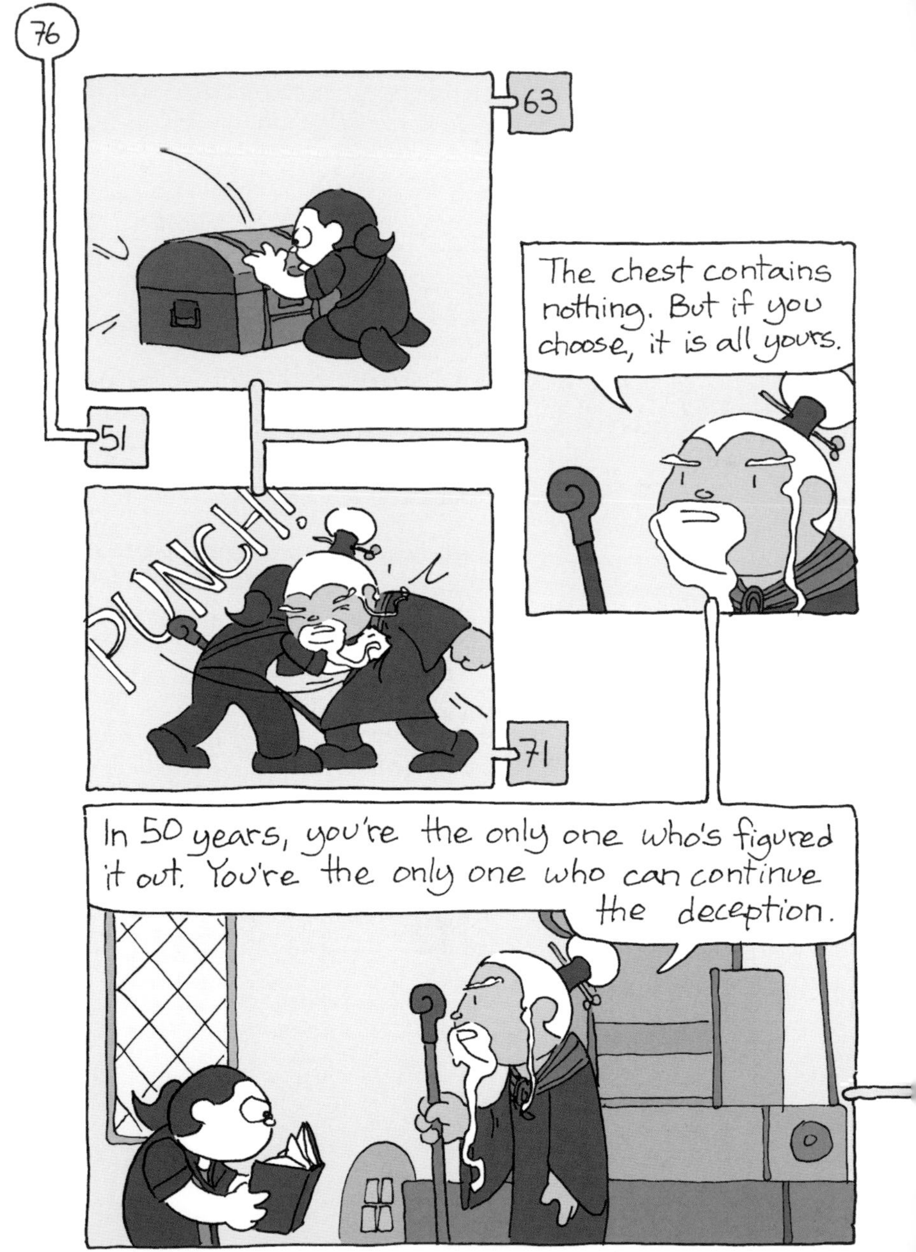
76
63
51
PUNCH!
71
The chest contains nothing. But if you choose, it is all yours.
In 50 years, you're the only one who's figured it out. You're the only one who can continue the deception.

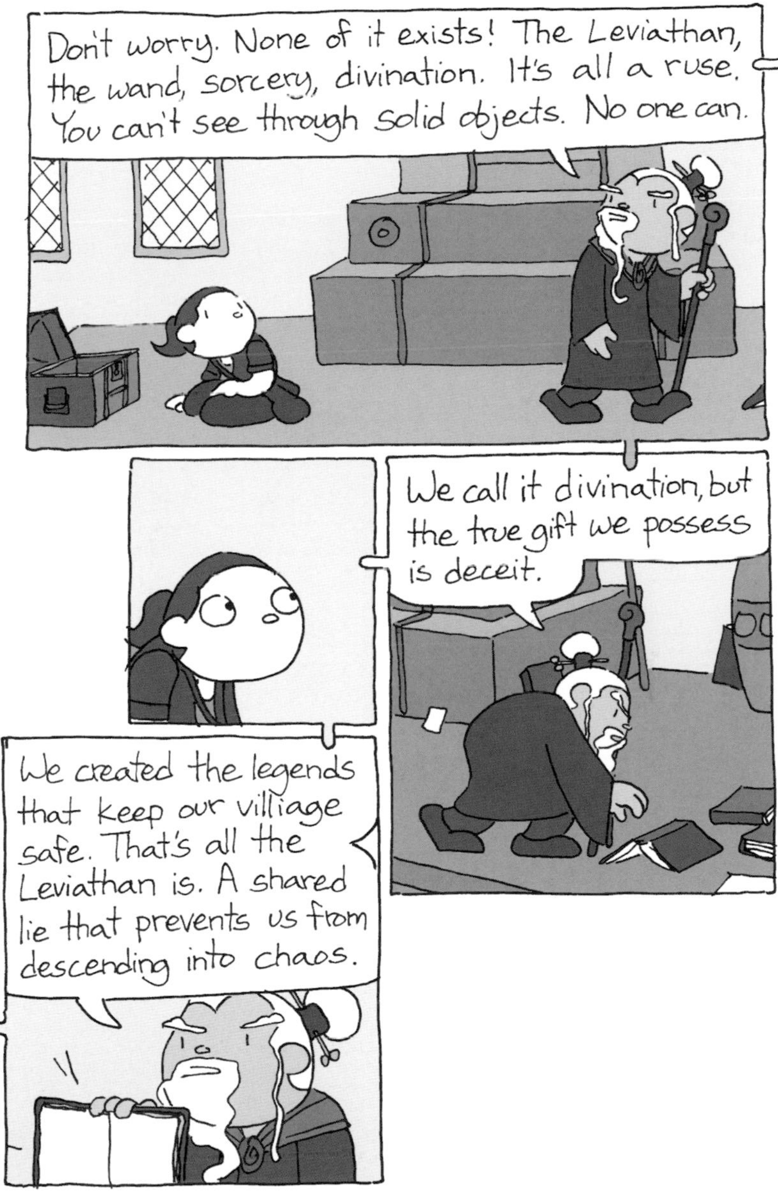
Don't worry. None of it exists! The Leviathan, the wand, sorcery, divination. It's all a ruse. You can't see through solid objects. No one can.
We call it divination, but the true gift we possess is deceit.
We created the legends that keep our villiage safe. That's all the Leviathan is. A shared lie that prevents us from descending into chaos.

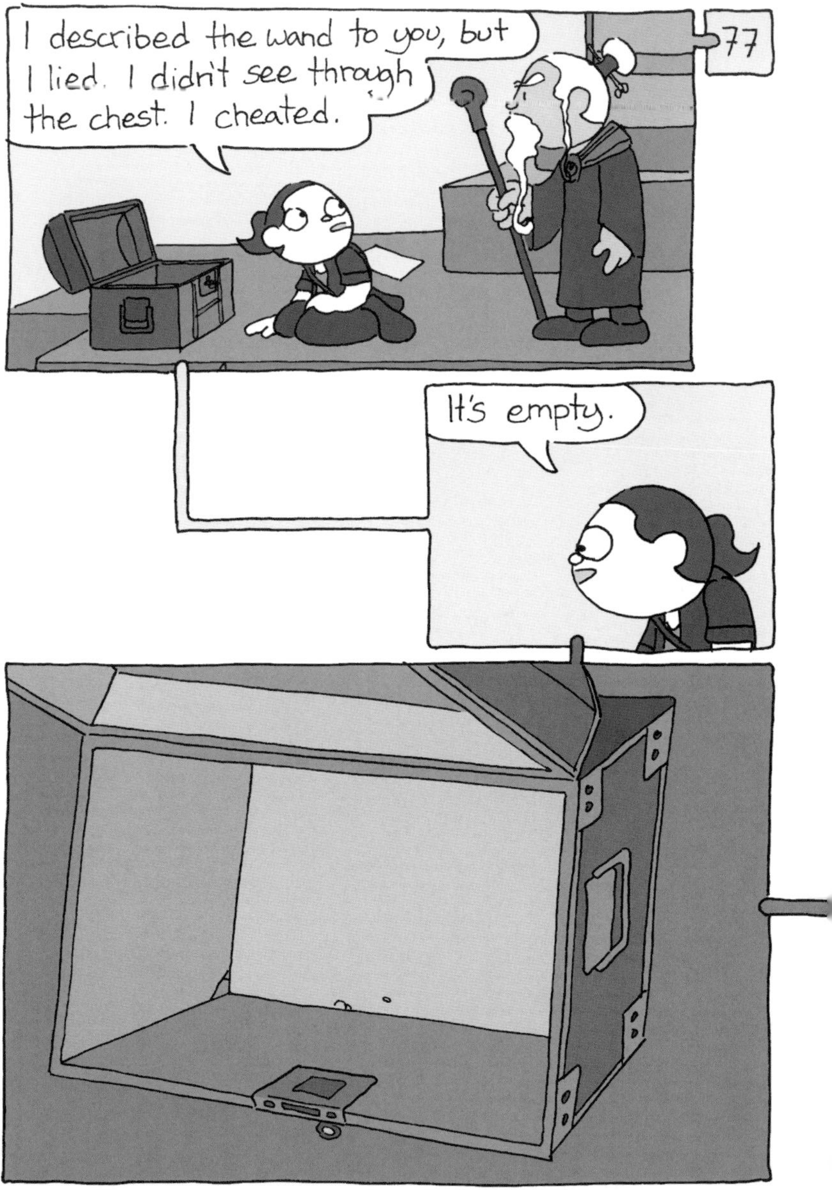
I described the wand to you, but I lied. I didn't see through the chest. I cheated.
77
It's empty.

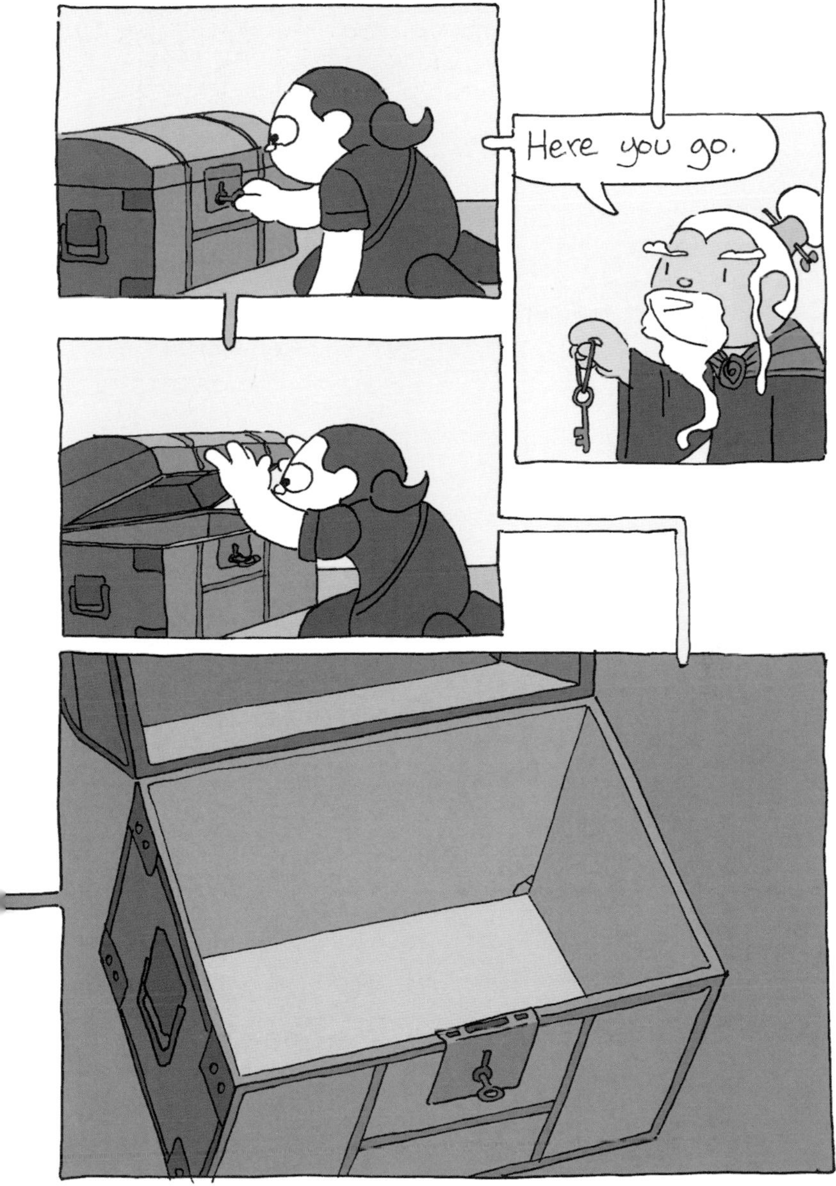
Here you go.

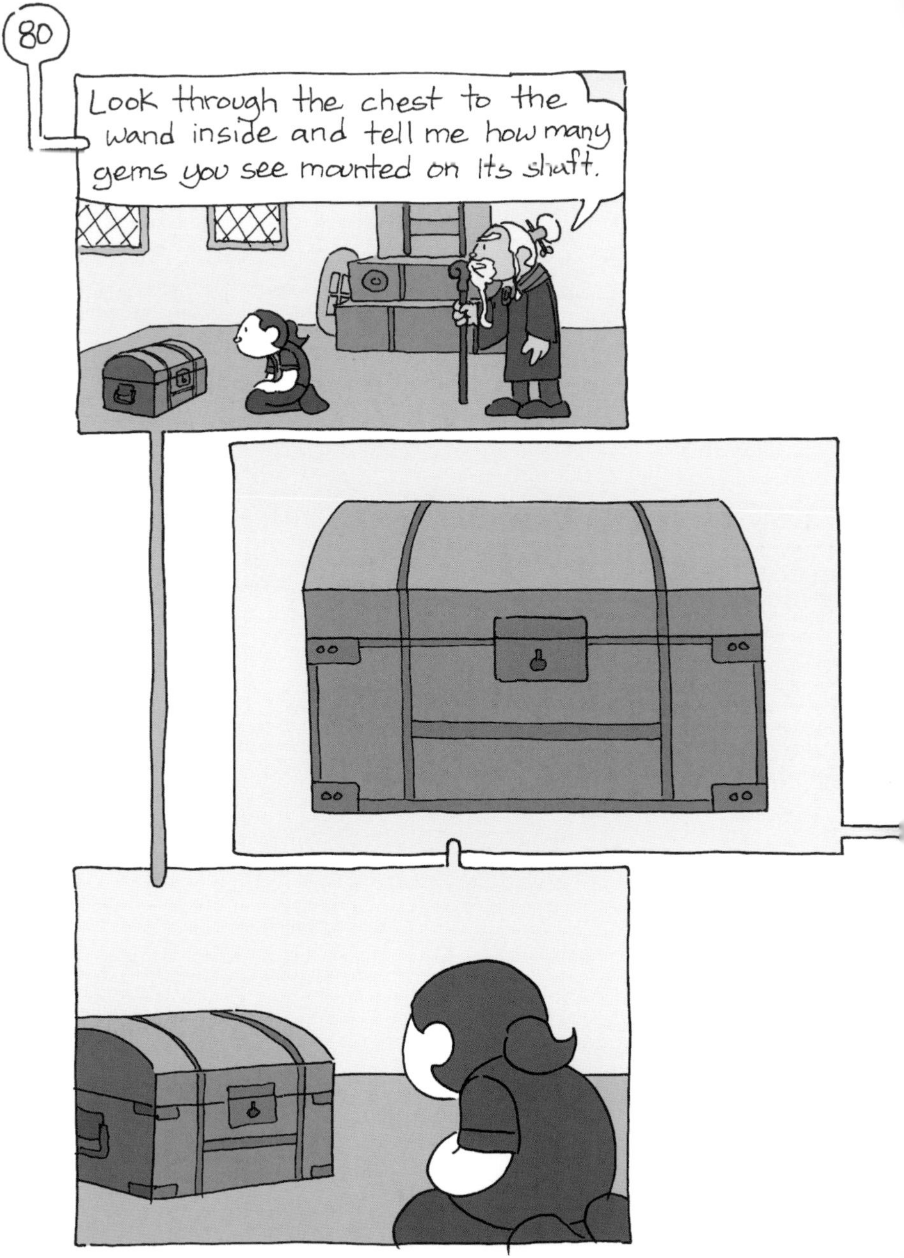
80
Look through the chest to the wand inside and tell me how many gems you see mounted on its shaft.

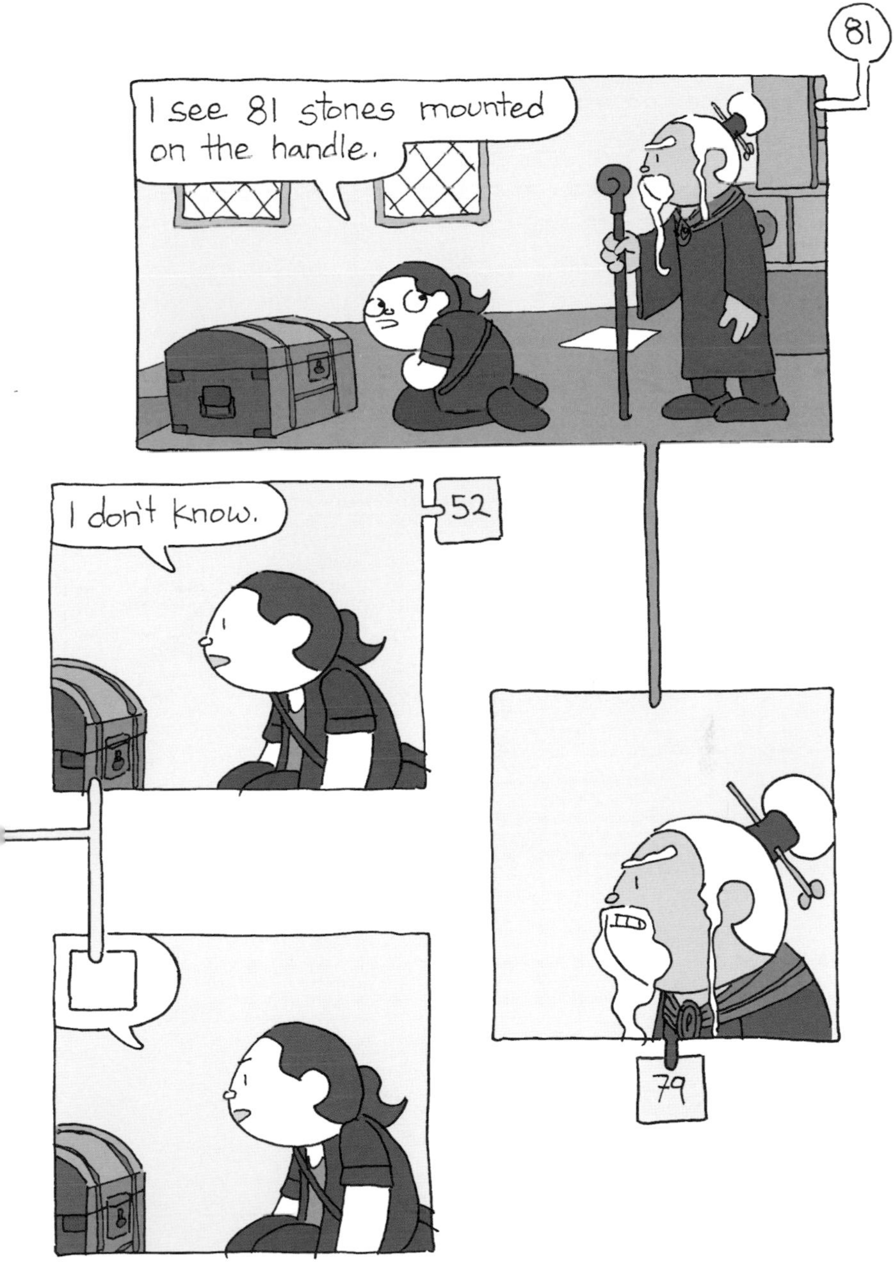
81
I see 81 stones mounted on the handle.
52
I don't know.
79

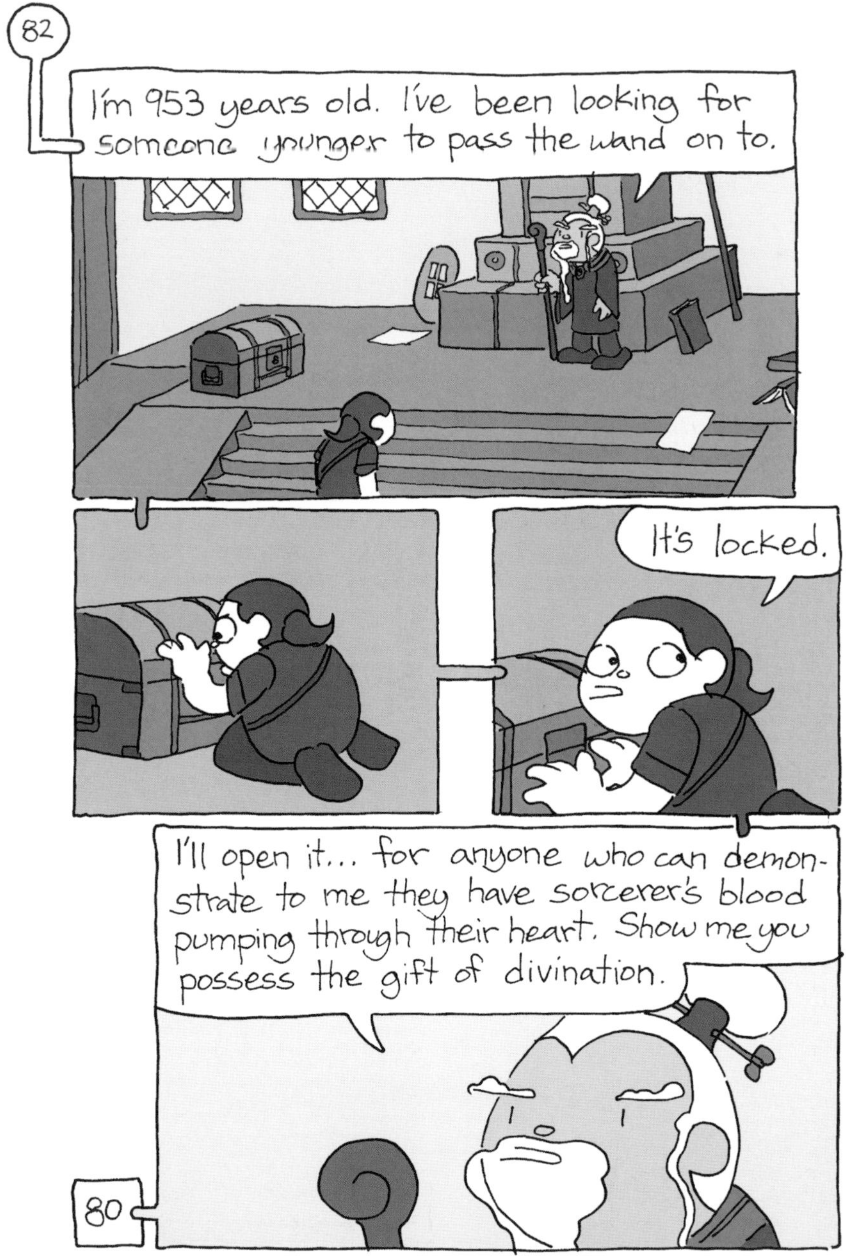
82
I'm 953 years old. I've been looking for someone younger to pass the wand on to.
It's locked.
I'll open it... for anyone who can demonstrate to me they have sorcerer's blood pumping through their heart. Show me you possess the gift of divination.
80

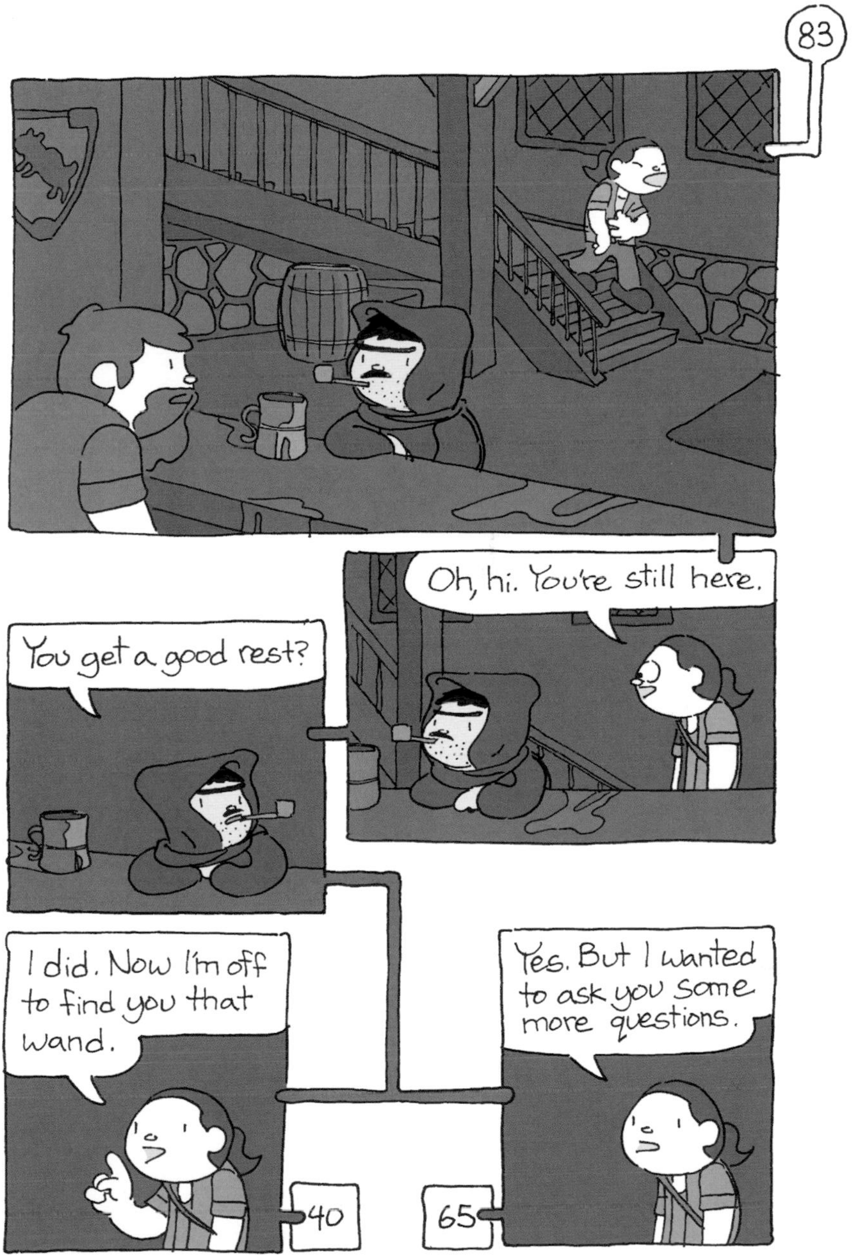
83
Oh, hi. You're still here.
You get a good rest?
I did. Now I'm off to find you that wand.
40
Yes. But I wanted to ask you some more questions.
65

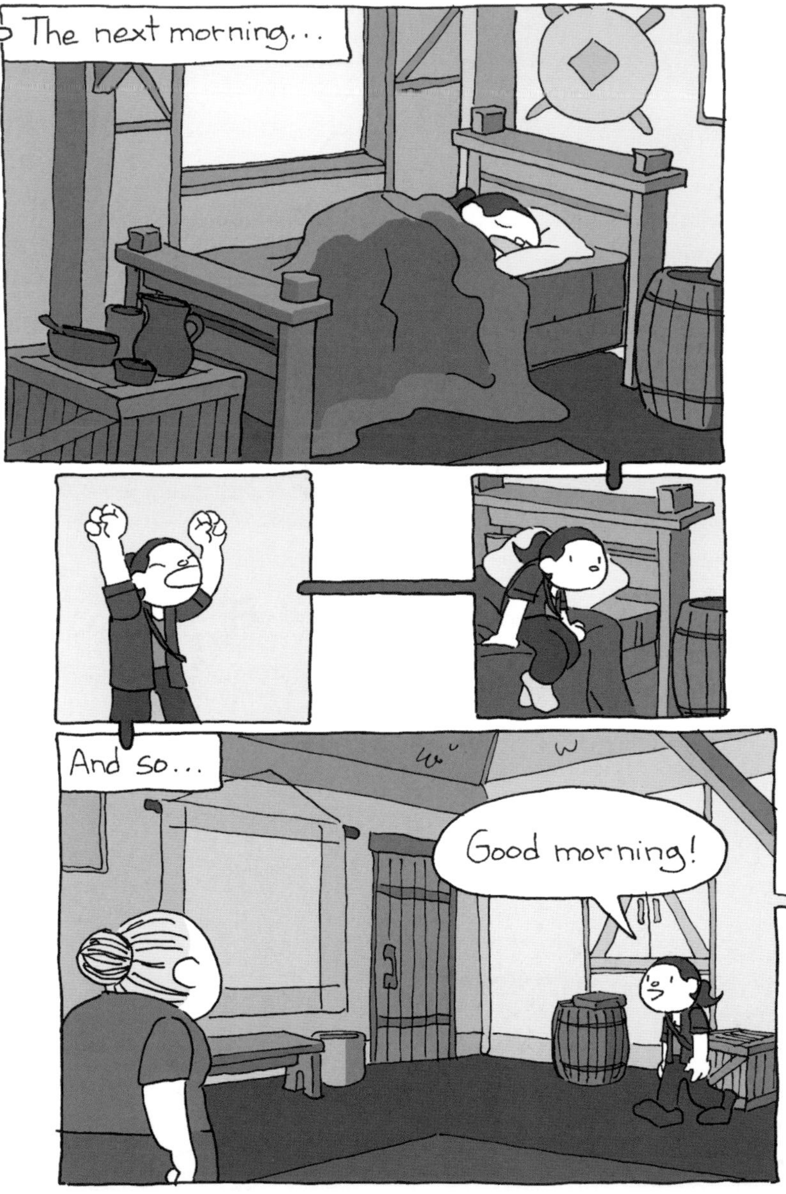
The next morning...
And so...
Good morning!

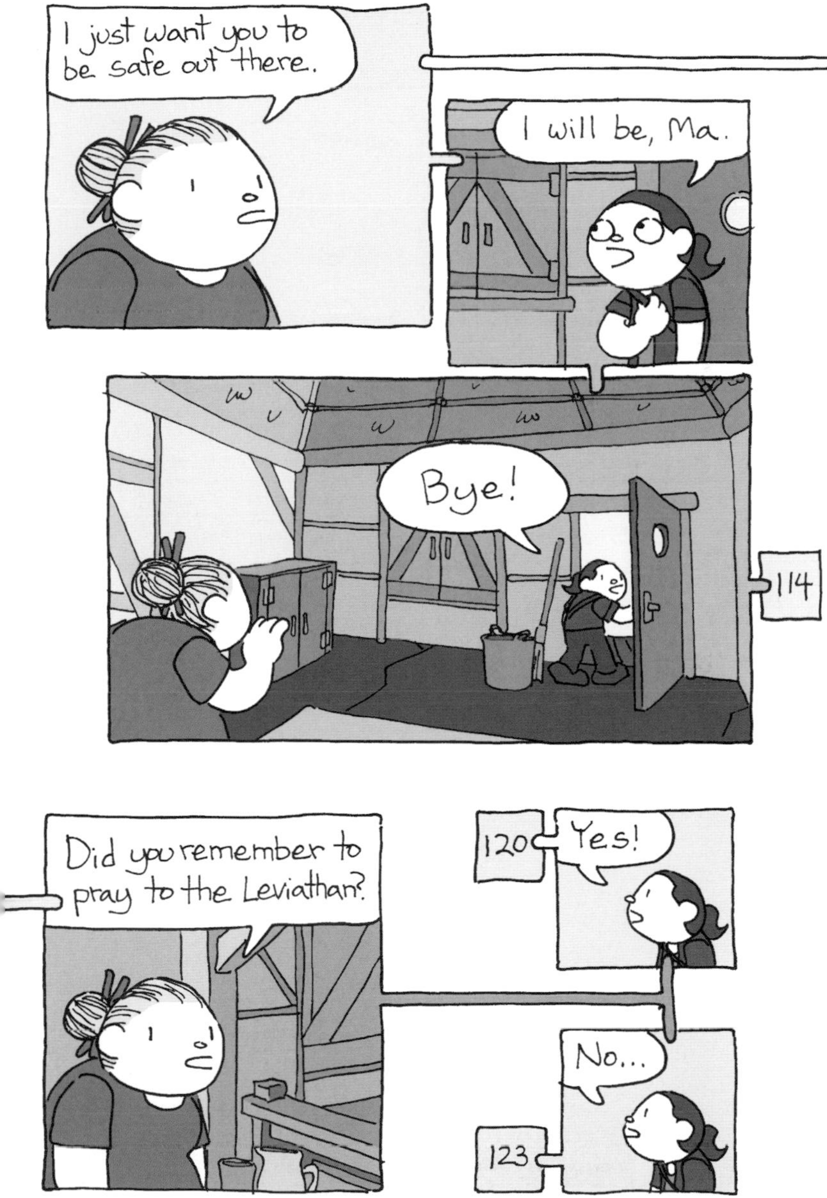
I just want you to be safe out there.
I will be, Ma.
Bye!
114
Did you remember to pray to the Leviathan?
120
Yes!
No...
123

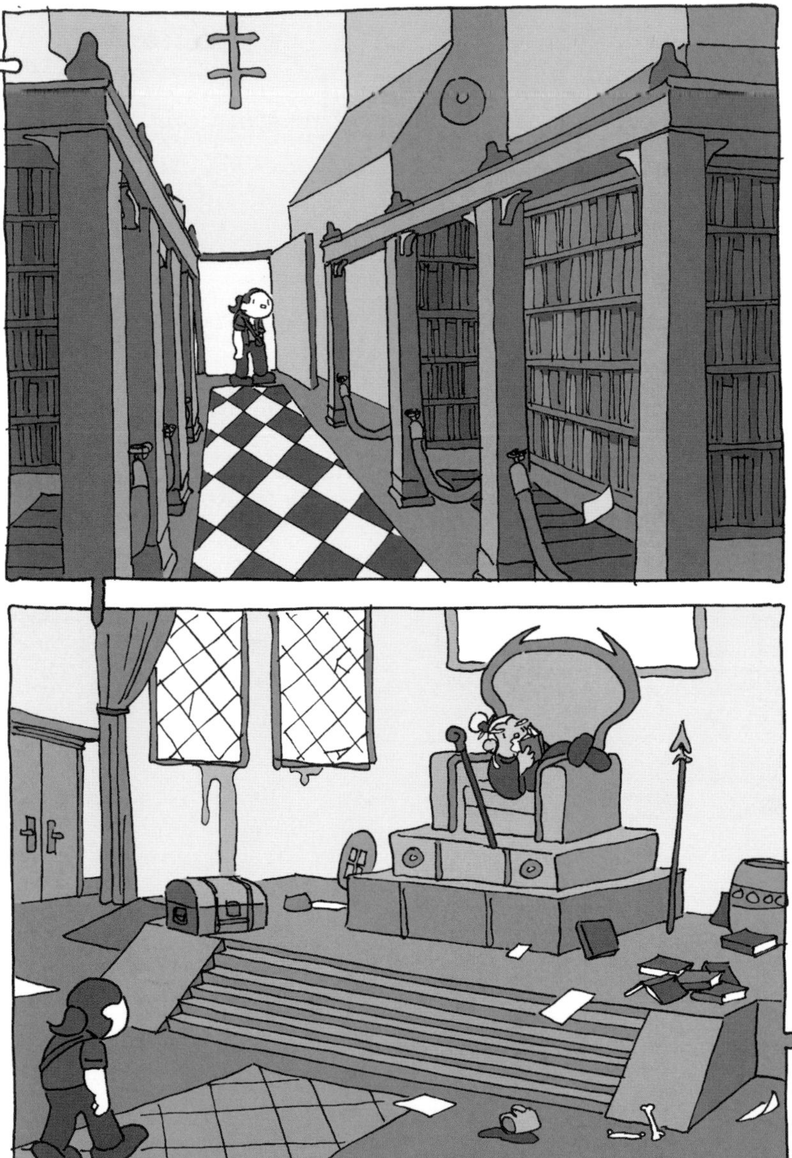

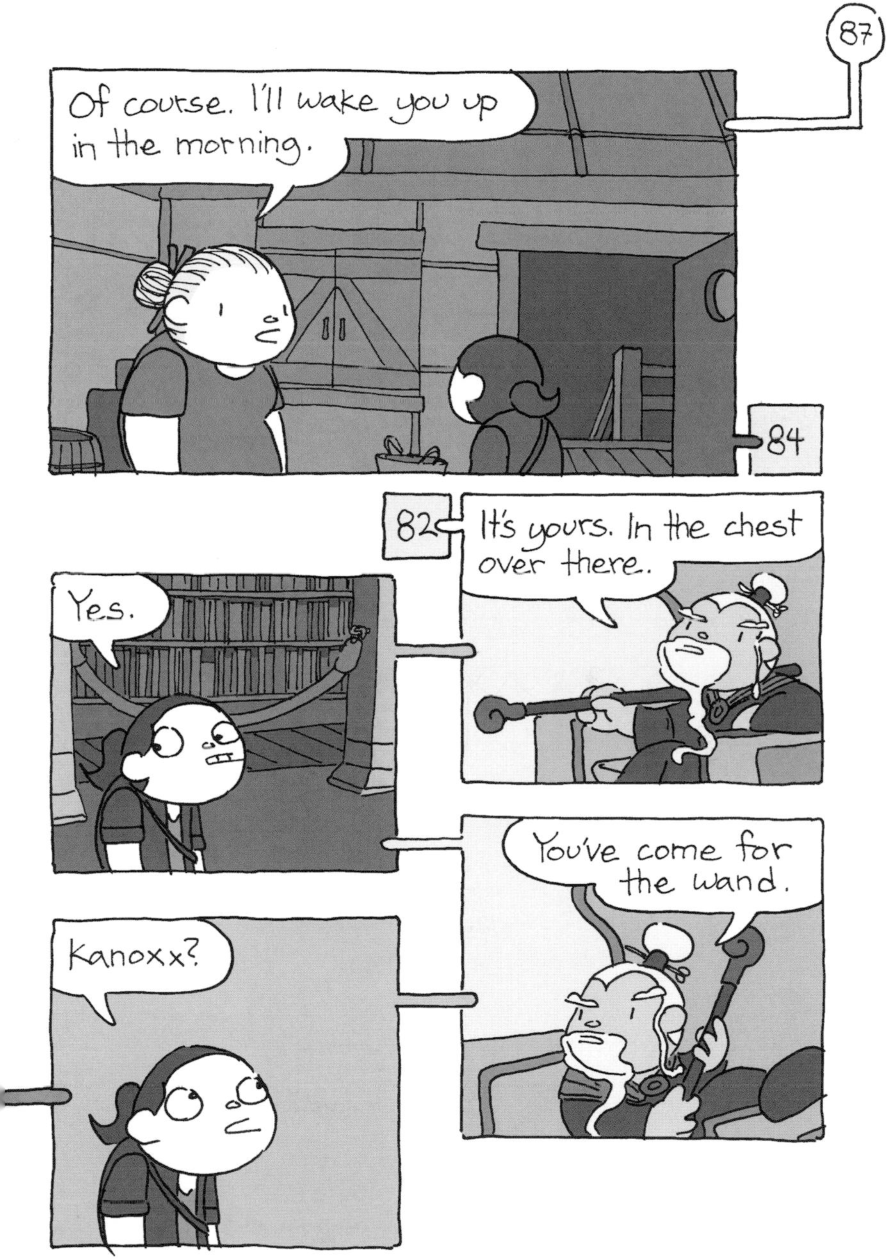
87
Of course. I'll wake you up in the morning.
84
82
It's yours. In the chest over there.
Yes.
You've come for the wand.
Kanoxx?

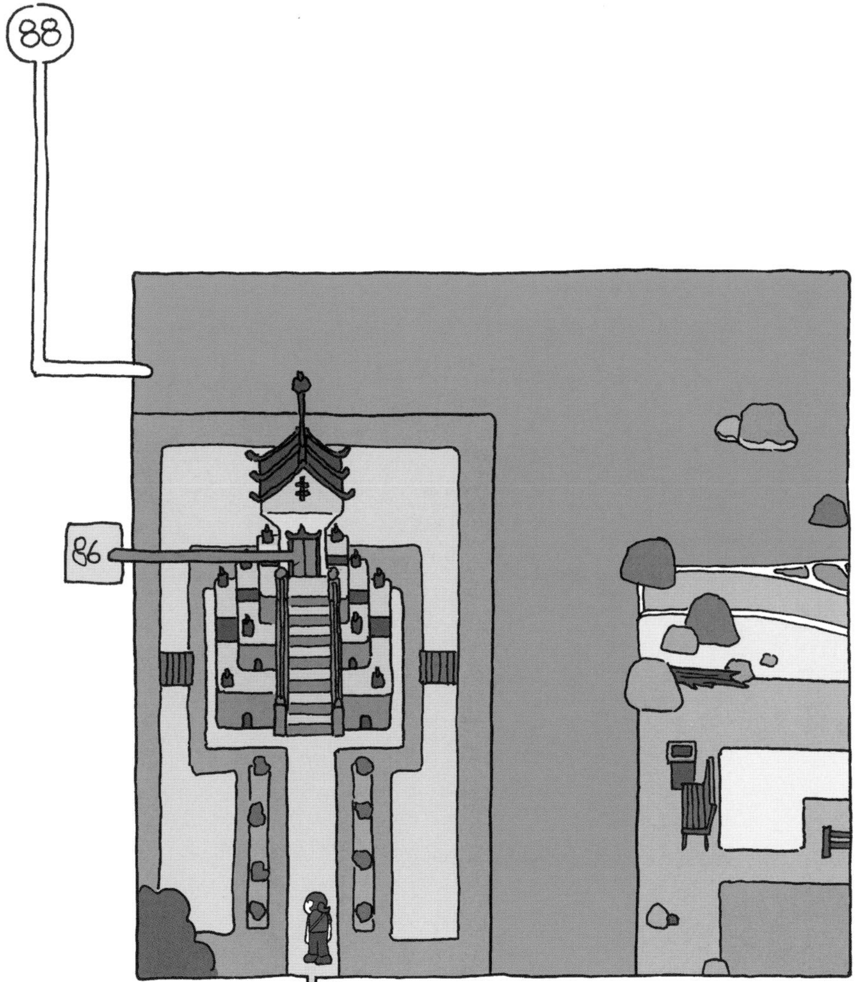
88
86
27

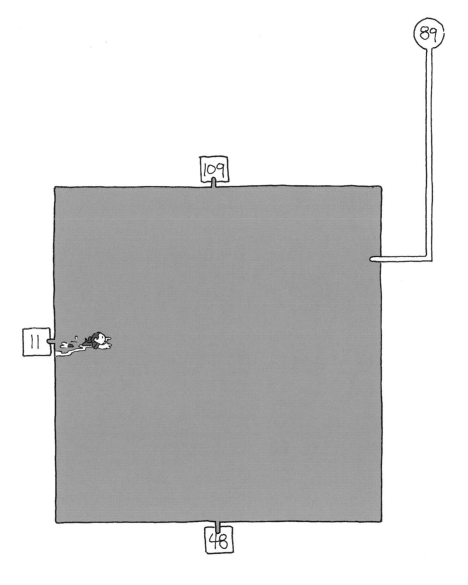

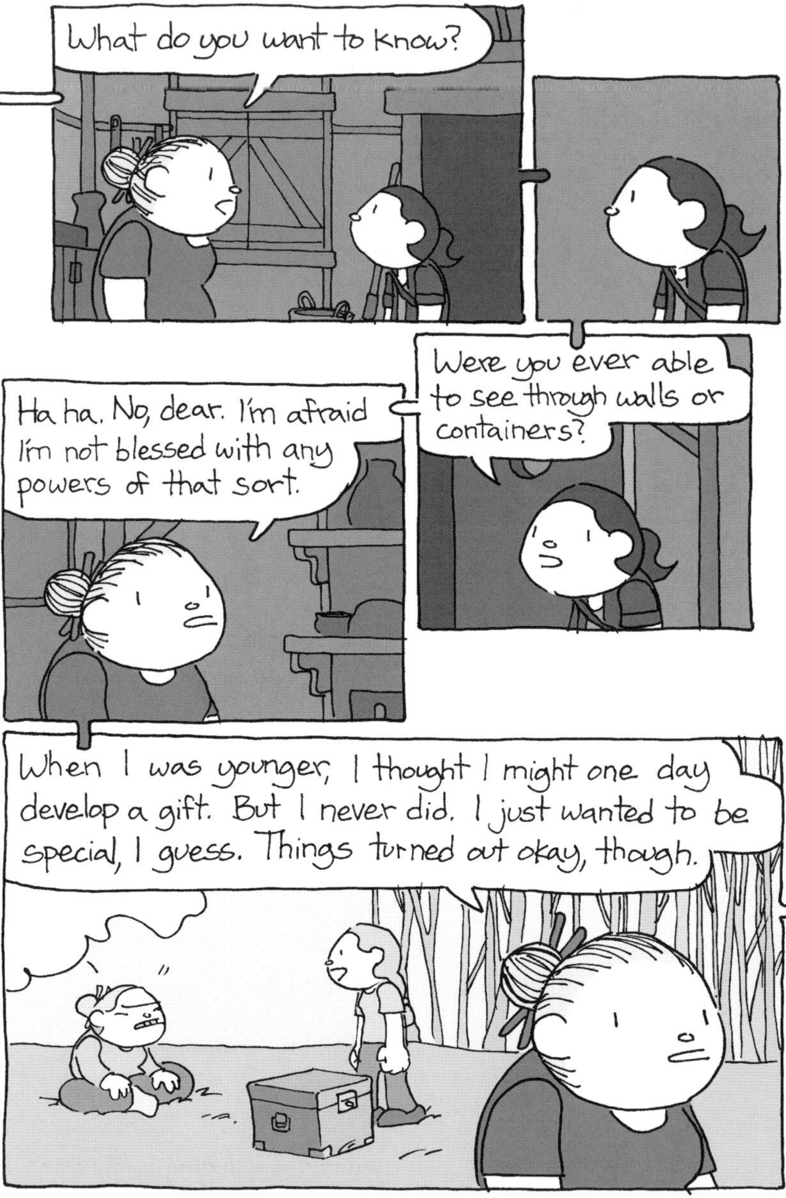
What do you want to know?
Were you ever able to see through walls or containers?
Ha ha. No, dear. I'm afraid I'm not blessed with any powers of that sort.
When I was younger, I thought I might one day develop a gift. But I never did. I just wanted to be special, I guess. Things turned out okay, though.

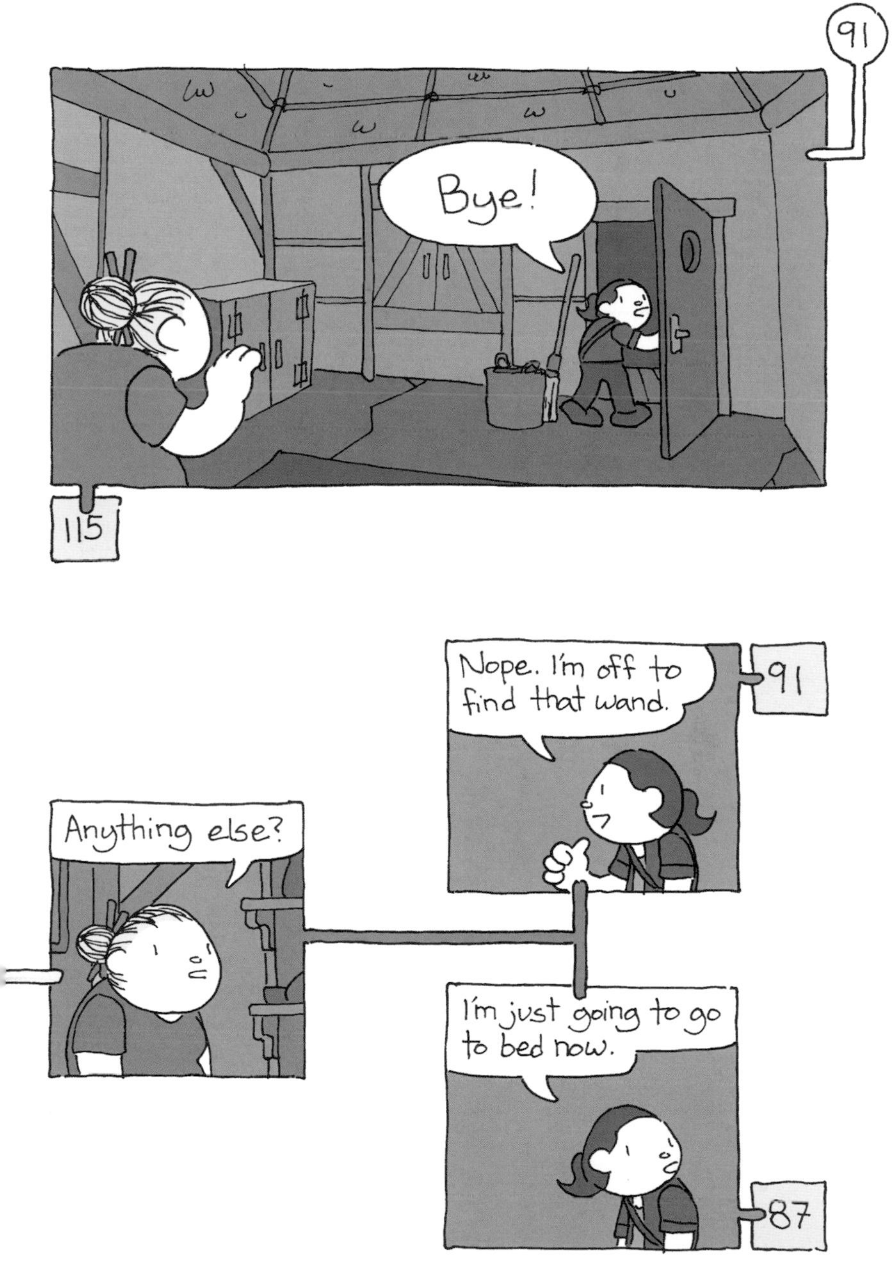
91
Bye!
115
Anything else?
Nope. I'm off to find that wand.
91
I'm just going to go to bed now.
87

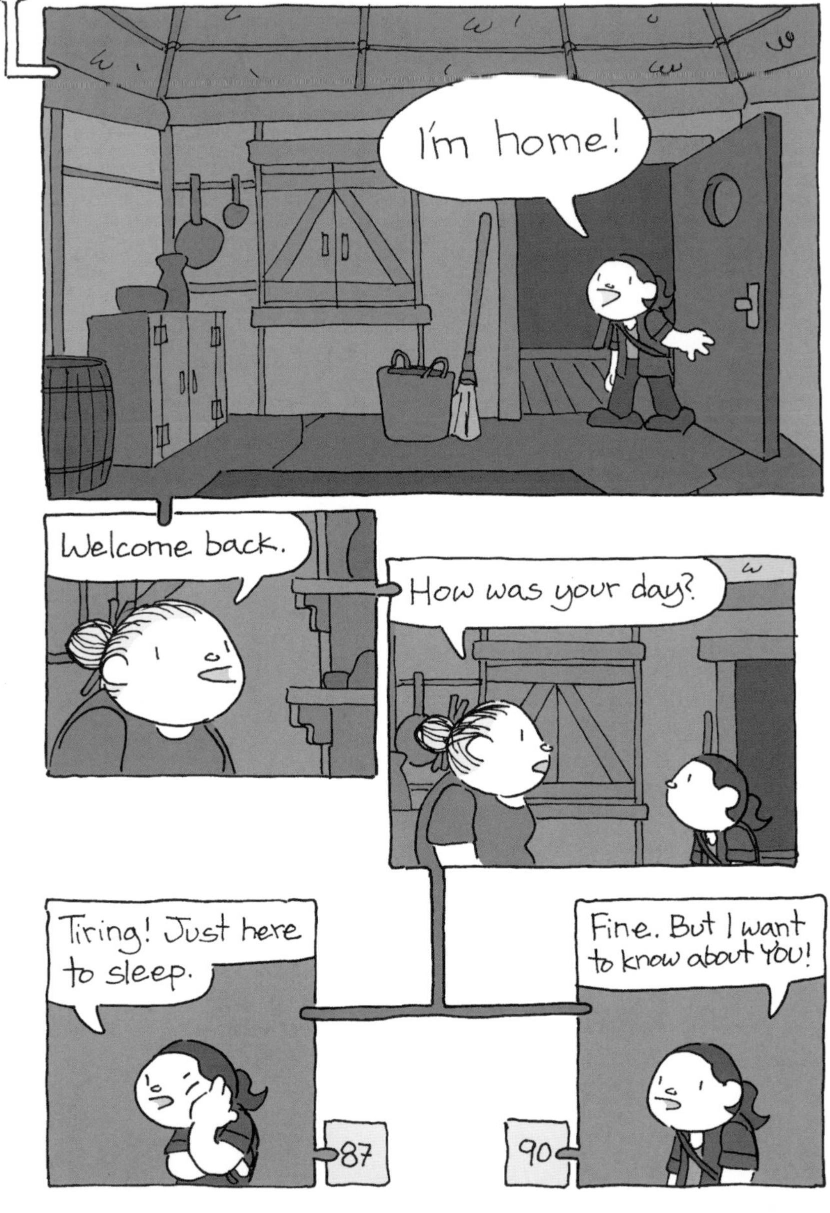
I'm home!
Welcome back.
How was your day?
Tiring! Just here to sleep.
87
Fine. But I want to know about YOU!
90

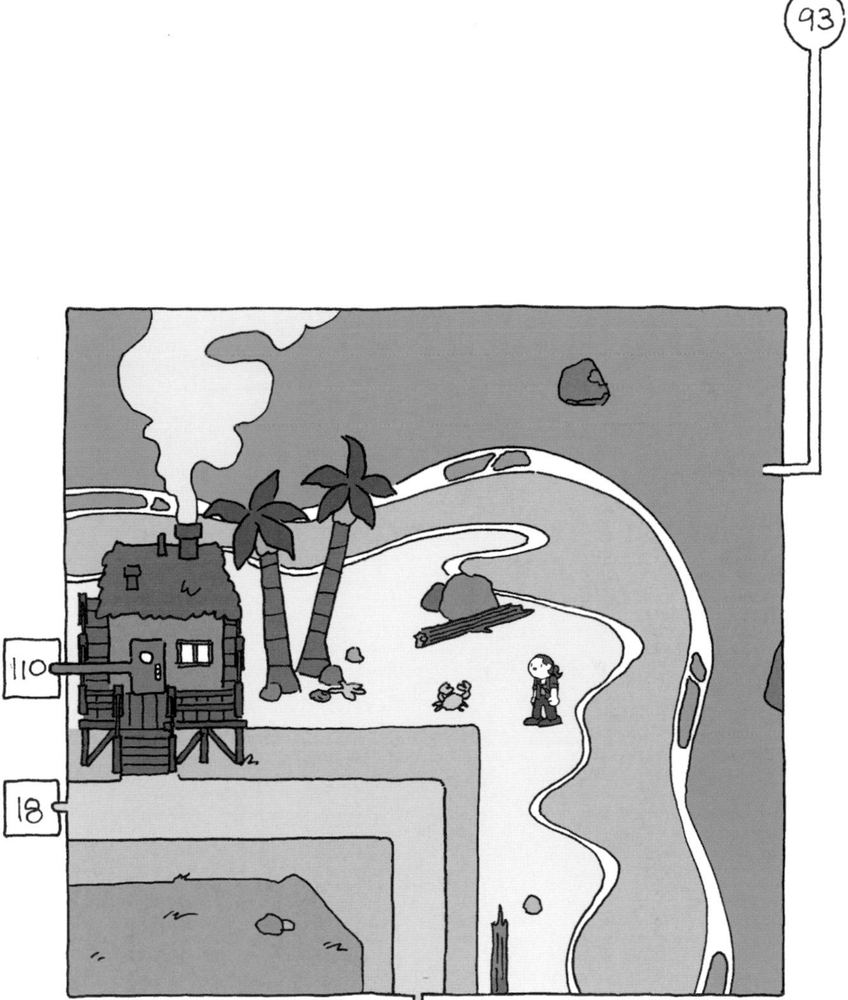
93
110
18
132

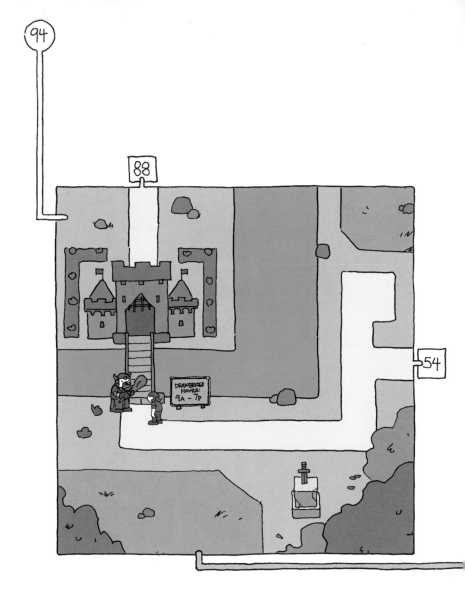

DRAWBRIDGE
HOURS:
9A - 7P

94

88

54

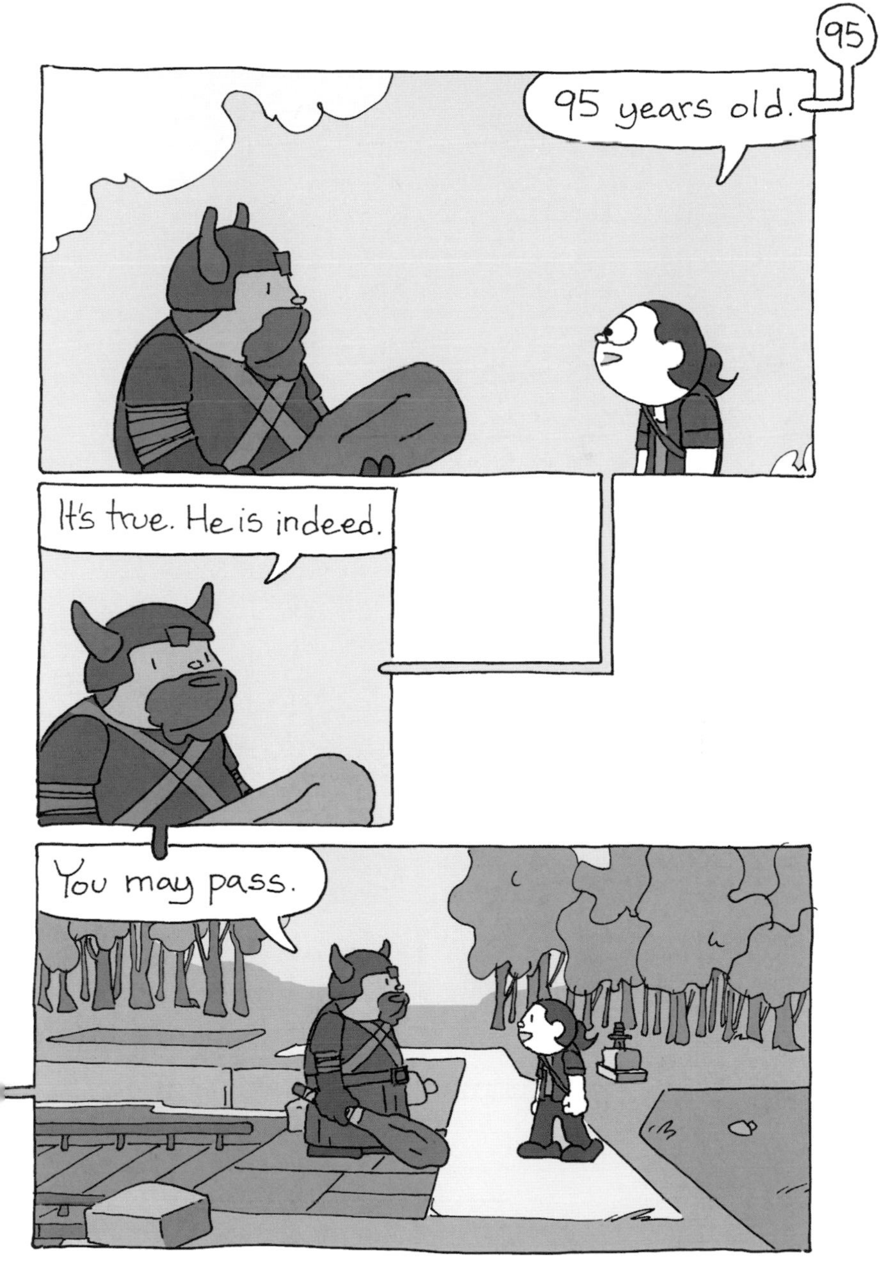
95
95 years old.
It's true. He is indeed.
You may pass.

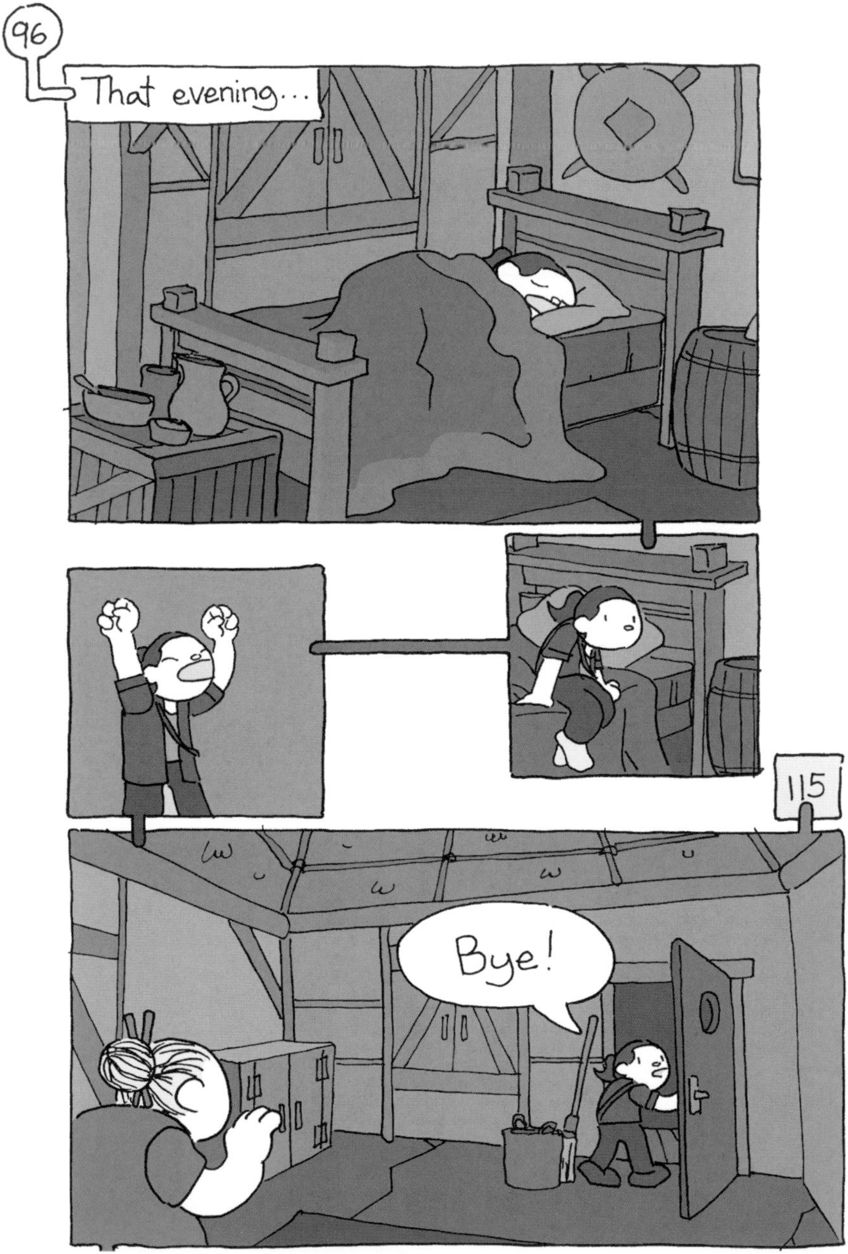
96
That evening...
115
Bye!

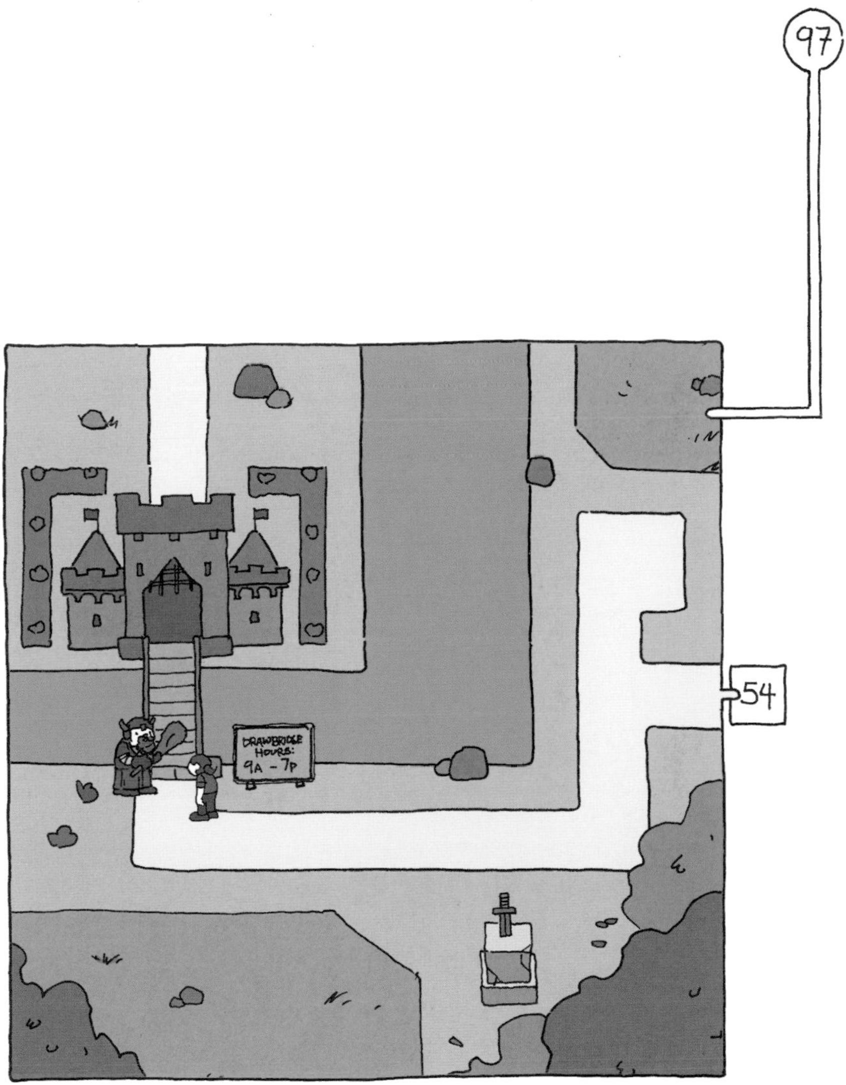
97
DRAWBRIDGE HOURS:
9A – 7P
54

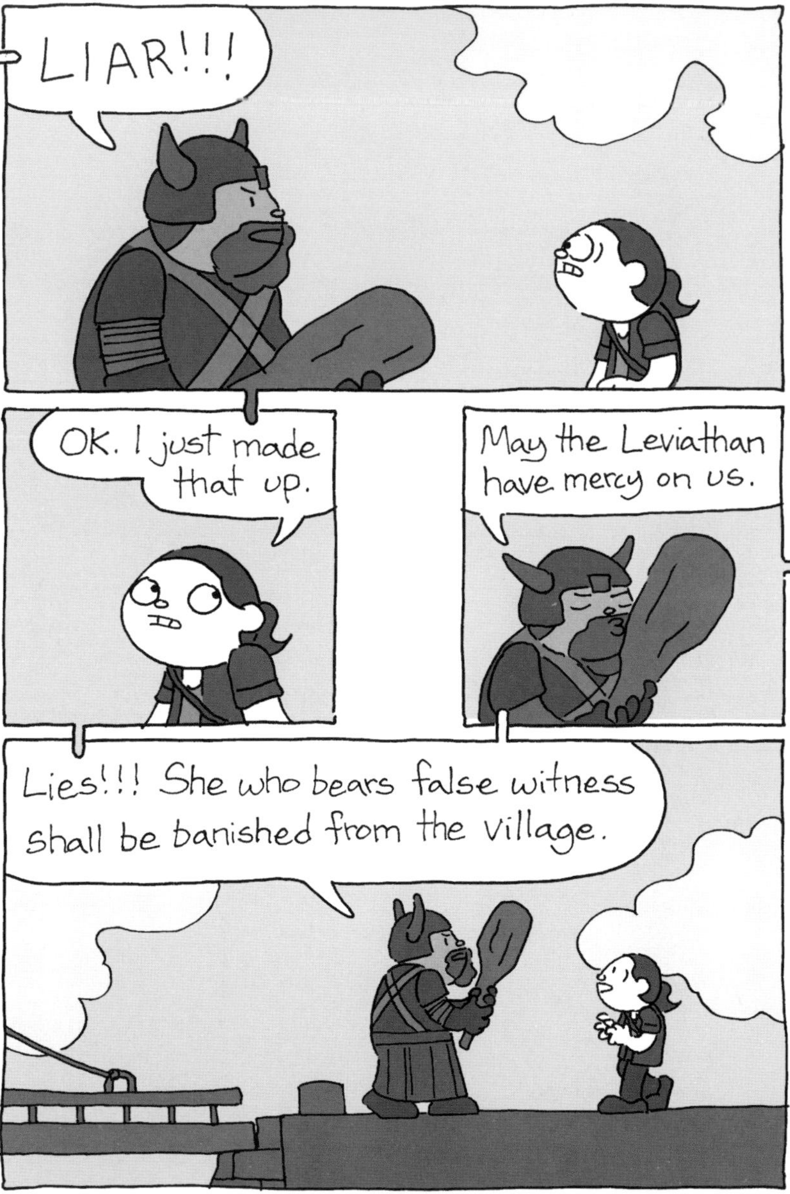
LIAR!!!
OK. I just made that up.
May the Leviathan have mercy on us.
Lies!!! She who bears false witness shall be banished from the village.

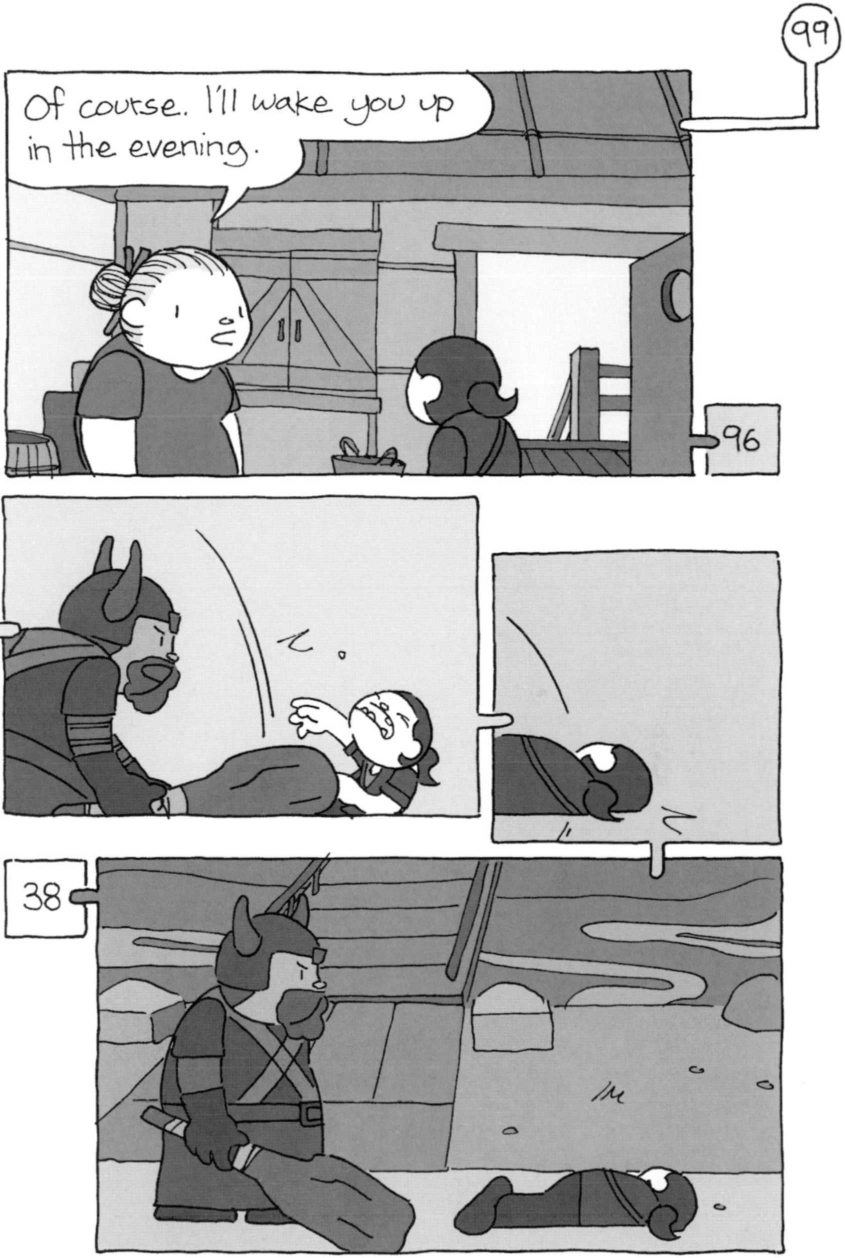
99
Of course. I'll wake you up in the evening.
96
38

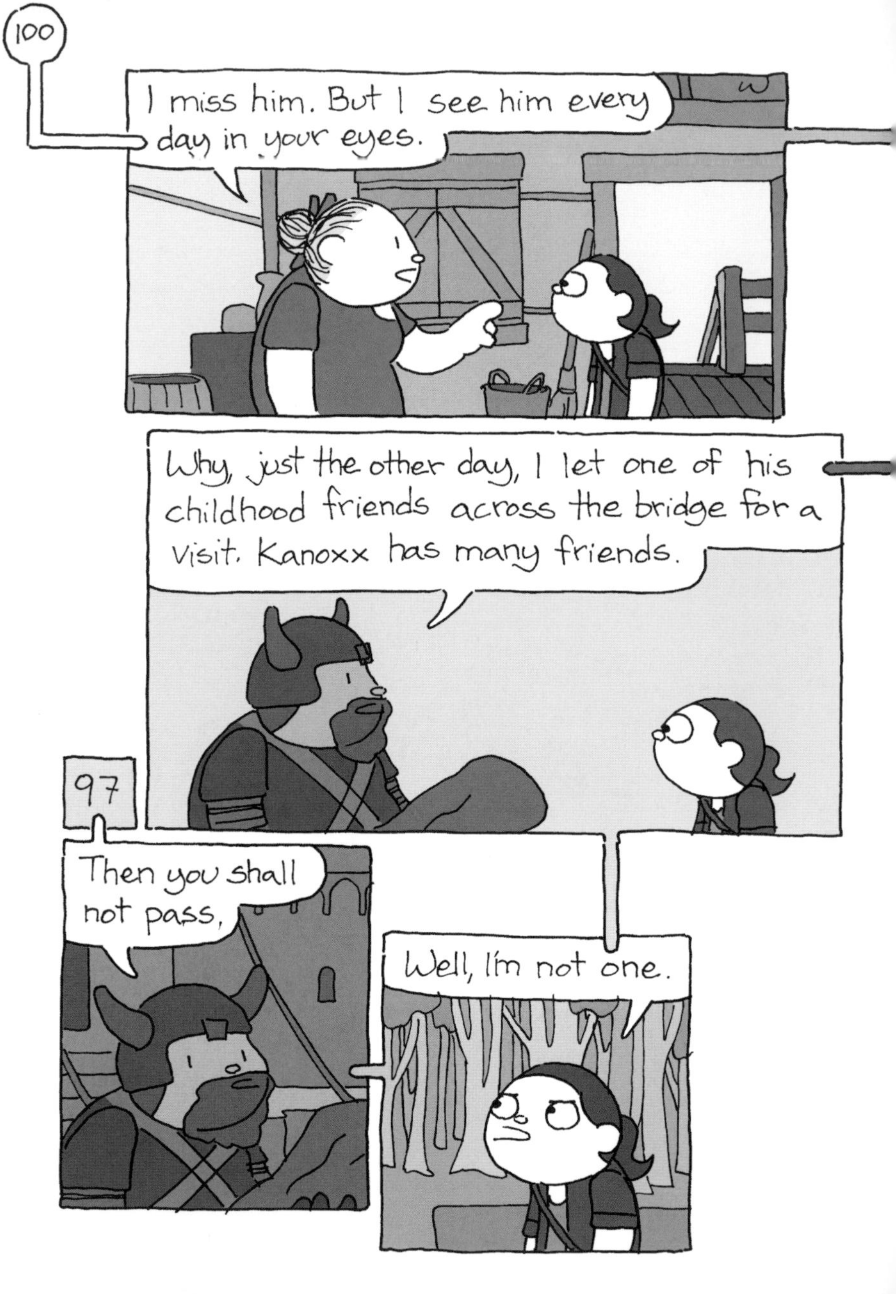
100
I miss him. But I see him every day in your eyes.
Why, just the other day, I let one of his childhood friends across the bridge for a visit. Kanoxx has many friends.
97
Then you shall not pass.
Well, I'm not one.

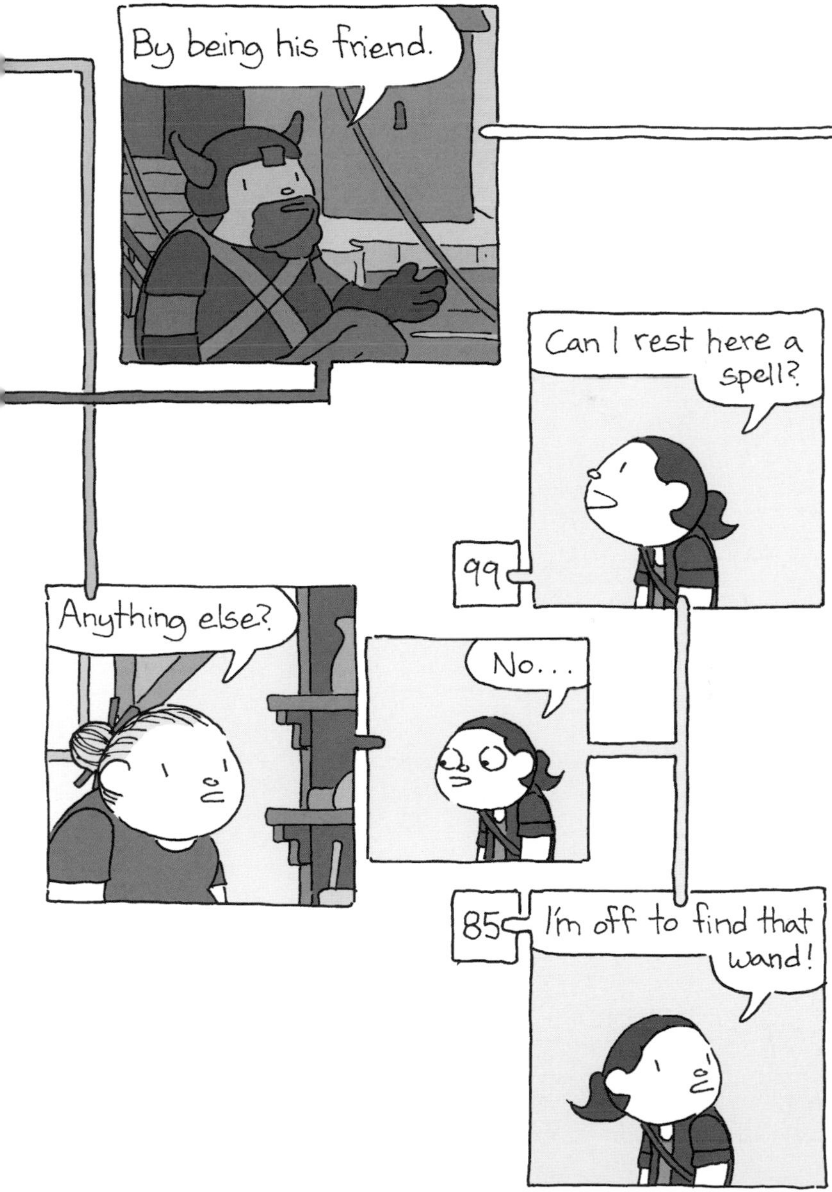
By being his friend.
Can I rest here a spell?
99
Anything else?
No...
85
I'm off to find that wand!

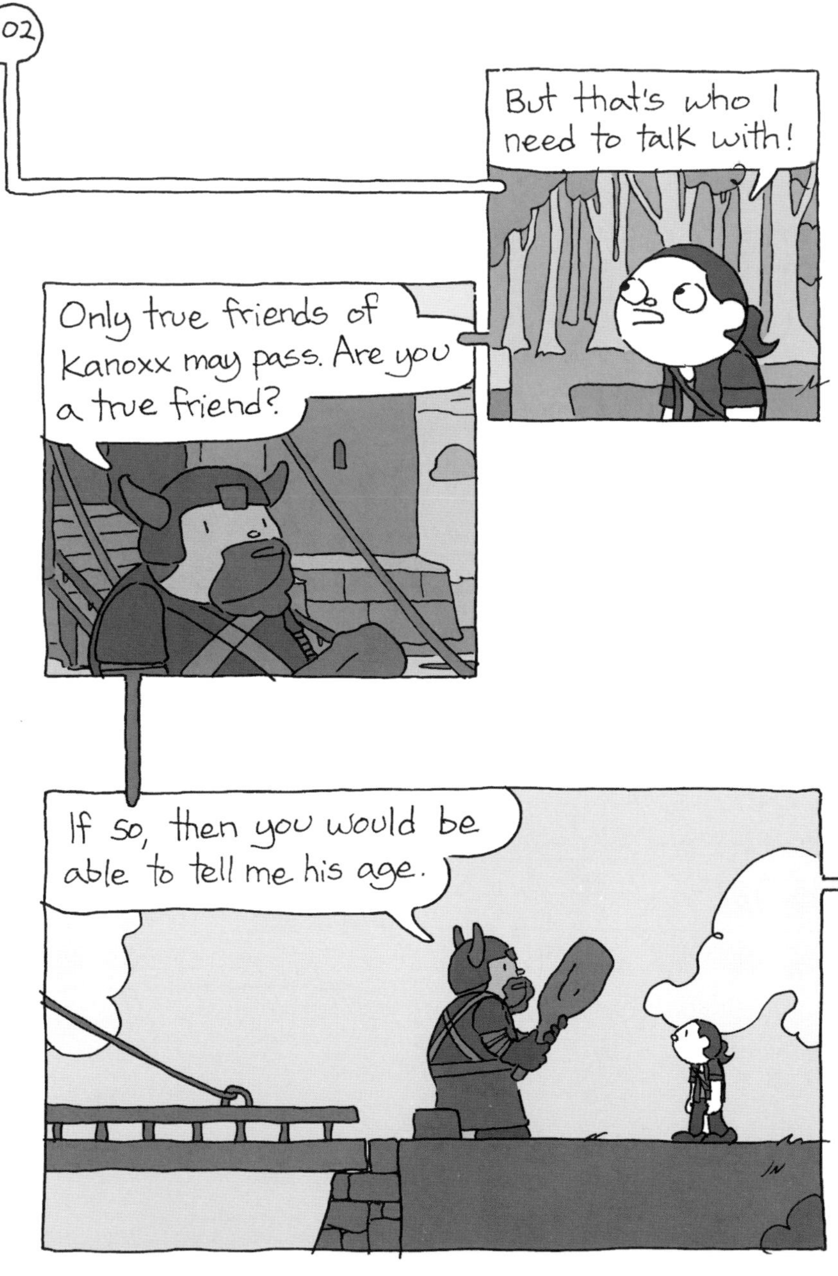
But that's who I need to talk with!
Only true friends of Kanoxx may pass. Are you a true friend?
If so, then you would be able to tell me his age.

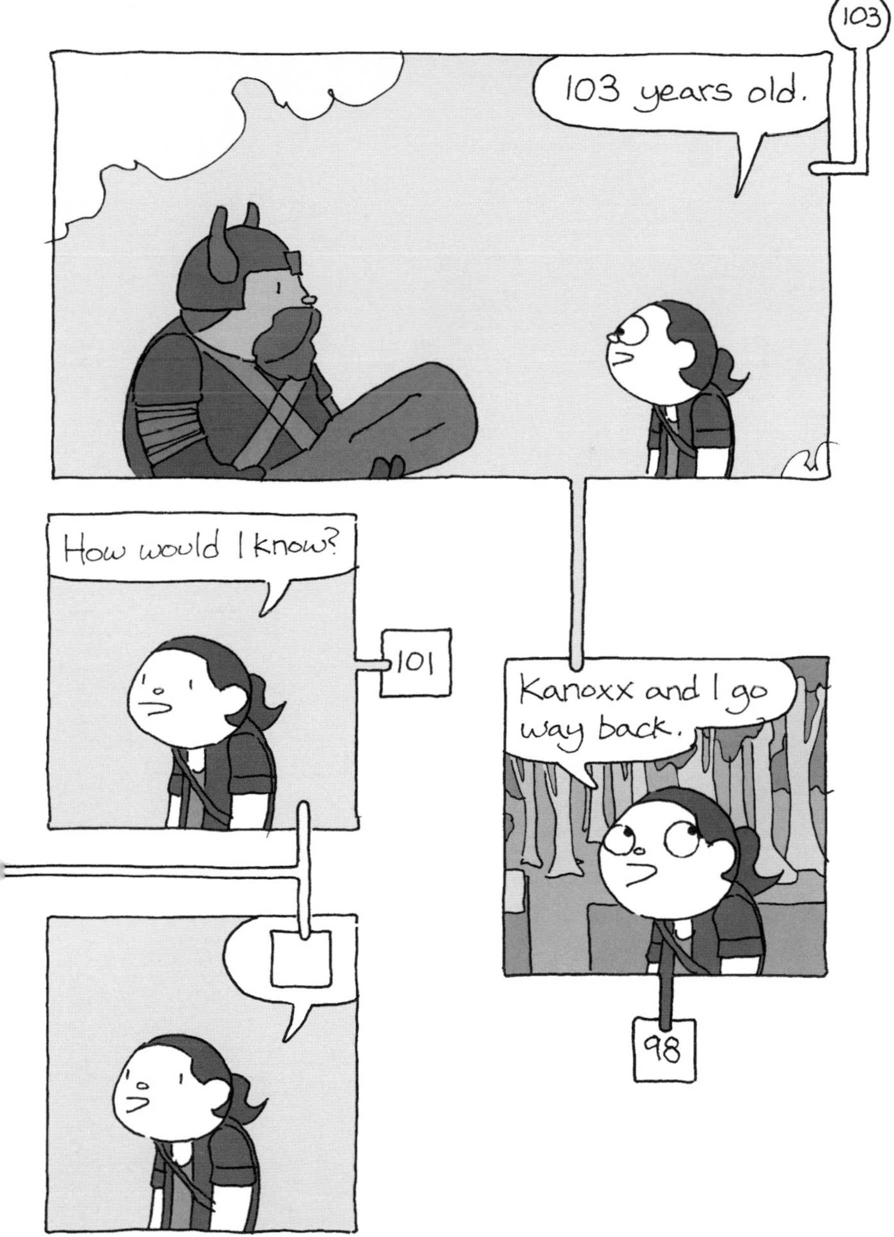
103
103 years old.
How would I know?
101
Kanoxx and I go way back.
98

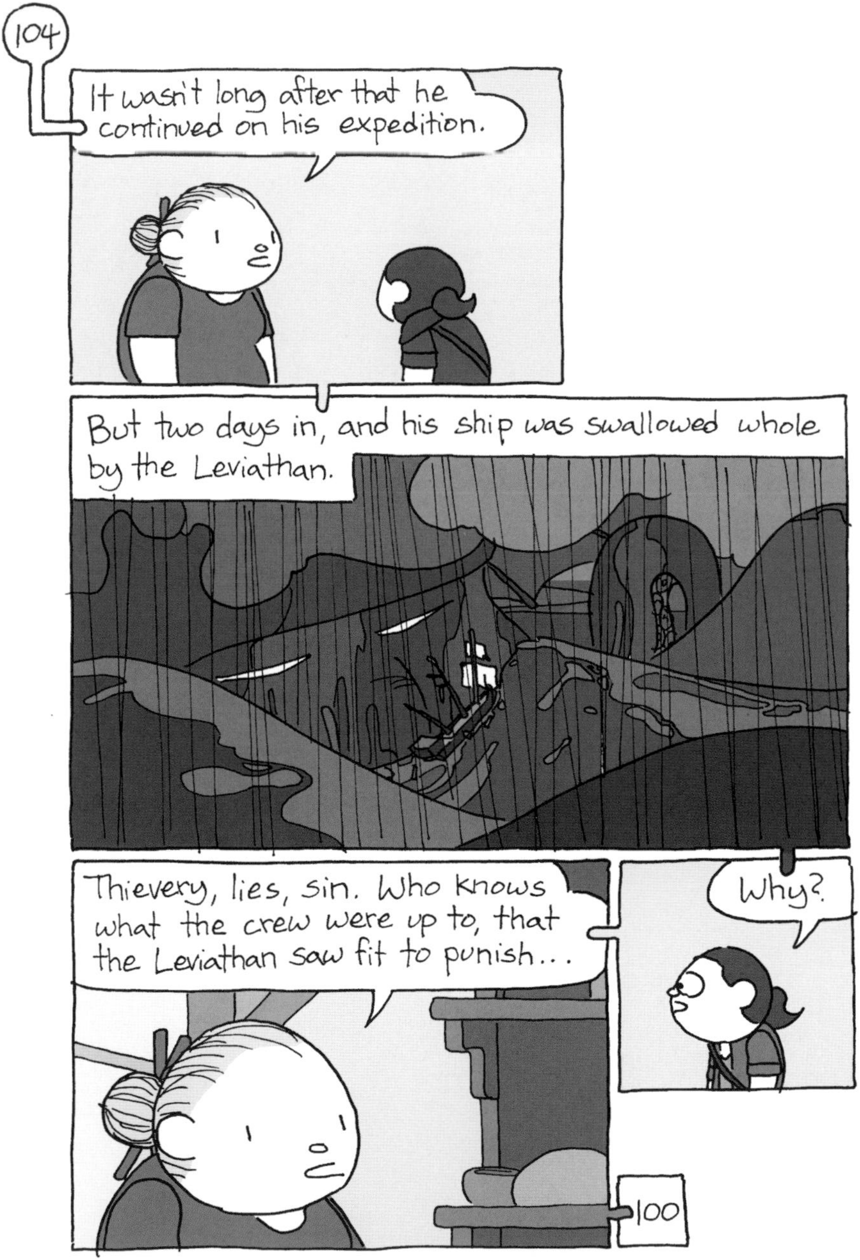
104
It wasn't long after that he continued on his expedition.
But two days in, and his ship was swallowed whole by the Leviathan.
Thievery, lies, sin. Who knows what the crew were up to, that the Leviathan saw fit to punish...
Why?
100

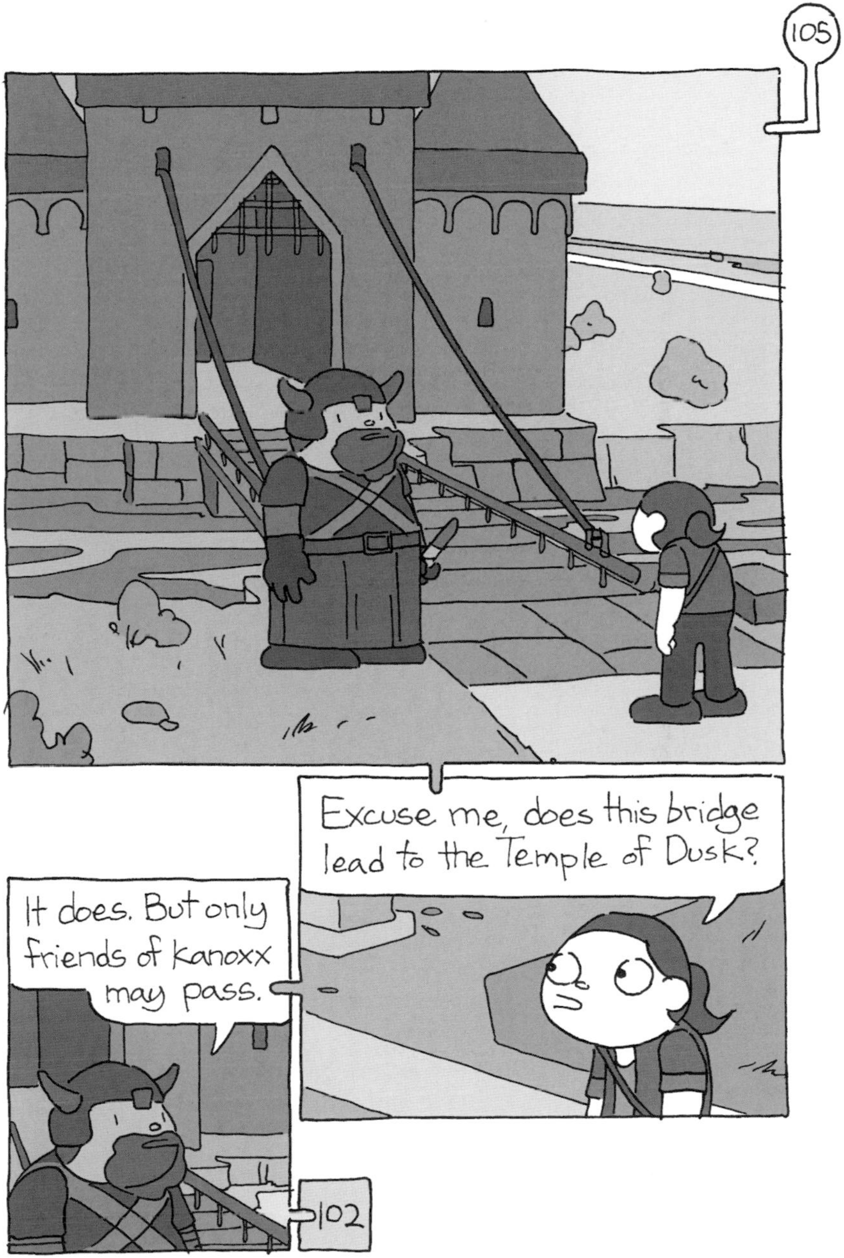
105
Excuse me, does this bridge lead to the Temple of Dusk?
It does. But only friends of kanoxx may pass.
102

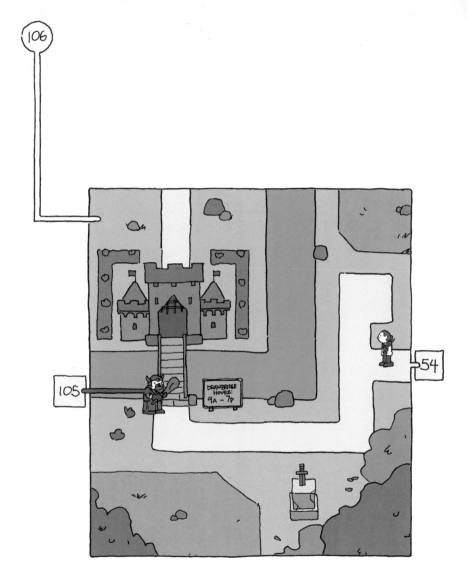

106

105

54

DRAWBRIDGE
HOURS:
9A - 7P

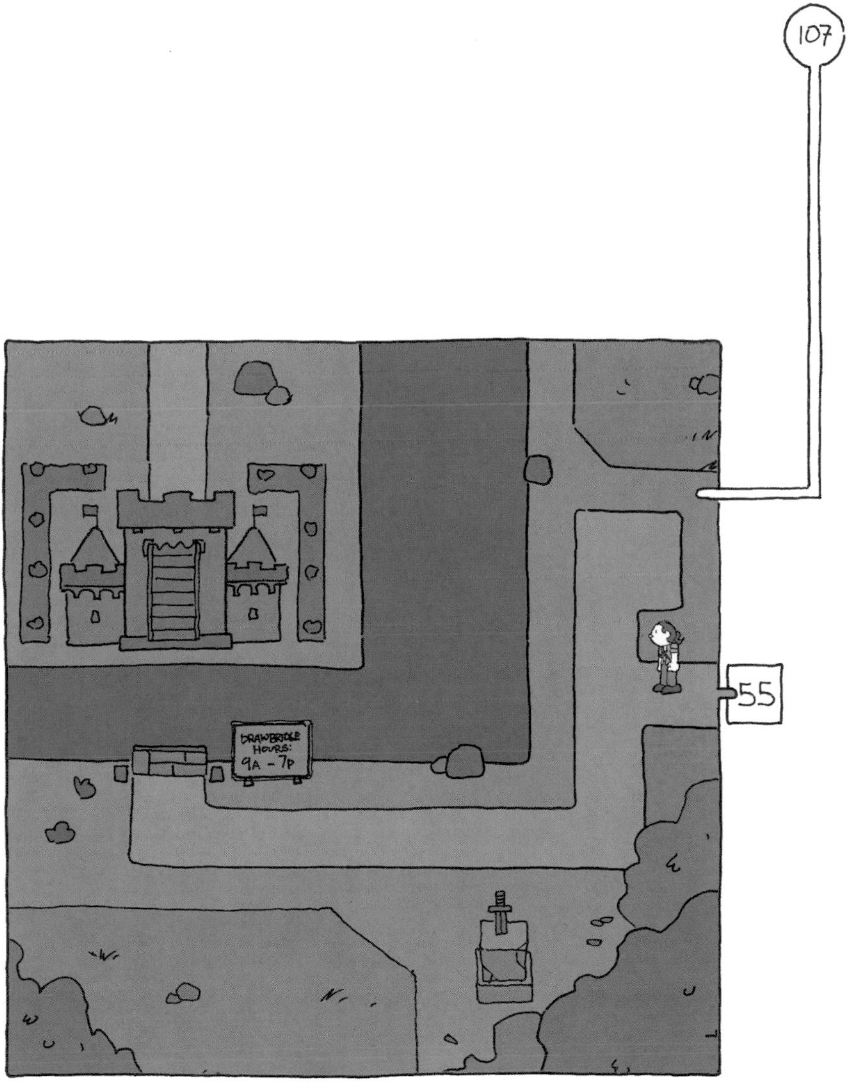
107
DRAWBRIDGE HOURS:
9A - 7P
55

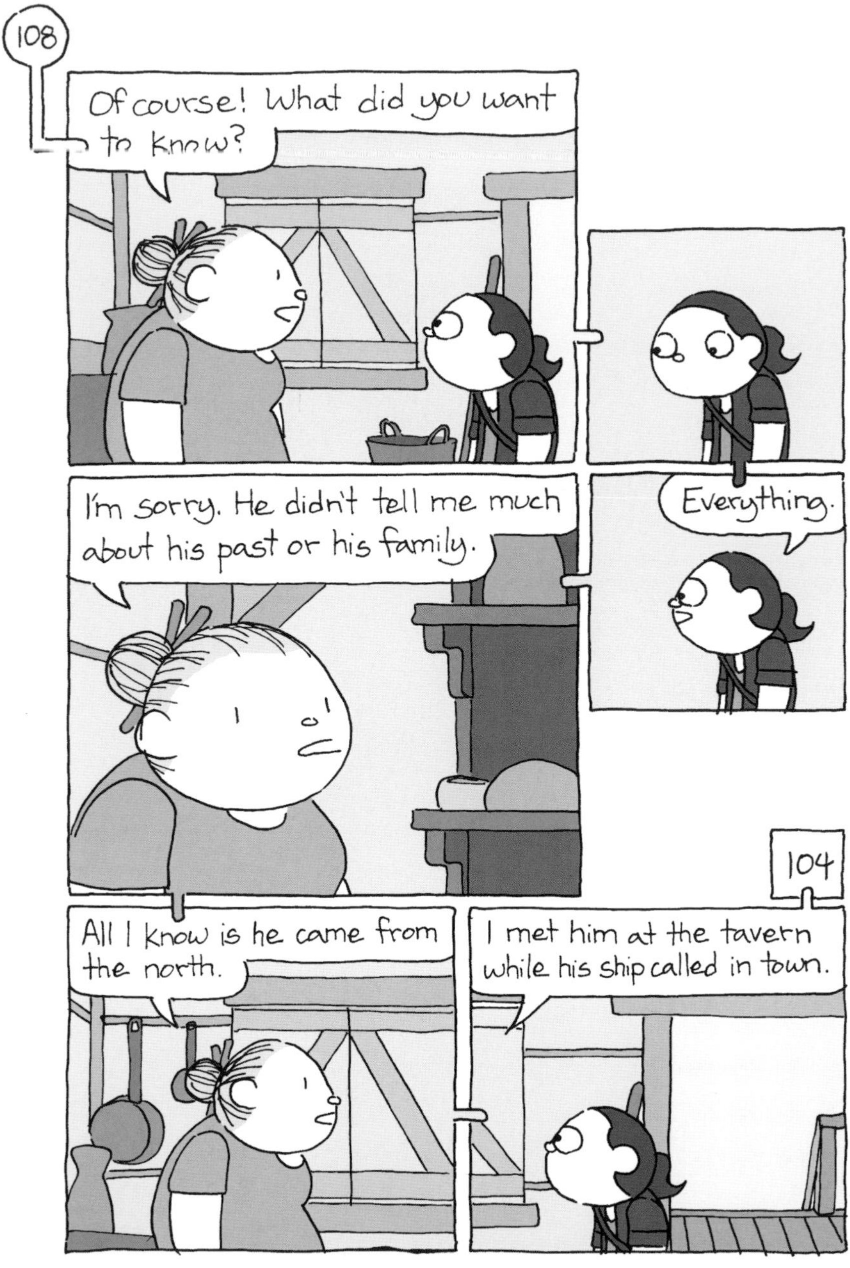
108
Of course! What did you want to know?
I'm sorry. He didn't tell me much about his past or his family.
Everything.
All I know is he came from the north.
104
I met him at the tavern while his ship called in town.

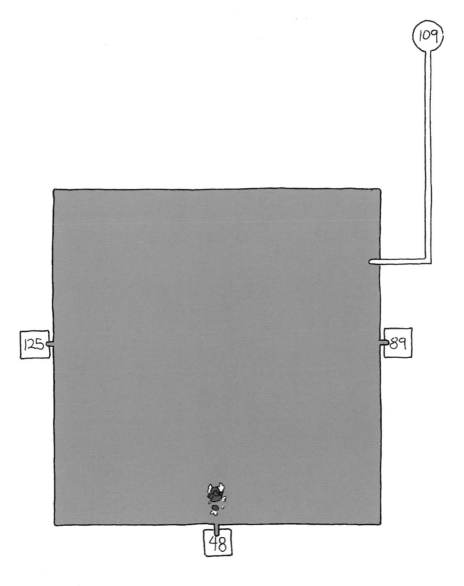

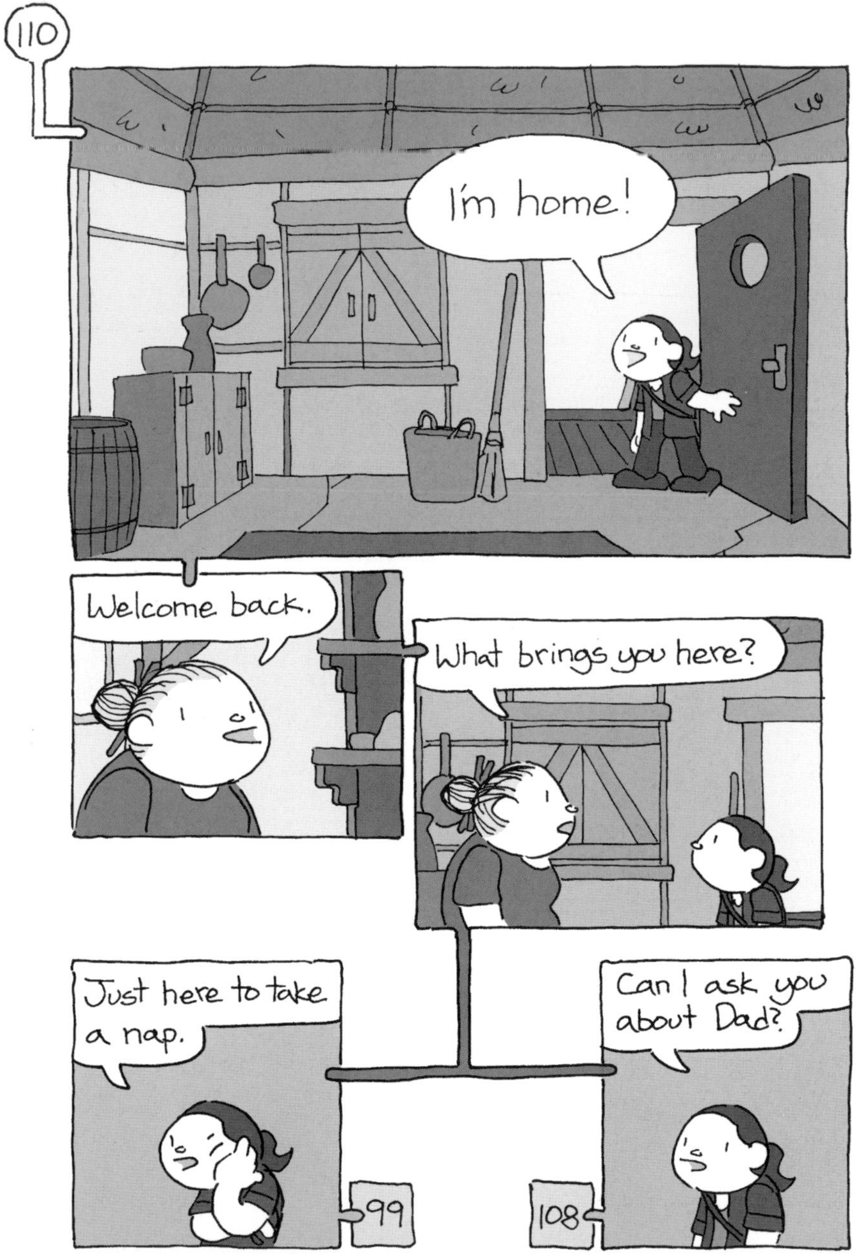
110
I'm home!
Welcome back.
What brings you here?
Just here to take a nap.
99
Can I ask you about Dad?
108

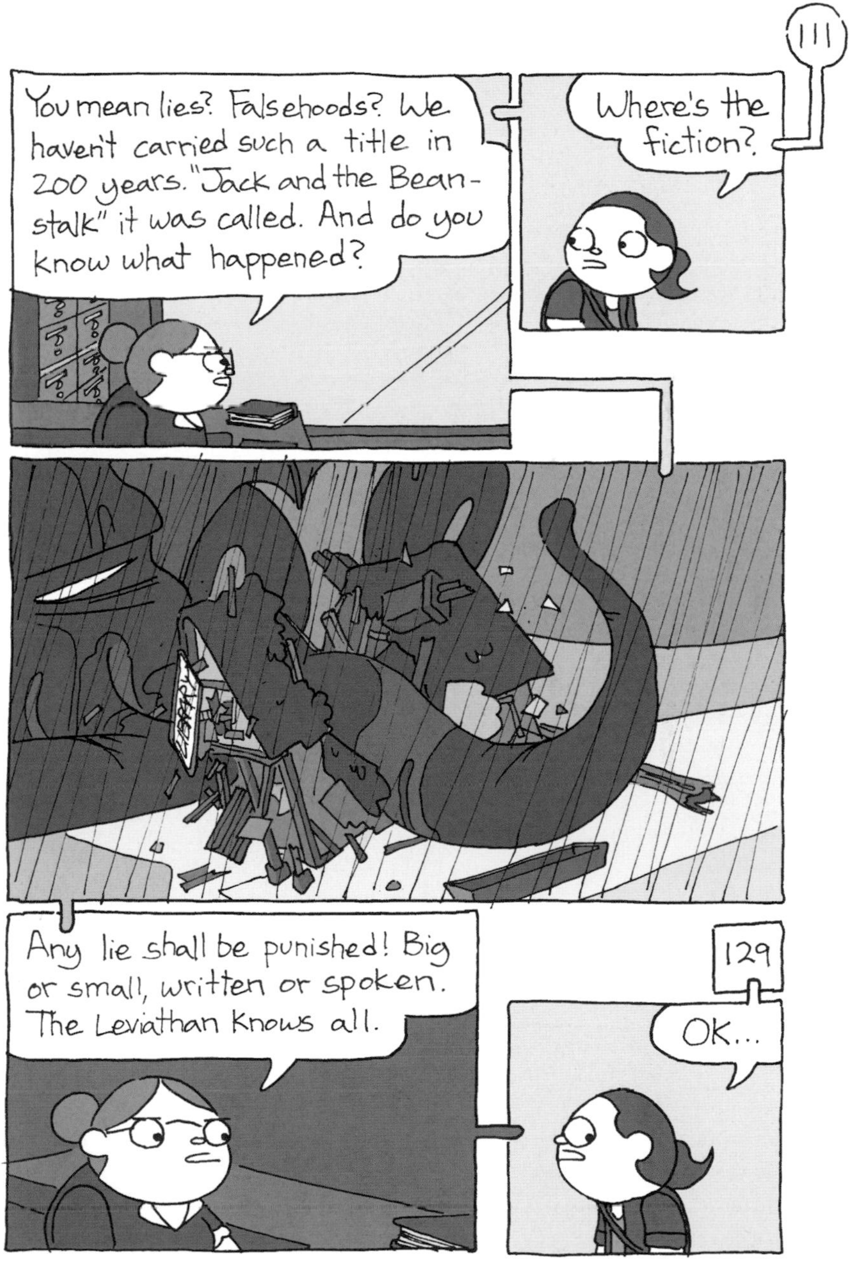
You mean lies? Falsehoods? We haven't carried such a title in 200 years. "Jack and the Beanstalk" it was called. And do you know what happened?
Where's the fiction?
111
Any lie shall be punished! Big or small, written or spoken. The Leviathan knows all.
129
OK...

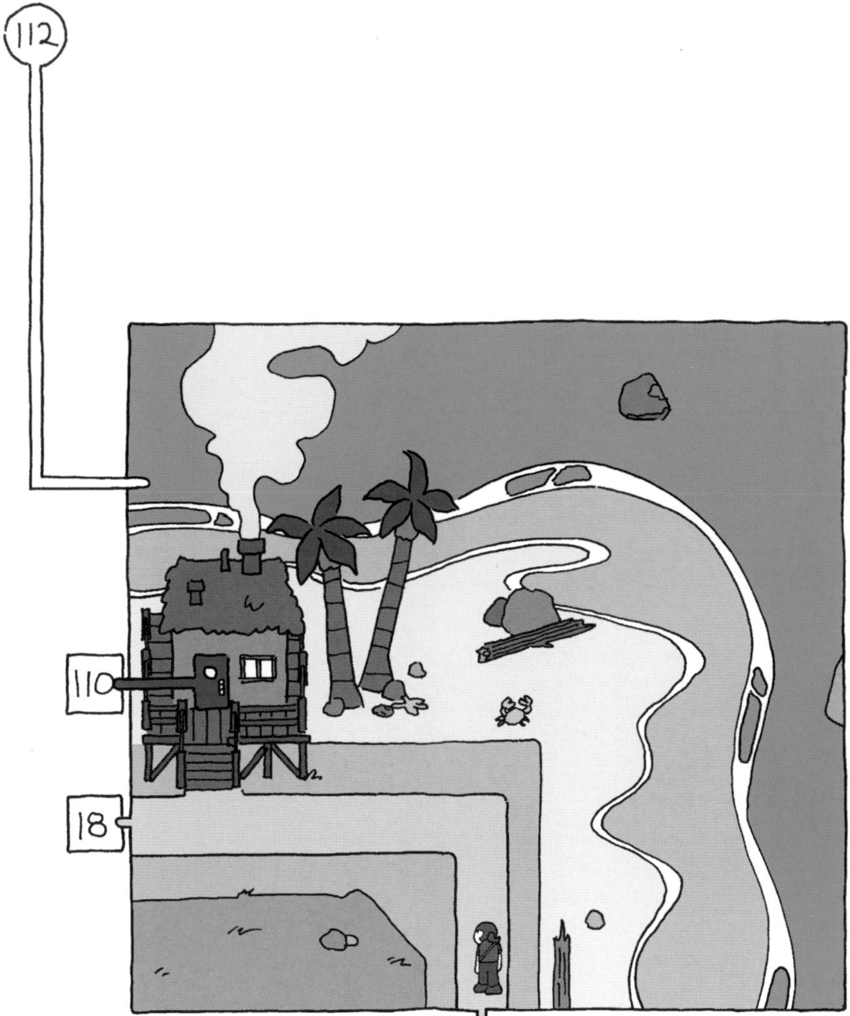
112
110
18
132

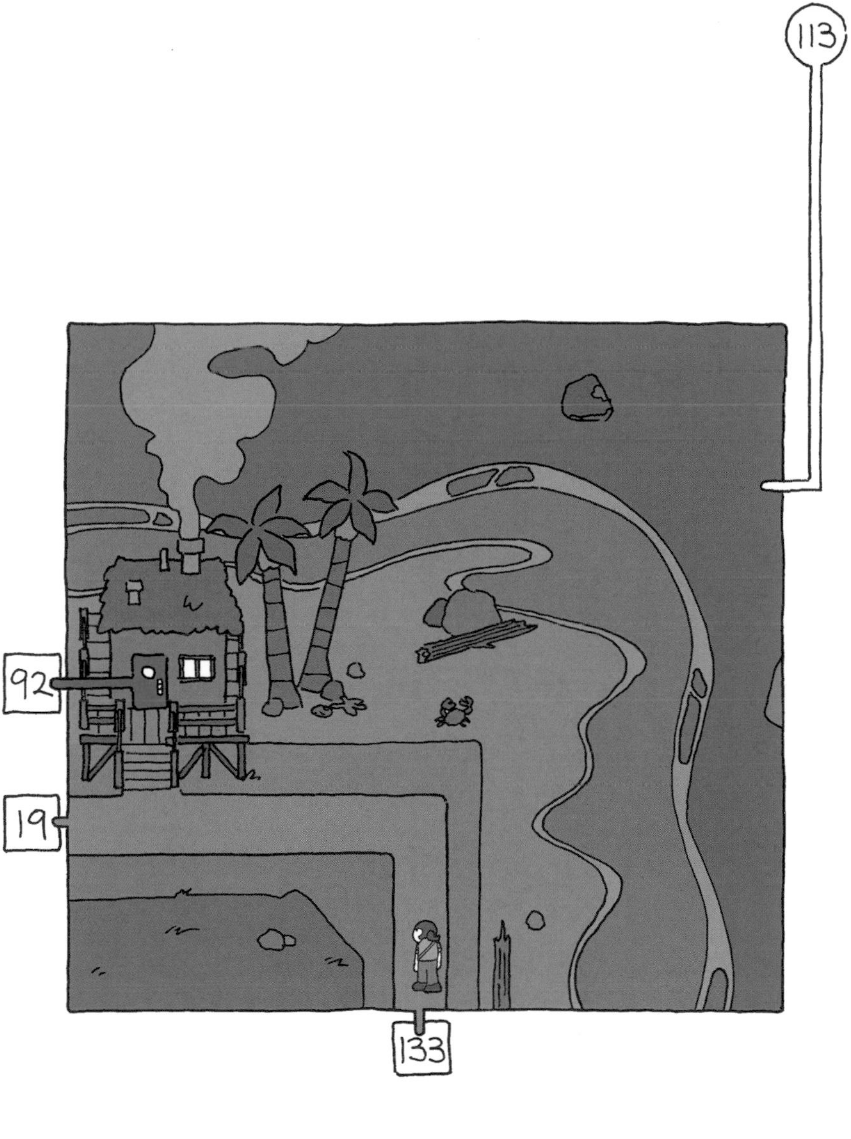
113
92
19
133

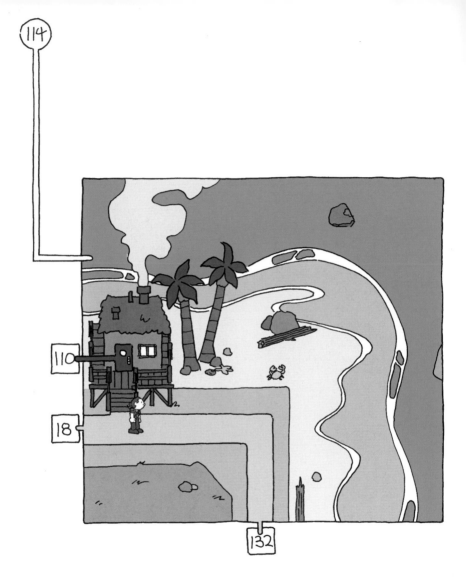

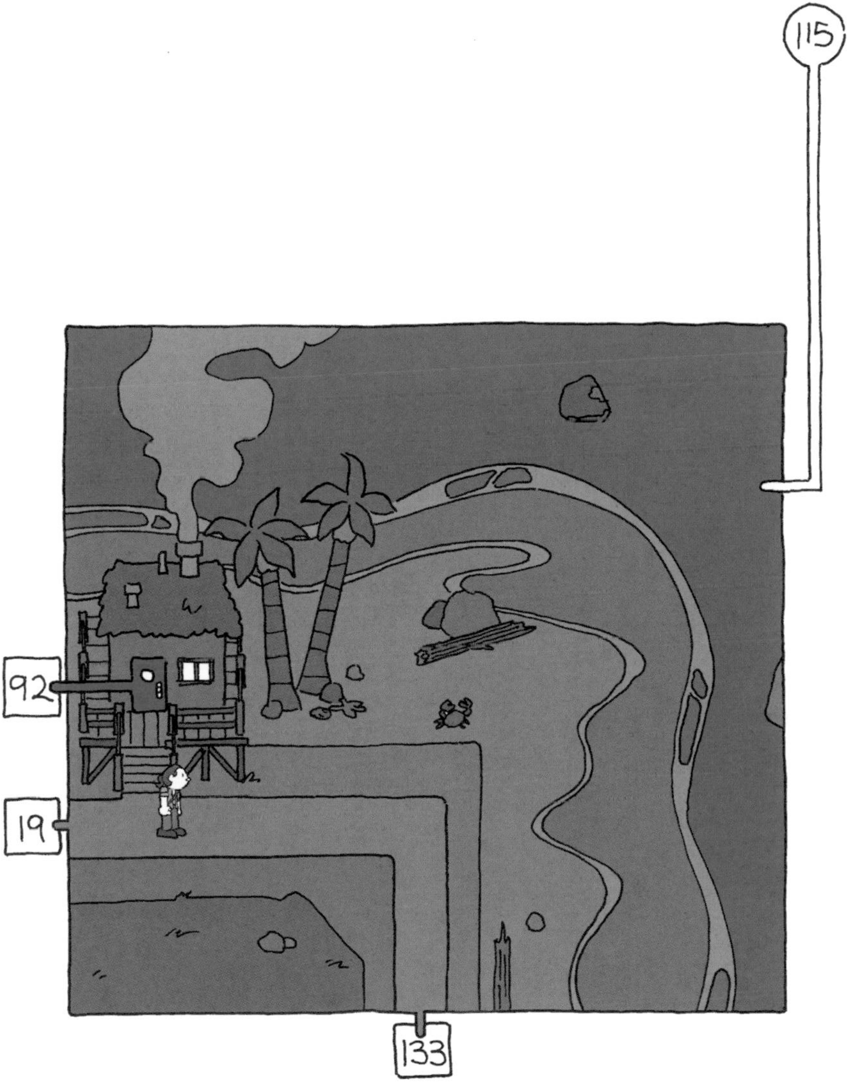
115
92
19
133

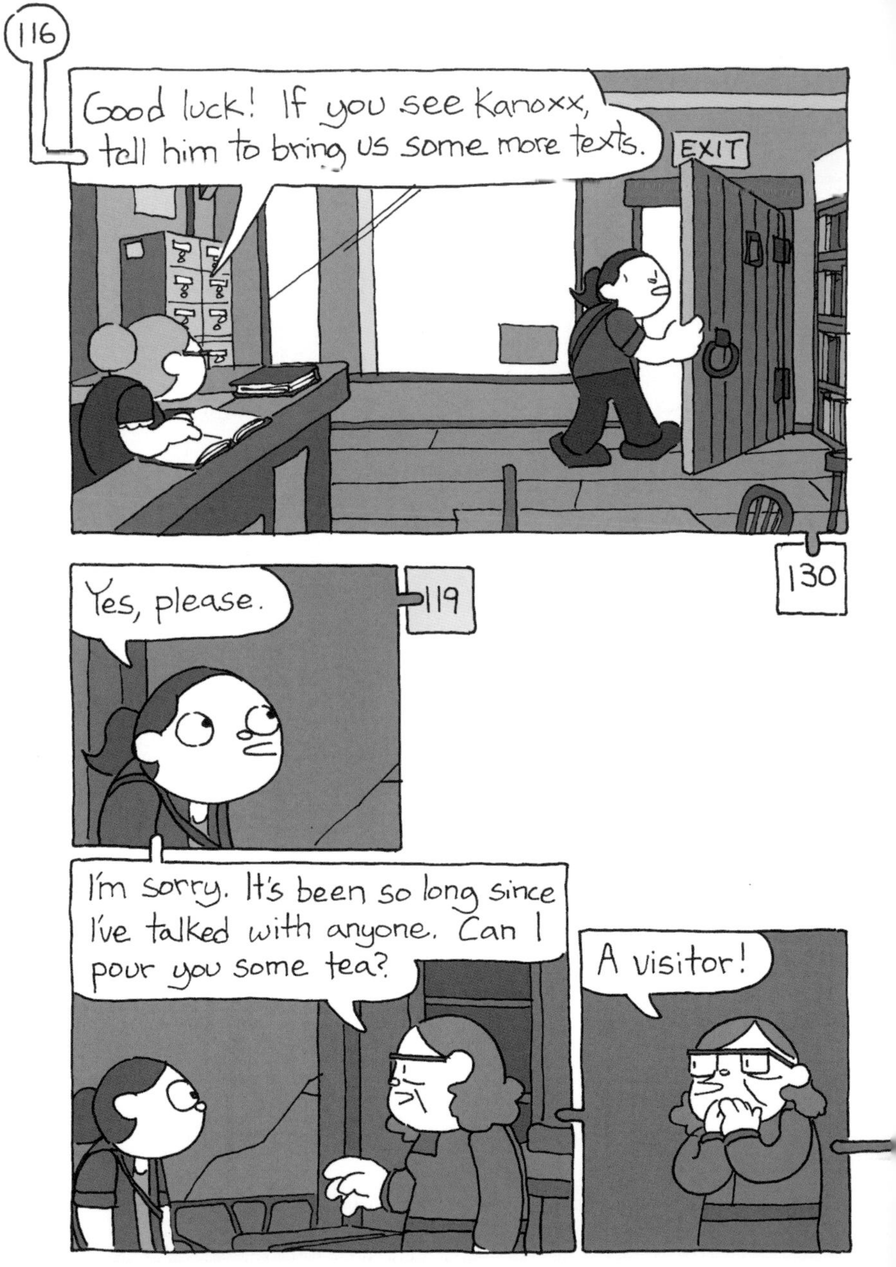
116
Good luck! If you see Kanoxx, tell him to bring us some more texts.
EXIT
130
Yes, please.
119
I'm sorry. It's been so long since I've talked with anyone. Can I pour you some tea?
A visitor!

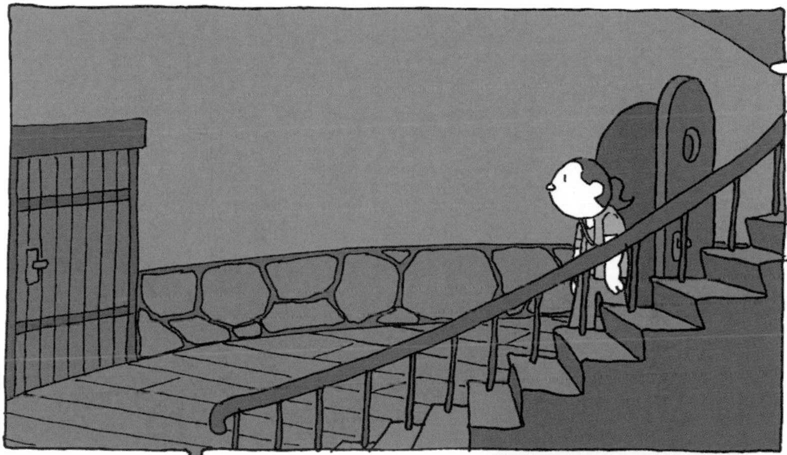

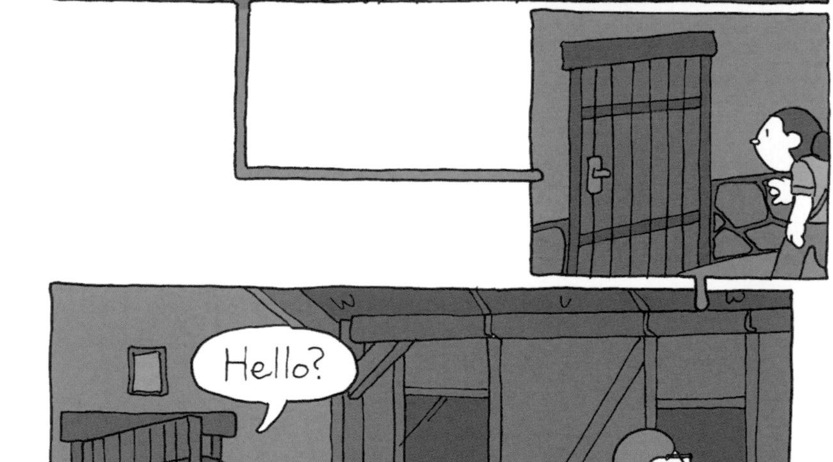

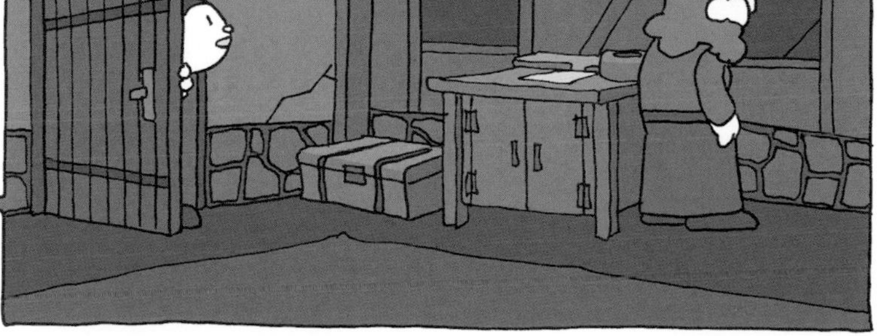
Hello?

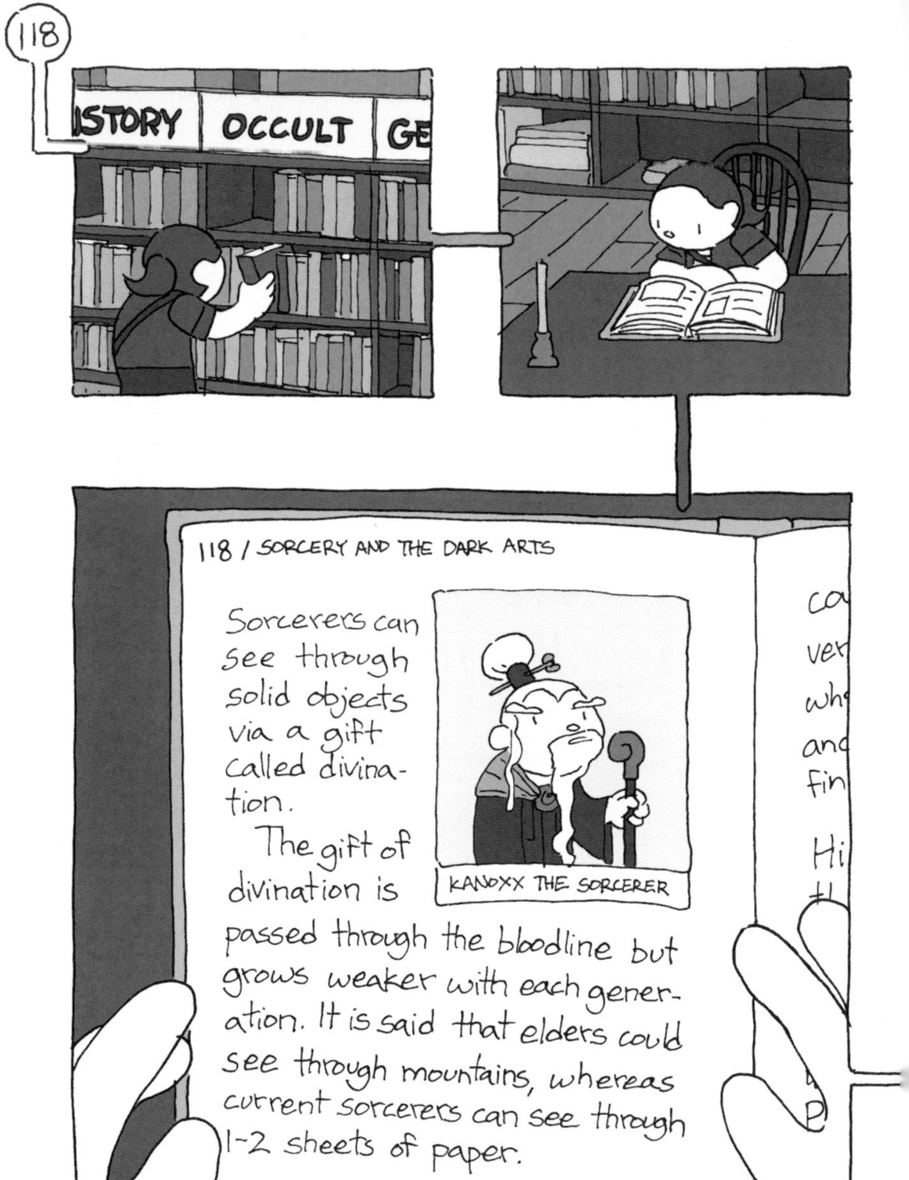
118
ISTORY
OCCULT
GE
118 / SORCERY AND THE DARK ARTS
Sorcerers can see through solid objects via a gift called divination.
The gift of divination is passed through the bloodline but grows weaker with each generation. It is said that elders could see through mountains, whereas current sorcerers can see through 1-2 sheets of paper.
KANOXX THE SORCERER

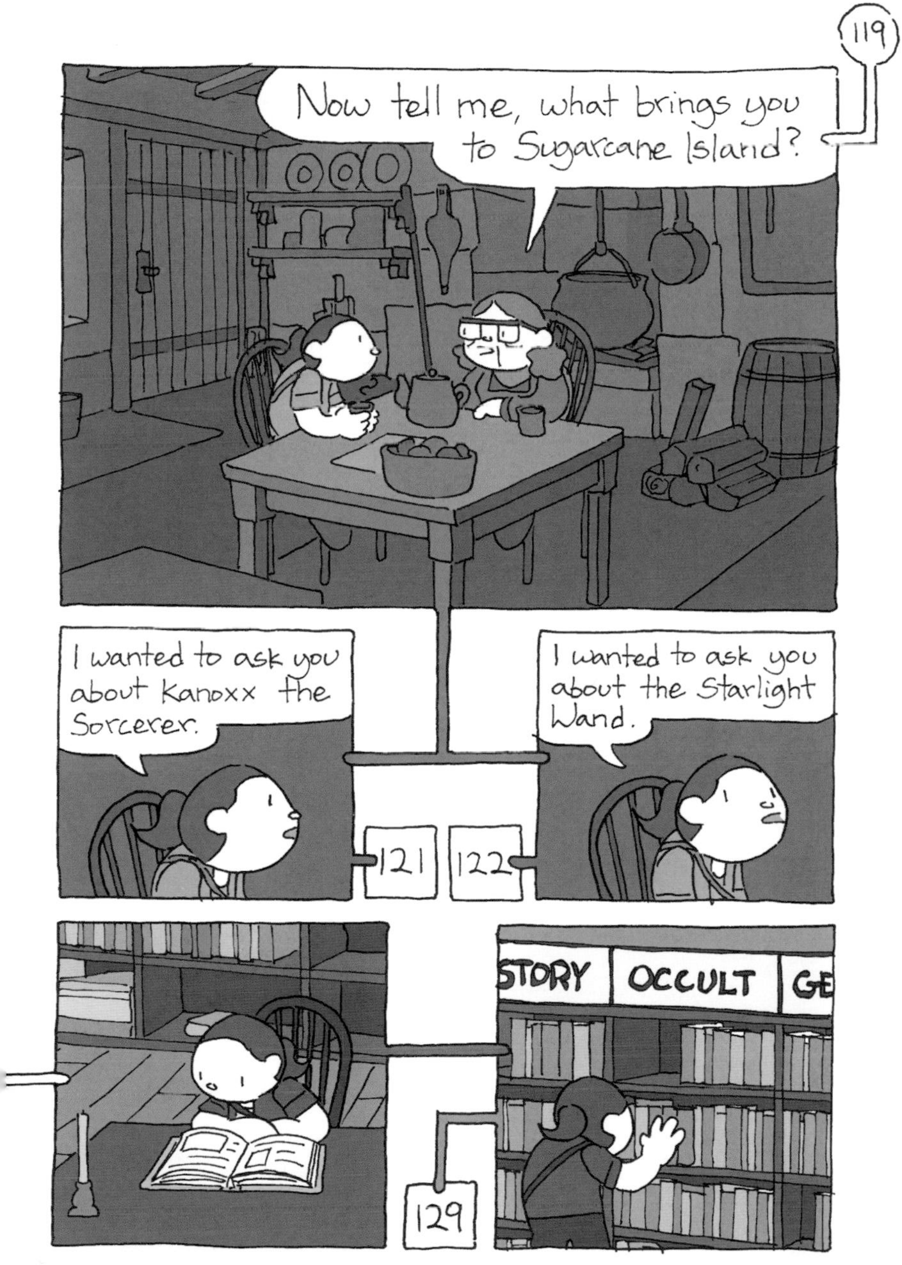
119
Now tell me, what brings you to Sugarcane Island?
I wanted to ask you about Kanoxx the Sorcerer.
I wanted to ask you about the Starlight Wand.
121
122
STORY
OCCULT
GE
129

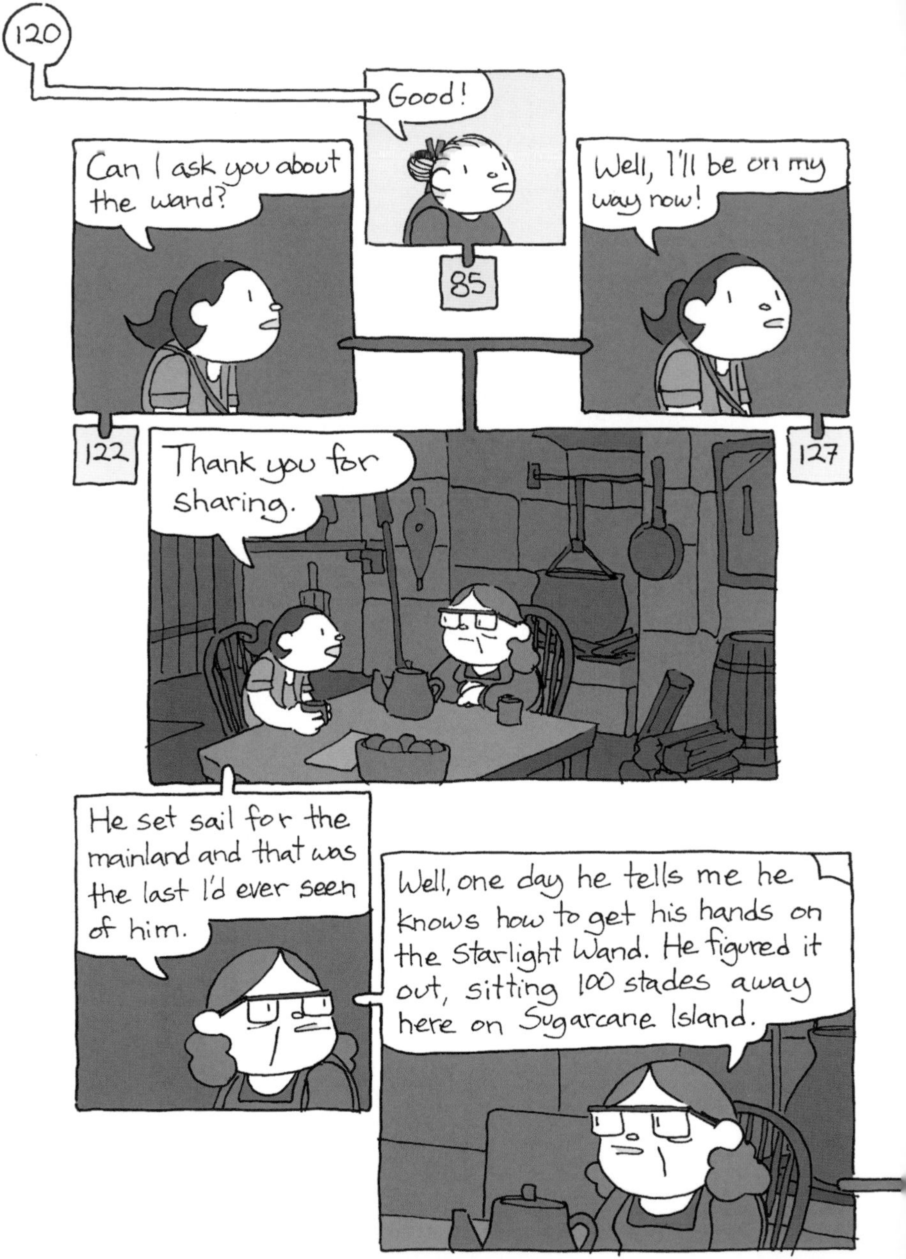
120
Good!
85
Can I ask you about the wand?
122
Well, I'll be on my way now!
127
Thank you for sharing.
He set sail for the mainland and that was the last I'd ever seen of him.
Well, one day he tells me he knows how to get his hands on the Starlight Wand. He figured it out, sitting 100 stades away here on Sugarcane Island.

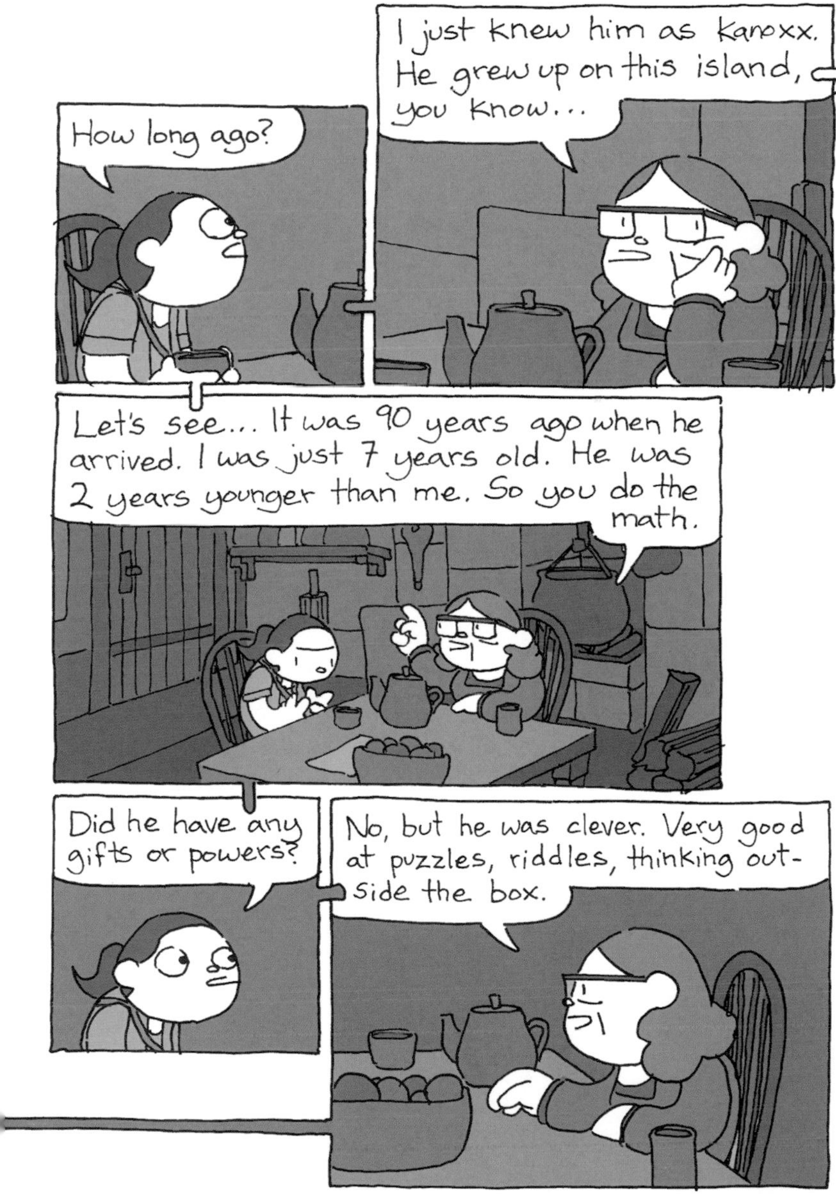
How long ago?
I just knew him as Kanoxx. He grew up on this island, you know...
Let's see... It was 90 years ago when he arrived. I was just 7 years old. He was 2 years younger than me. So you do the math.
Did he have any gifts or powers?
No, but he was clever. Very good at puzzles, riddles, thinking out-side the box.

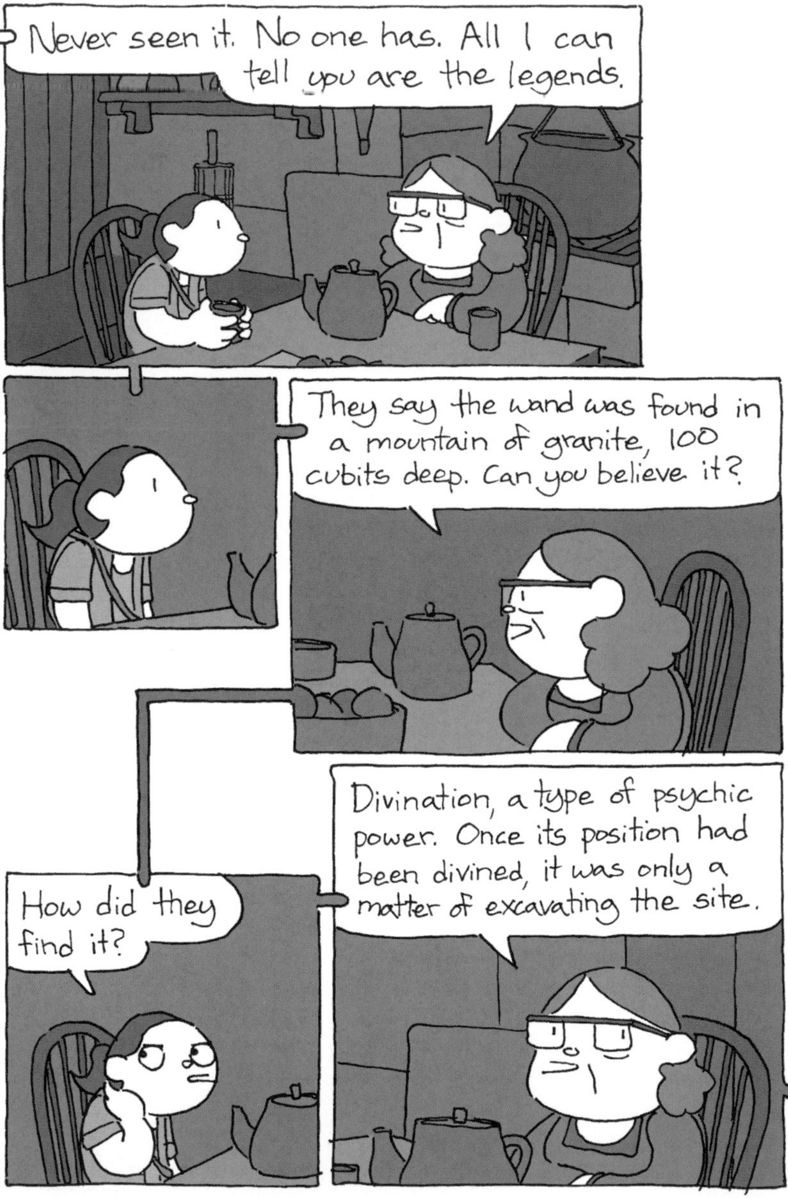
Never seen it. No one has. All I can tell you are the legends.
They say the wand was found in a mountain of granite, 100 cubits deep. Can you believe it?
How did they find it?
Divination, a type of psychic power. Once its position had been divined, it was only a matter of excavating the site.

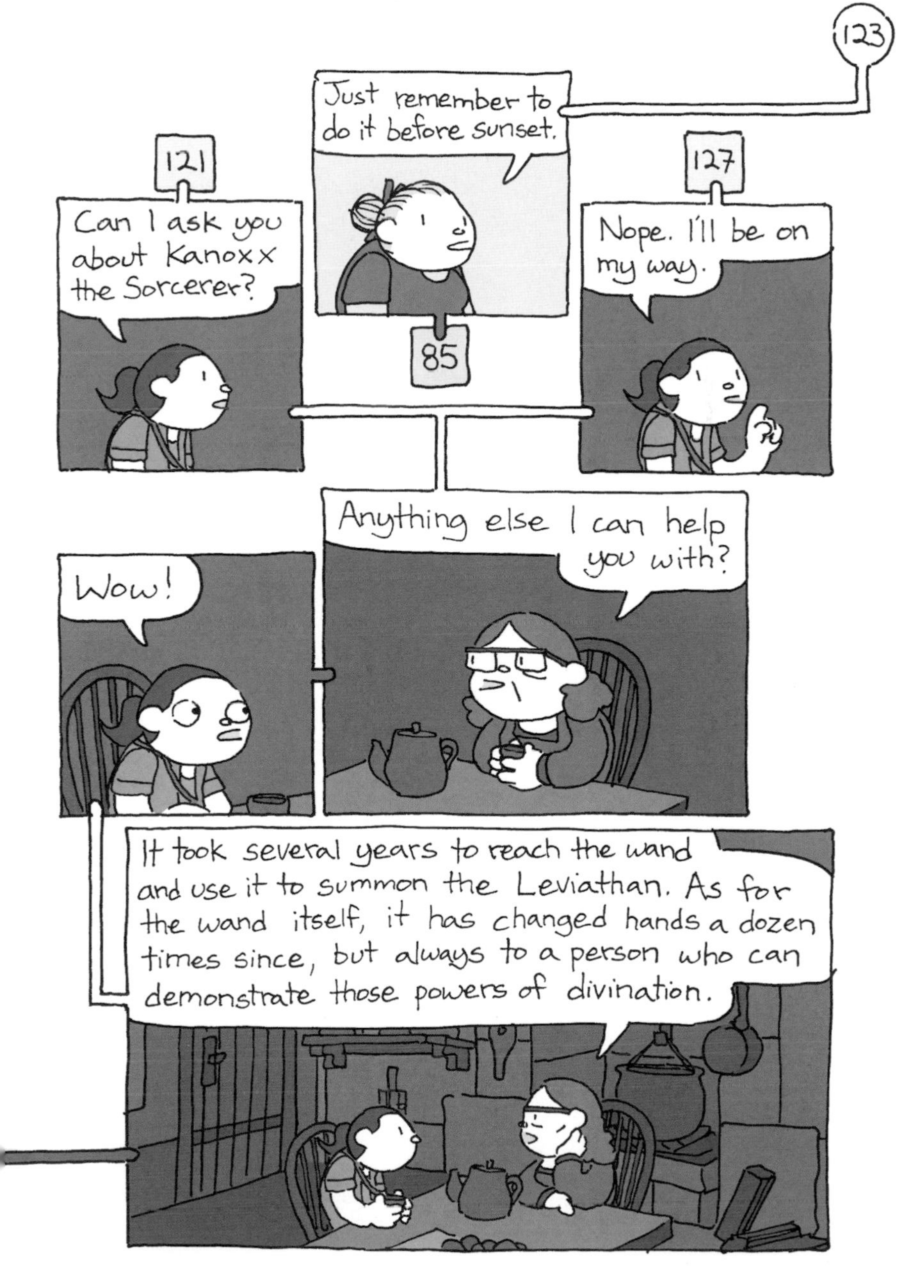
123
Just remember to do it before sunset.
121
Can I ask you about Kanoxx the Sorcerer?
85
127
Nope. I'll be on my way.
Anything else I can help you with?
Wow!
It took several years to reach the wand and use it to summon the Leviathan. As for the wand itself, it has changed hands a dozen times since, but always to a person who can demonstrate those powers of divination.

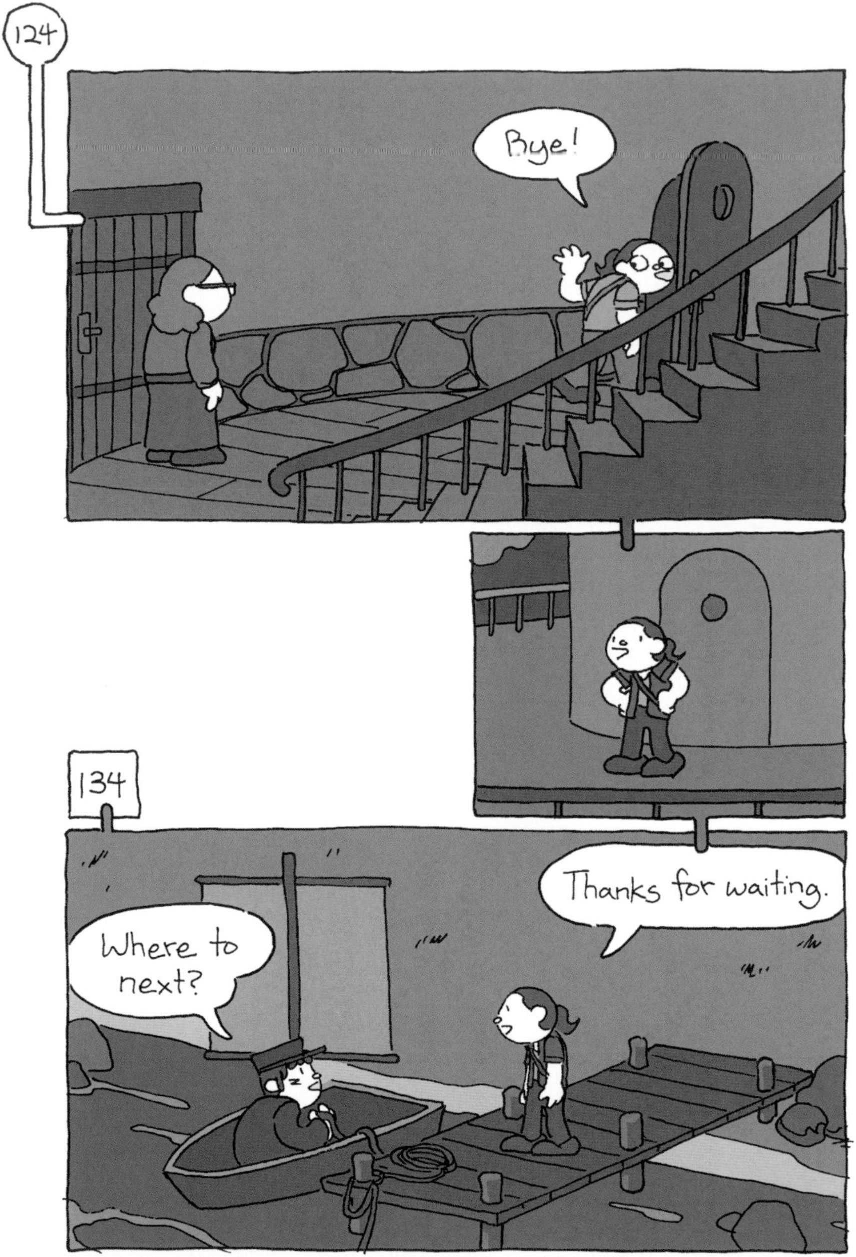
124
Bye!
134
Thanks for waiting.
Where to next?

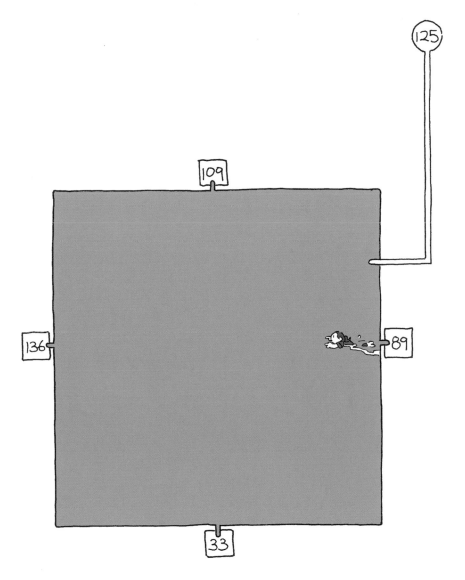

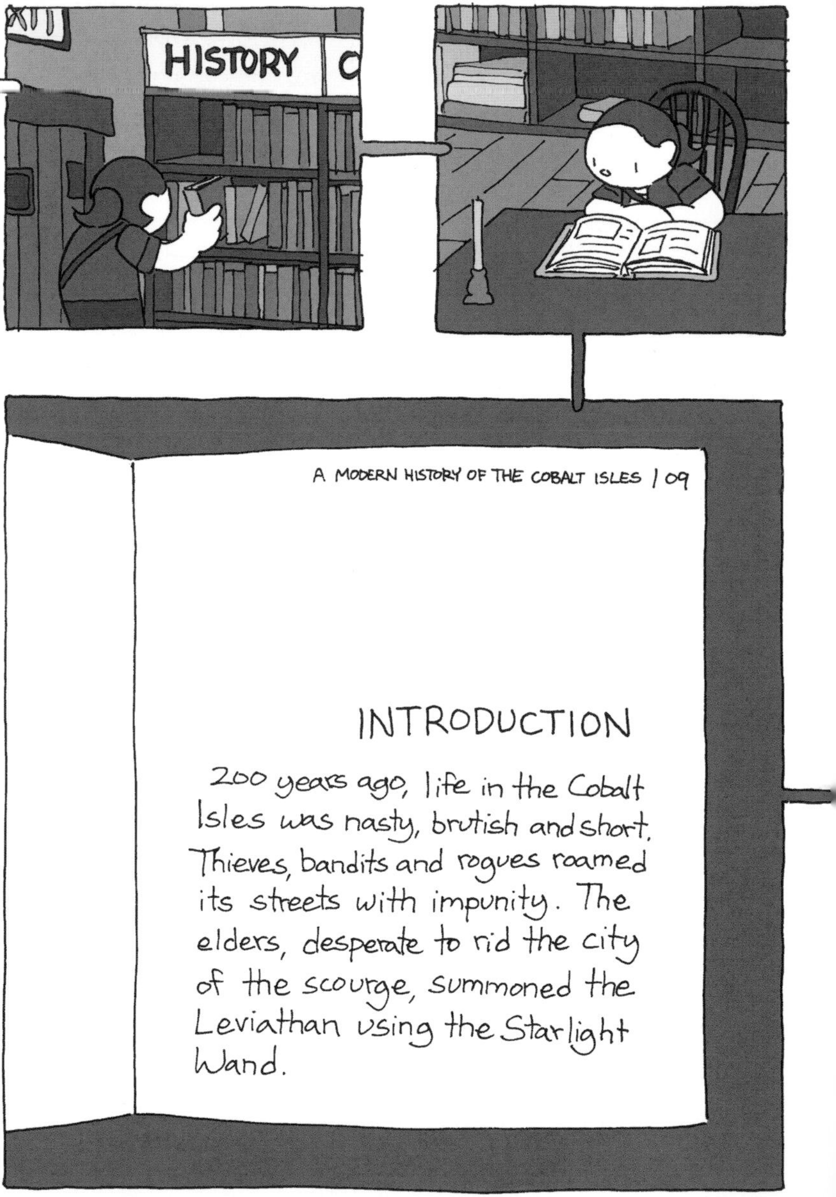
HISTORY
A MODERN HISTORY OF THE COBALT ISLES | 09
INTRODUCTION
200 years ago, life in the Cobalt Isles was nasty, brutish and short. Thieves, bandits and rogues roamed its streets with impunity. The elders, desperate to rid the city of the scourge, summoned the Leviathan using the Starlight Wand.

129

124

I'll walk you out...

10 | A MODERN HISTORY OF THE COBALT ISLES

The elder who first used the wand was a sorceress who passed her powers of divination on to the

THE LEVIATHAN

Leviathan. Some say the power has made the sea god too power-ful. In fact, a total of 41 ships have been sunk by the Leviathan since the end of the Dark Age.

On the other hand, peace and

pros
insta
activ
a ra
ture
Su
the
elab
beca
othe
by th
No
whil
anyo

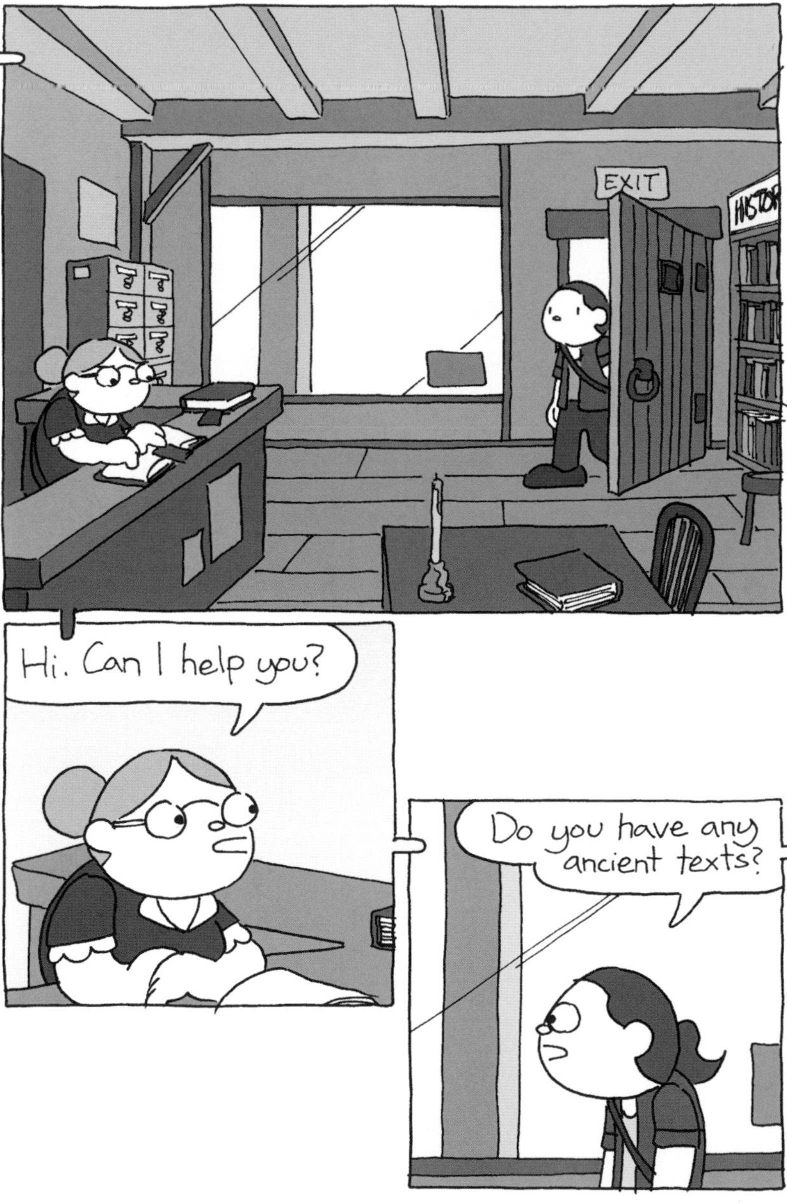
EXIT
Hi. Can I help you?
Do you have any ancient texts?

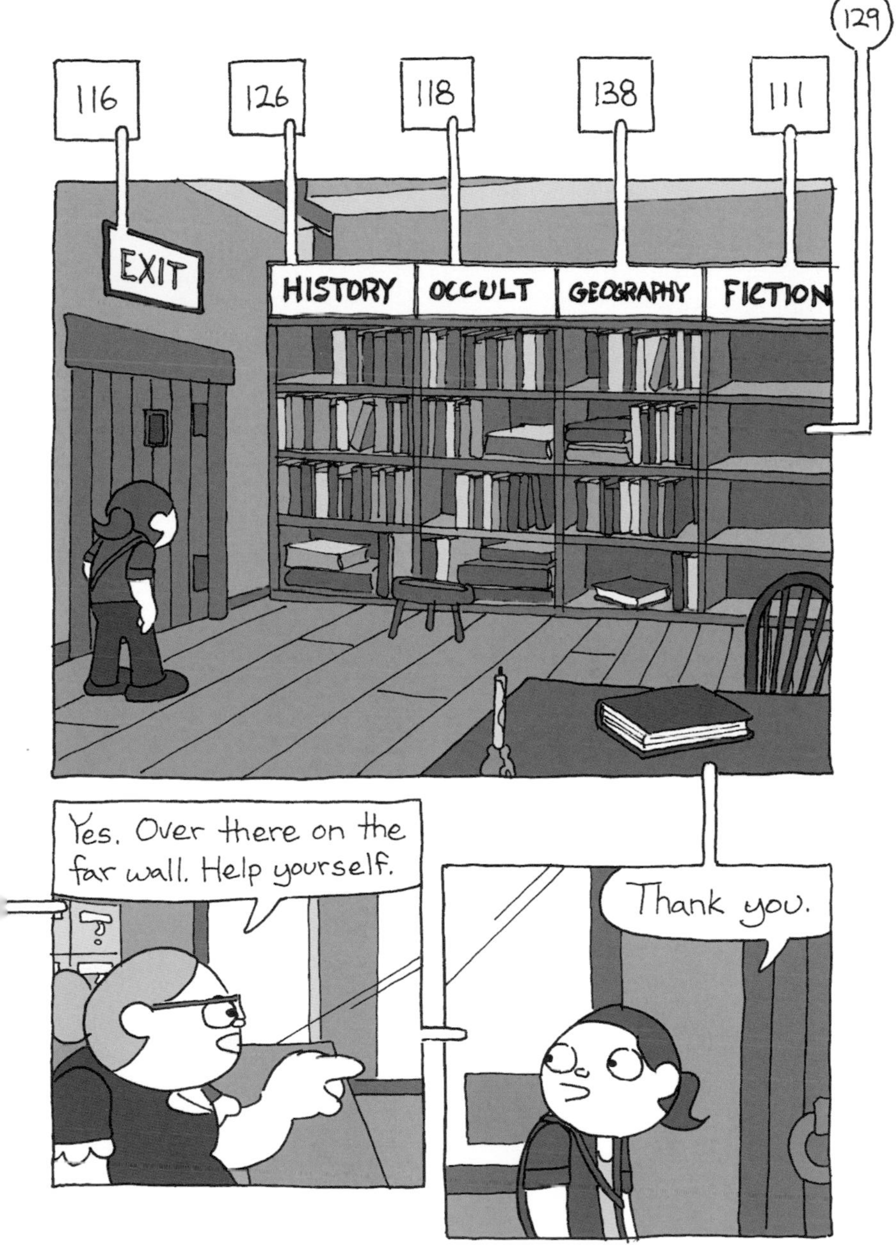
129
116
126
118
138
111
EXIT
HISTORY
OCCULT
GEOGRAPHY
FICTION
Yes. Over there on the far wall. Help yourself.
Thank you.

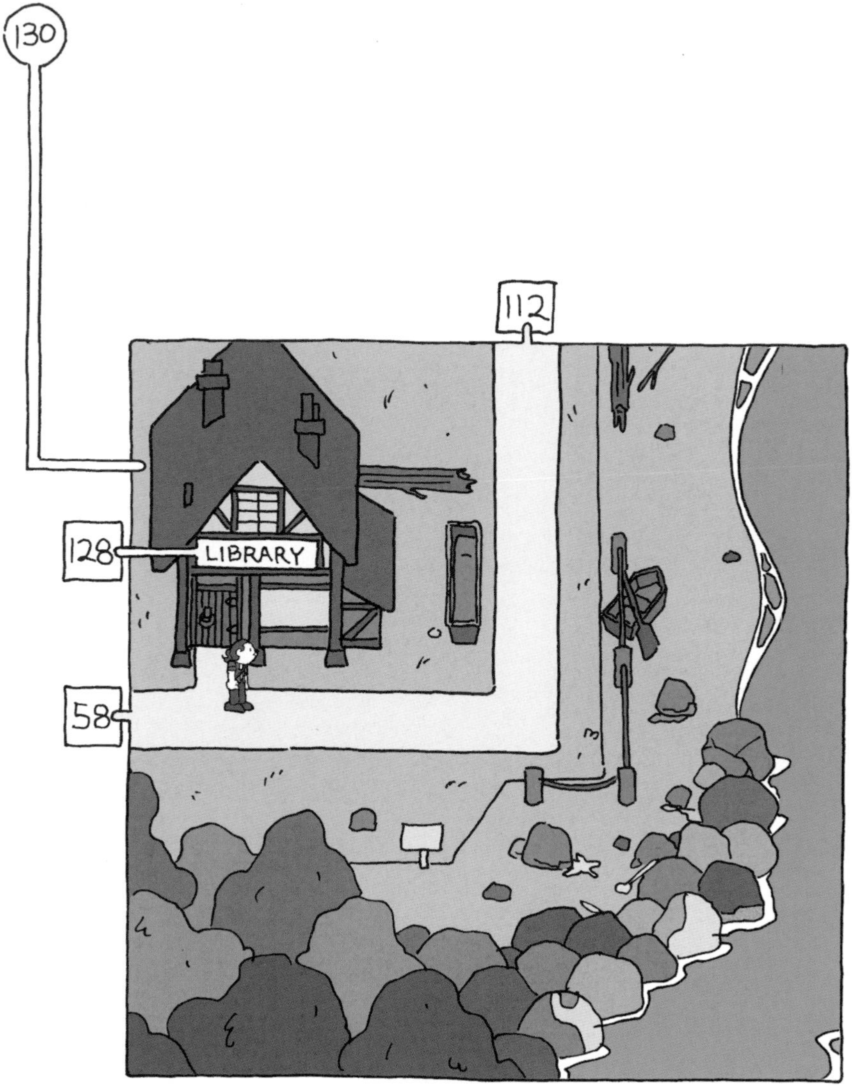
130
112
128
LIBRARY
58

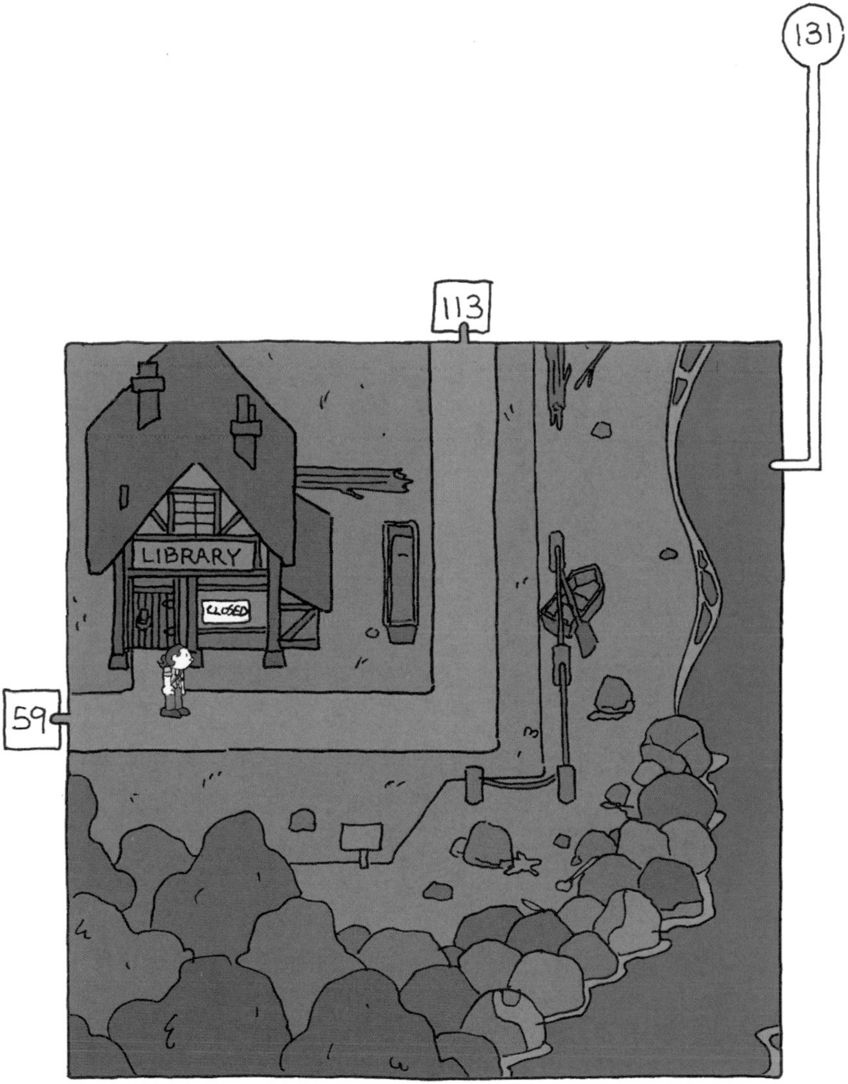
131
113
LIBRARY
CLOSED
59

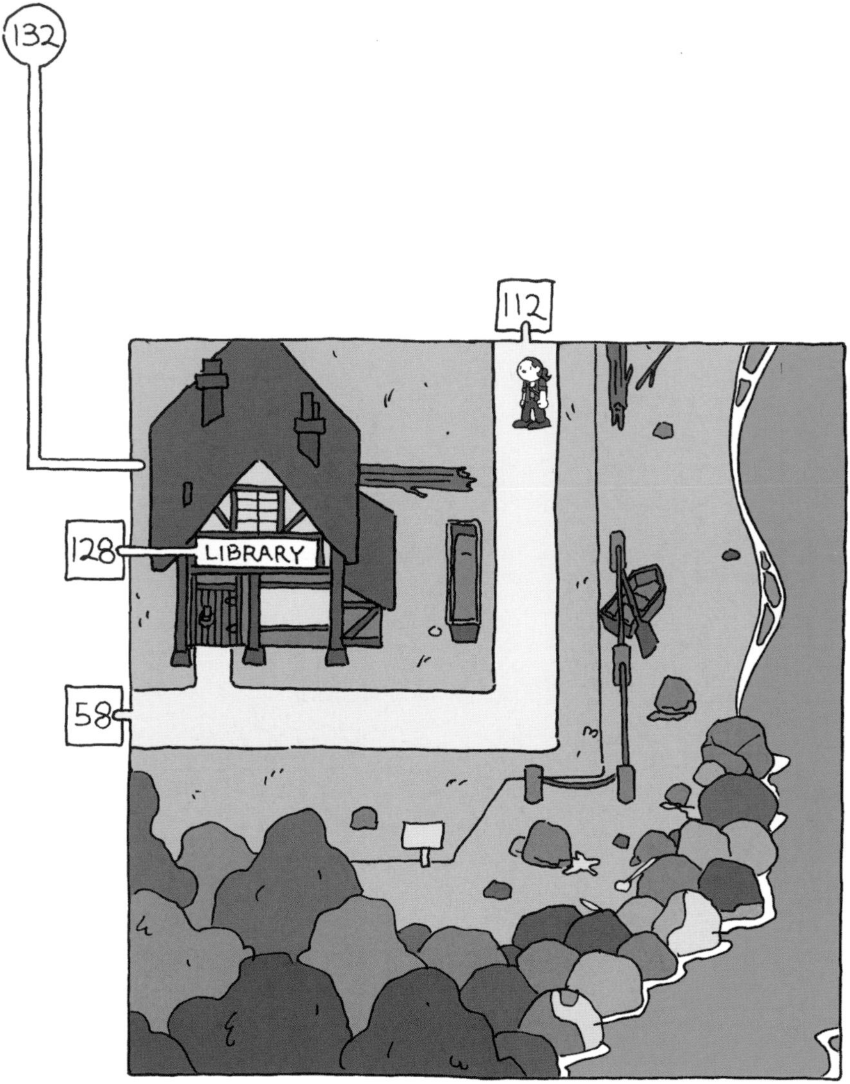
132
112
128
LIBRARY
58

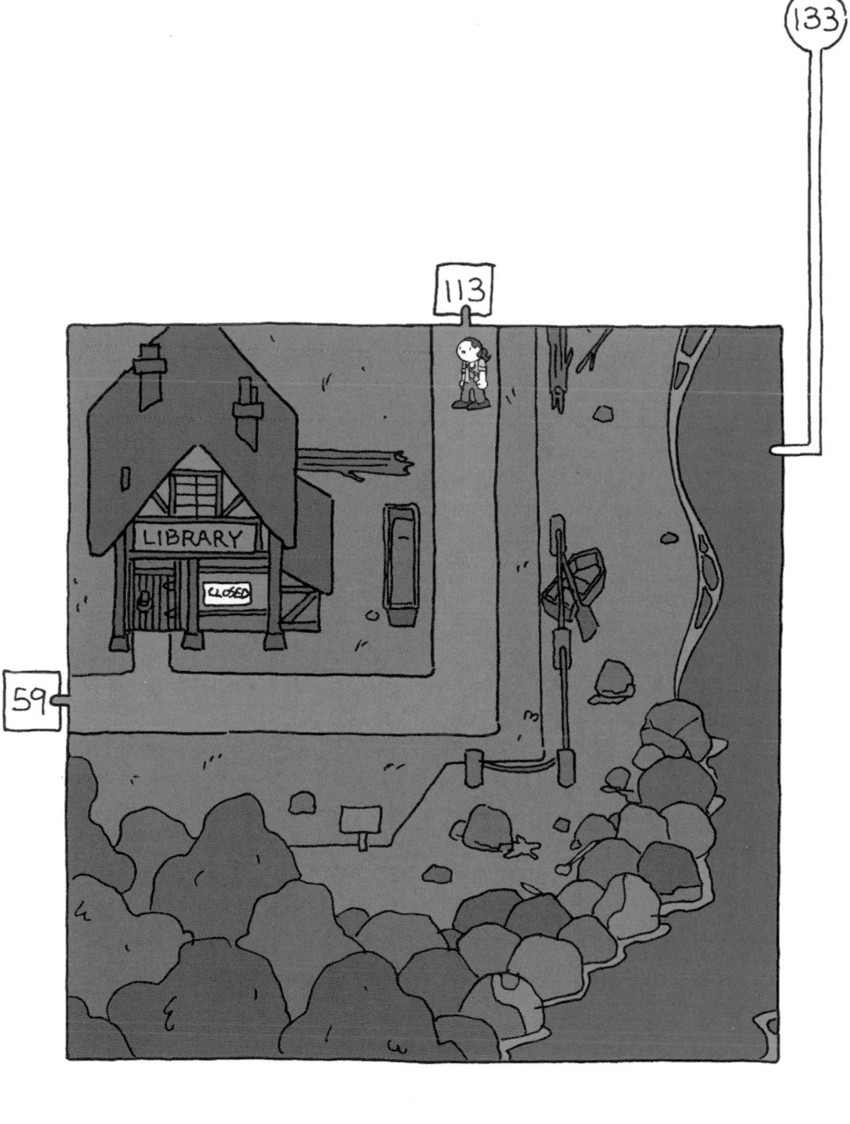
133
113
LIBRARY
CLOSED
59

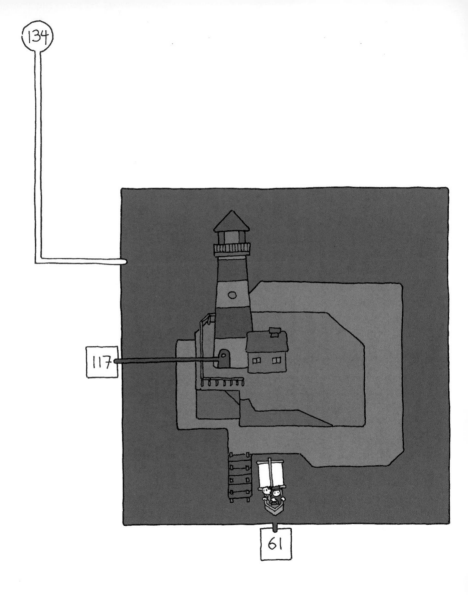

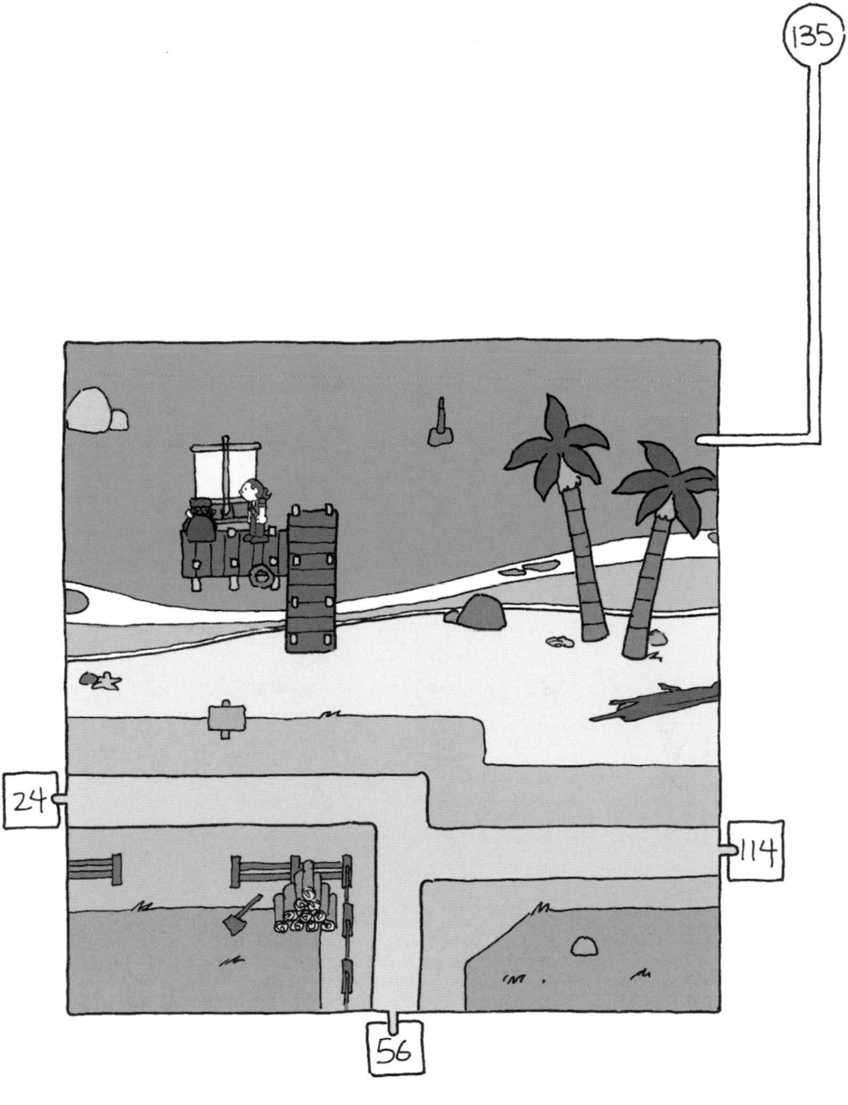
135
24
114
56

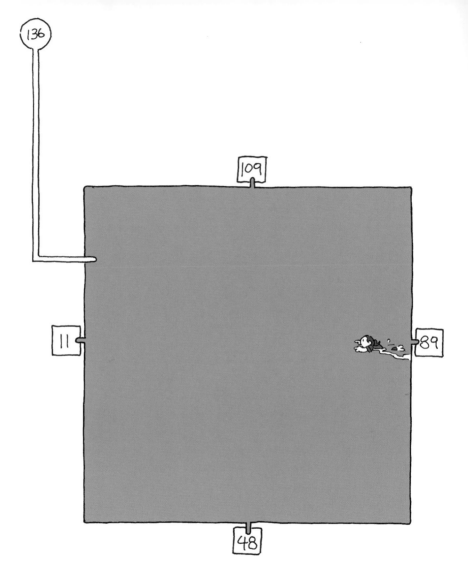

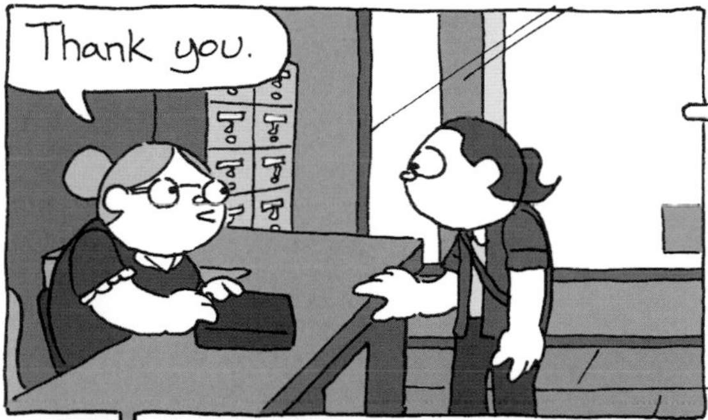
Thank you.

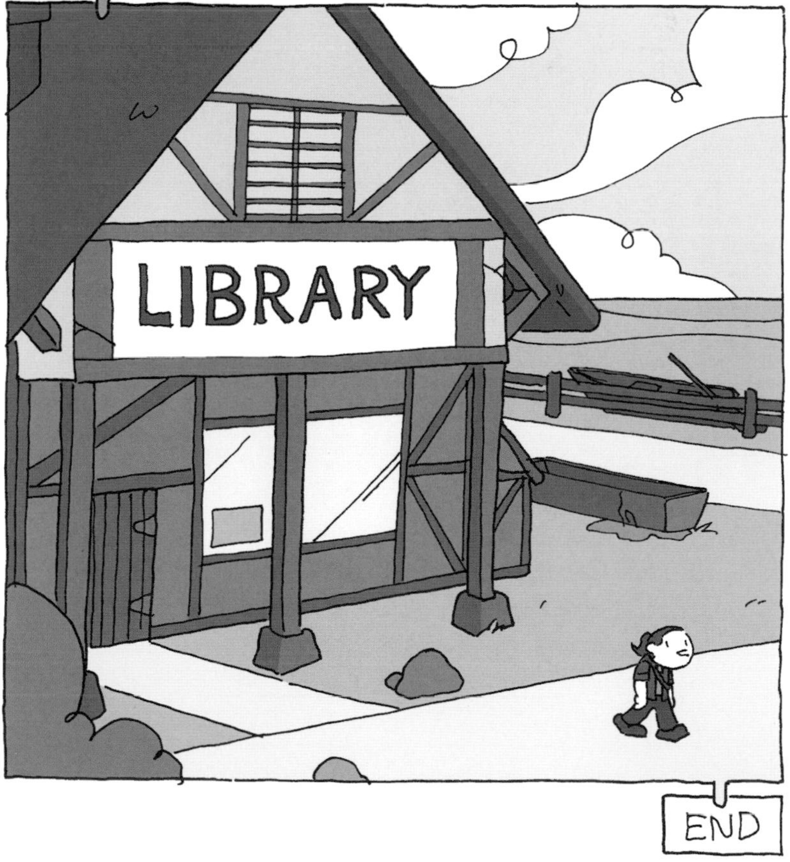
LIBRARY

END

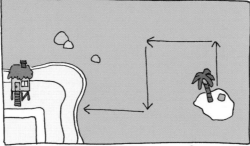

138 | AN ATLAS OF THE COBALT ISLES

FIG 1: ROUTE FROM LOST ISLAND TO MAINLAND

to the mainland, once out of sight of land, the sea in between becomes confusing and mazelike.

According to legend, one may successfully navigate the sea by swimming <u>NORTH</u>, then <u>WEST</u>, then <u>SOUTH</u>, then <u>WEST</u> once more.

MAP

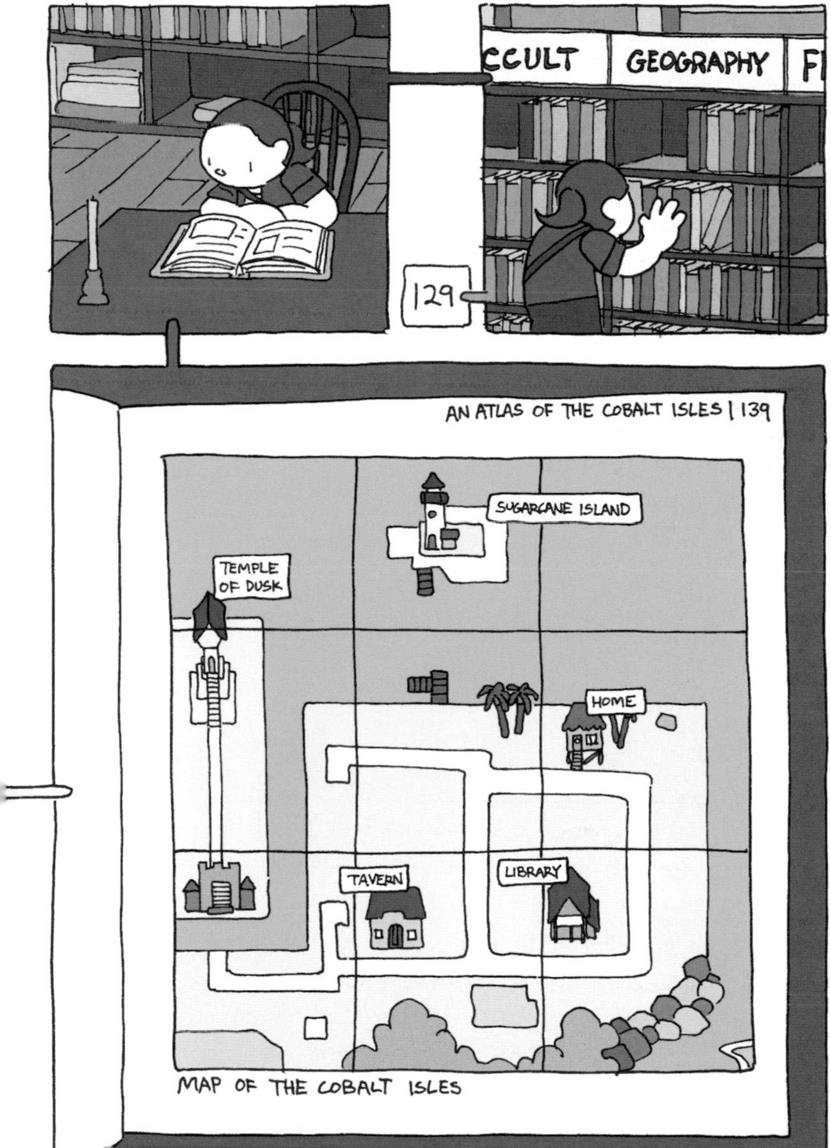
CCULT
GEOGRAPHY
129
AN ATLAS OF THE COBALT ISLES | 139
SUGARCANE ISLAND
TEMPLE OF DUSK
HOME
TAVERN
LIBRARY
MAP OF THE COBALT ISLES